2084: THE SISTERHOOD

Printed in Australia
First printed March 2023
This edition first printed 2024

Ben Hastings Publishing

Cover design by Melinda Childs
Typeset by Jessica Chaplin

Paperback ISBN 978-0-646-70685-6
eBook ISBN 978-0-646-70686-3

2084: THE SISTERHOOD

BEN HASTINGS

PROLOGUE

4th April 2024,

As I sit here writing I know they can kill me before I finish my next sentence.

But they haven't.

The threat is real; the fear never goes away.

But I've learnt to be good.

What else has this old man learnt?

I never question the motives and wisdom of Big Brother. I have come to understand that to achieve stability and order and to protect the Party society must embrace conformism and accept that rationing, subjugation, suppression and surveillance are for our benefit.

I am thankful for the independent States of Eurasia, Eastasia and our own Oceania. We must embrace war with a zest akin to life itself. It provides an environment ripe for enforcing discipline, suppressing society, preventing tedium and redirects resentment and aggression into positive channels. Let us acknowledge that death and destruction serve a greater purpose. War prevents overpopulation whilst creating perpetual demand for manufacturing and consumption.

I am frustrated by the stalled growth of the language of Newspeak as the transmission from parent to child fails.

I am most thankful for my wonderful wife Mary, our son Brien, his wife Jane, and our precious little granddaughter Sonya.

I have also learnt that life is making the best of what you've got.

The Party is right.

Two plus two is five.

I have been cured.

Winston Smith

PART I

2039 – 2049

|

The dark, still silence of early morning was pierced by the harsh tone of a man's voice that goaded Sonya awake. If she were not out of bed within the next 30 seconds, the face on the Telescreen would start yelling at her. Sonya stretched out into the cold, blueish glow of his gaze and flicked the lamp switch to turn on another day. Her squinting eyes gradually adjusted to the light as she stumbled her way to the bathroom for a shower. The water was lukewarm as usual. She was moving too slowly and there was no time for breakfast, just a gulped, weak coffee and a dry biscuit on the run. As she ventured out on her one-kilometre walk to work, it was another bleak, foggy morning and the air tasted dirty. It always felt like it was about to rain – maybe it was the polluted haze that darkened the sky, like pregnant storm clouds about to burst. A pair of pale grey overalls hung loosely on her slender frame and she had to pull the collar in tight to keep out the chilly breeze. In the filtered dawning light, her breath appeared in gusts of mist as she hurried along the rubble-strewn path.

Sonya was a member of the Outer Party and had graduated two years ago, securing her first job in the Assessing Department of the Ministry of Health. Like all government buildings, her place of employment was large and imposing, and although undoubtedly constructed long ago, its exterior displayed obvious strength. It was a multi-storey structure made of light-coloured stone that had darkened over time, being stained by the grimy air. Its few dusty windows of framed mirror-glass kept out prying eyes.

Daybreak arrived as Sonya stepped inside the cavernous reception area. She sidled past the snaking queues that were already formed in front of a long counter where Ministry staff registered each visitor. The patients were then told to sit in the waiting area until a staff member came to escort them to the Assessing Department. Unnecessary eye contact was avoided and other than the whispering echoes of conversations between staff and the forlorn unwell, the place was soundless.

Sitting at her workstation, Sonya had an unhindered view of the waiting area. During the day, she often glanced across the floor to see how busy the Ministry was, although it was always full. Checking was merely a habit to see if there was anyone in the queue she recognised. The constantly bloated corral of patients was a comfort to her. It meant her twelve hours at work would seem to pass quickly. There was nothing she dreaded more than the fear of being idle.

A sober-looking attendant brought forward her first patient before silently receding. Sonya left the file she was studying and stood to greet him with a confident, outstretched hand and friendly smile.

'Hello, Comrade Jacobson, please take a seat,' Sonya said. 'It looks like we might get some rain.'

'Thanks. You could be right about the rain,' he replied.

Jacobson was a middle-aged man who, prior to his illness, had worked in another Outer Party Ministry, the Ministry of Truth. Although Sonya was content with her position, it didn't stop her wondering what it was like to be employed by one of the other Ministries, especially this most secretive one. He wasn't supposed to talk about it, but he found Sonya so unusually approachable, he couldn't stop himself when she questioned him during their previous appointment. His working life had been filled with writing history and rewriting history. As Jacobson described his job, Sonya gradually came to realise that most of what she had ever read had been reworked many times over by the Ministry of Truth. The news bulletins, economic accounts and war reports were constantly being updated and yes, changed, but it was best to unthink it. Sonya loved reading and books were scarce, although she had managed to collect several old classics on a bookshelf at home.

'Now tell me how you're feeling this morning?' Sonya asked.

'Double plus ungood. Since my last visit, my dizziness has grown worse. I've had night sweats and regular bouts of severe abdominal pain,' he said, looking more uncomfortable. She peered into his foggy grey eyes as he spoke. He was agonisingly thin and looked to be aging prematurely. His skin was dry and colourless, and his vacant stare only emphasised his poor health.

'Are the pains becoming more frequent?'

Jacobson gasped as he nodded to confirm and groaned as he slumped further into his chair.

She tapped on her computer tablet as she quickly read the screen before glancing over at the open file amongst the piles on her desk. 'I have your test results here, Comrade Jacobson,' she said, now studying his grim face. 'Your blood work and biopsies indicate that your condition is terminal. I didn't expect your decline to be so speedful,' she added. 'What we need to do is make arrangements to transfer you to Area 15.'

'Oh, thank you, Comrade,' Jacobson said. His breathing was laboured and he struggled to blow his nose into a crinkly brown handkerchief. 'I am sure that will be the best for me.'

Sonya entered the necessary notations into the computer tablet, completed some documents and handed Jacobson a light-scribe. He feebly scrawled his signature across the bottom of the screen.

'Here, take this Deliciyum. It will ease your pains and relax you,' she said, putting a spoonful of the yellow powder into a small cup of water and handing it to him. Dispensing the drug was an important function of the Ministry of Health. He took hold of it slowly and tipped the sour drink down his throat.

'If you would like to follow me, Comrade Jacobson, I'll show you the way to the Transportation Department.'

'You mean I'm going right now? Don't I have to pack some belongings?'

'Oh, no. There is no need to worry about any of your personal possessions. We will take care of everything and have them waiting for you when you arrive,' Sonya reassured him as she took up his file and headed towards the door.

Although Jacobson was extremely surprised by how suddenly the arrangements were made for him, he accepted what he was being told. There was nothing else he could do or wanted to do for that matter. He shakily arose from his chair and as he faltered, Sonya swiftly stepped over to support his arm. Apart from the tapping of their footsteps on the hard, grey-tiled floor, it was ghostly quiet as they walked down the brightly lit corridor towards two large, heavy doors. Through them, they passed into a large sterile room that made you feel cleansed upon entering, and where the intense dazzling white glare made your eyes instinctively squint. It was crowded with men, women and children sitting in rows of stiff chairs facing a large, shiny counter that had two serious men perched behind it, their eyes darting about on the screens in front of them. The hush was only broken by the feverish clicking on their touch screens and the occasional whimper of a small girl. There were several people already being attended to at the counter. Sonya and Jacobson waited for their turn.

The waiting area in the Transportation Department was an impersonal space. It was not only obviously full of pain, which Sonya could see on the crowd of frowning faces, but also of anticipation. *Thank goodness for Area 15. We are so lucky to have it,* she thought. She didn't know much about the mysterious location. Apart from being commonly described as a 'paradise', it promised recuperation, rehabilitation, or at least palliative care for the ill, the damaged, the dying and the criminally insane. One thing was certain, though: no one ever returned from Area 15.

'Good morning, Comrades. It looks like we might get some rain,' chirped the bureaucratic assistant behind the counter. He looked

Jacobson up and down without smiling as they approached.

'You could be right about the rain,' Sonya offered in reply. Now turning to Jacobson, she said, 'This is Comrade Mack. He will look after you from here and attend to all of your further arrangements.' She handed the documents to Mack. He gave them a cursory glance. As she watched him, she was impressed by how well he feigned interest. She looked at Jacobson and nodded to him with a weak smile.

'Okay, Comrade Jacobson, please take a seat and wait until you are called,' Sonya heard Mack say as she turned to leave.

She had only known Jacobson for a short time but already felt empathy towards him. Pity for his pain, but also optimism for his recuperation at Area 15. Sonya cared and always tried to find the positives in any situation no matter how small they seemed. An extremely rare personality trait in these times that had to be kept hidden away and this only added to her solitude. She wondered how many others there were just like her, guarding their secrets.

Sonya exited the Transportation Department and as she walked briskly back to the compact yet functional cubicle that contained her desk and examination table, she observed her busy Ministry of Health comrades diligently attending to the sick and waning. However, they nor she could provide any therapeutic treatment, substantial medical assistance or even convalescence. Nothing but basic injury care, pain relief and referral to Area 15. The progress of medicine had been abandoned long ago because it was counterproductive to waste resources on prolonging life when the world suffered from overpopulation.

Her next patient was a man whom she didn't recognise. He had a badly ulcerated ankle that needed to be cleansed of the foul-smelling, thick greenish mucus that oozed from the wound. She looked at him and tapped the examination table, indicating he should lie there.

Sonya gleaned his file and noted he was a garbage collector from East Anglia.

'Where do you live?' she asked as a conversation starter.

'In East Anglia, about two kilometres away, in what was my parent's house,' he answered.

'Was?'

'Yes, up until last year. My father was sent to Area 15 when he got too ill to stay at home. I hope to see him again one day, but you know what they say. No one ever returns from Area 15.'

'That they do,' she agreed as she worked on the ankle.

'After Father left, my mother's health started to decline and she died only a month later whilst sitting at the dinner table one night. So speedful. We were eating our meal when she suddenly fell forward, her face landing directly in the bowl, splashing her soup everywhere,' he said.

'That must have been a terrible shock!' Sonya imagined the poor woman coated in the brownish watery sustenance.

'Yeah,' he said, with a slow nod. 'The next day I struggled to carry her all the way here. She was placed on a gurney and I had to wait until someone came and wheeled her away. When they told me I could leave, I did, and I've lived alone ever since.'

'East Anglia is one of the nicer areas,' she said.

Sonya finished with the ankle, bandaged it with a clean dressing, and he was gone in under an hour.

Whilst completing his file as she sat in the firm but comfortable plain white chair behind her desk, the reception doors burst open and caught her attention. A man carrying a limp girl of about five years old came ambling through, requesting urgent help. Sonya stood up and beckoned him towards her with a wave. The tall man with a furrowed brow and watery blue eyes headed straight for her, bypassing the queues, and laid the unconscious child on the table in front of her. She checked the small girl's pulse and breathing and knew from the look of her badly broken left leg that she had been in some sort of horrible accident. Of more concern was the patch of deep reddish purple expanding across her bulging lower abdomen. It meant internal injuries far beyond Ministry capabilities.

'What do you think, Comrade?' the man pleaded.

'Double plus ungood. I can only recommend she be sent to Area 15,' she said, unemotionally.

'But she's so young and I'll never see her again,' said the man in disbelief.

'Please don't worry, they'll take good care of her,' she said.

I know we have Area 15, but I wish I could do more, she thought without changing her expression – it would be dangerous to do otherwise. But she only knew basic wound care. Of course, in an environment of unsanitary living conditions that encouraged bacteria and where infections flourished like mushrooms in manure, this treatment was helpful. However, she longed to do more. She could splint and bandage a broken limb but even this simple therapy was prone to failure and Deliciyum was of no use to this poor girl. Her mind was racing. *Why can't I cure diseases and treat serious injuries?*

Sonya sighed and sat back at her overloaded desk, tucking some loose strands of long blonde hair back behind her ear. She opened another file in preparation for receiving her next patient. It was only 7.42 a.m.

A dull headache was creeping up on her and turning her thoughts to a dose of Deliciyum when the Department Supervisor suddenly poked his head into her station.

'Could you please come to my office, Comrade?' he asked, then walked away, not waiting for an answer. Sonya looked up from her work, a little startled by the request. In all her years working at the Ministry she had only ever experienced cold greetings from him and could count on one hand the number of times they had spoken. Her heart skipped a few beats before starting to thud heavily as she immediately got up and followed him.

Her Supervisor was a tall man with lean features, a workaholic who expected nothing less of those around him. His dark narrow-set eyes seemed too close together and emphasised his hollow cheeks and sharp jawline. As Sonya observed the balding spot on the back of his head, it crossed her mind that she had never seen him smile, a stark reminder of the bitter disenchantment that choked society. He sat down at his desk and whilst considering the messy pile of papers scattered in front of him, he began speaking.

'Comrade Smith, your diligence has been noted by the Inner Party and they have decided to promote you to Section Manager effective immediately. A departmental announcement will be issued within the hour. Could you please be ready to vacate your desk and move into management station 44C.' He looked up, handed her a single sheet of pale pink paper, and said, 'Congratulations,' before rubbing the corners of his closed eyes with his right thumb and forefinger. By the time he resumed typing on his illuminated screen, she was gone.

Sonya packed up her meagre collection of personal effects whilst waiting for the announcement. In a small brown box, she carefully placed a pale blue ceramic cup with a slightly chipped handle, a collection of some prized pencils, a favourite light-scribe, a small paperweight made of clear glass encasing a fragment of ancient pink coral, and a picture frame housing a photo of her pet bird: a petite grey-and-white skittish finch with a vibrant red beak whom she had named Hope.

Then there it was, a simple message scrolled across the screen on her desk and on every other one in the Ministry:

…Comrade 60792 Smith S. is relocating within the Ministry due to promotion …

At the age of nineteen Sonya had excelled amongst her peers in the Ministry; even so, her promotion was sudden and unexpected. There was no need for her to do anything with the files she was currently working on. She rose from her chair and quietly left the station she had occupied for just over two years. Striding to her new location, Sonya passed the cubicles of her busy co-workers. She knew only a few of their names, and one was Comrade 59849 Robinson B. For a fleeting moment, her radiant blue eyes found his and she returned Billy's faint smile with her own as she walked by. Not long after she had vacated, a small, thin woman with mousey-brown hair would arrive to occupy her old cubicle.

Following the bright white corridor which served windowless management stations on both sides, Sonya checked their numbers until she came to the one designated 44C. It was less cramped than her previous cubicle, but not as big as an office. She created a space on the crowded desktop to place her box and found a job description memo. It said she was now in charge of overseeing the workload of everyone in her section of the Assessing Department and went on to list her tasks and responsibilities.

Sonya stared at the words and they began to swirl around the page as her mind grappled with the concept that she would no longer be dealing directly with patients. This was the part of her previous work she enjoyed the most, conversing with people and absorbing their stories, their lives. She would dearly miss the daily interactions with her patients like the man with the ulcerated ankle with whom she had spoken for nearly an hour. It felt as if she had been redeployed just as she had begun to develop and extract deeper sentiments and emotions from her role. However, nothing could dampen the gratification she received from being promoted. She didn't like to admit it, but she was proud of her ambition. Sonya smiled to herself briefly. It was the first time she had felt this delighted in a long while. Moments later, she was reviewing the Department's latest processing statistics.

II

Waking from a restless sleep, Billy Robinson recoiled at the thought he was due at the Ministry of Health, until the Sunday messages of Love for Big Brother coming from the Telescreen began to resonate in his drowsy mind. The day of respite from the working week calmed him. He climbed out of bed, a young man in his early twenties, tall, slim, and able-bodied. After the morning fifty push-ups and sit-ups, he sat, feeling hopeless, at the dining table in his small gloomy living room, looking down at a bowl of thin, tasteless soup with his mop of black curls dangling over his pouting face. He knew he'd still be hungry after he finished it. Indeed, he had forgotten what it felt like to not be hungry. And the rumours about the Inner Party having luxuries and privileges ordinary people could only dream about just inflamed his frustration once again. An involuntary shudder shimmied down his spine; such thoughts were illegal and dangerous.

As he nibbled on a hard piece of stale crust that had to be washed down with a swig of Gin, he glanced over at the Telescreen, mindful of its ever-present eyes and ears. Its electronic mouth was spewing incessant monotonous monologues of government announcements, continually spruiking all kinds of facts, but *what the hell is in these cans of soup that everyone eats at least once a day?* he wondered. If only he could switch it off or dim the sound, just for a while, maybe it wouldn't be so grinding on his nerves. The oppression fuelled by fear and propaganda lingered unseen and weighed on Billy like gravity.

Then he remembered that the Ministry of Plenty was at his local market today distributing scarce extra rations of cabbage, coffee powder, small portions of chocolate and maybe even some razor blades. That shifted his mood and probably saved him from stirring the ire of the Ministry of Love Thought Police who no doubt were spying through his Telescreen. A quick shower and shave allowed a hastened departure to get to the marketplace before it sold out.

A cool gust whipped through Billy's front door as he stepped outside and flecks of dirt caught in his eyes. He frantically blinked as he set off briskly on his trek and looked up occasionally at the squalid, filthy housing of his neighbourhood that was in a constant state of disrepair. A lot of buildings were at risk of collapse and streets were strewn with rubble from crumbling facades and only through experience had pedestrians carved the safest path. Many people lived in fear of being injured or even killed by the dilapidated ruins they called home. Billy started running towards the electric shuttle, the only form of public transport circulating the city, as it approached the nearby pickup point. There were other markets but venturing too far beyond the boundary of your local area was prohibited (except for Inner Party members, of course) by the Ministry of Transport. This branch of the government implemented the travel restrictions, dismantled infrastructure, and enforced the policy to terminate the manufacture, use and ownership of all forms of motor vehicles. Initially introduced as an emergency measure aimed at reducing the life-threatening levels of greenhouse gases saturating the atmosphere, it soon became just another accepted constriction of society. Aviation was outlawed entirely soon after. For ordinary people, holidays became distant memories, then fanciful dreams. As the shuttle jolted to a halt, Billy climbed aboard and found an unoccupied steel bench near the door that he could collapse onto and catch his breath.

* * *

Sonya's head was still fuzzy with her dreams of chocolate as she got dressed. It had been weeks – or was it months? – since she'd tasted her last piece and there was no way she was going to miss the opportunity of getting some more today. Little feathered Hope zealously tweeted in his rusty cage suspended from the ceiling in the corner of the living room to remind Sonya that he would like some more birdseed.

The murky sky held patchy grey puffs and although the breeze was cool Sonya decided to walk the short distance to the market. There was a crowd when she arrived, but she had seen busier times. There were still plenty of high rows of large timber crates filled with cabbages which meant she could head straight for the chocolate. It was always in short supply. Fortunately, the queue was only a dozen deep and after scanning her identity card to deduct payment from her account, she was chuffed to have a small block of the silky brown substance wrapped in foil tucked in her bag.

When she found her way back to the cabbage stalls, the maximum limit allowed had been reduced from two per person to only one. It was added to her bag and then she obtained some salt, pepper and two tiny bundles of rosemary.

A congested congregation in the far end of the market signalled that coffee was being distributed. Nothing attracted a swarm like that bitter dried powder. Standing amongst the bodies, Sonya first noticed the luscious nest of curly coal-black hair on the tall man standing a couple rows in front of her. She hustled sideways past a short, pudgy gentleman whose breath reeked of stale Gin and discreetly squirmed forward between a couple of women so that she came to stand shoulder-to-shoulder with Billy.

'Hello. Comrade Robinson, isn't it? I've seen you at work,' Sonya said. She turned to look at him briefly.

'Well, hello, Comrade Smith. Running low on coffee too, huh?' he replied with a polite grin.

Sonya nodded as she stared straight ahead, a little surprised but mostly flattered that he recognised her. They didn't speak further as they approached the men taking payments and handing out the small brown paper bags.

'Are you now finished shopping for today?' Billy asked as they each bought a ration of coffee and turned to walk away.

'Almost, I just need to find some birdseed,' Sonya answered.

'Ah, you've got a pet bird. That's nice.'

'Yes, a little finch called Hope.'

'I can help you look.'

'Thank you, Comrade, but you don't have to,' she said coolly, grateful for his company but careful not to show it.

'I know,' he replied.

They began strolling together whilst trying not to look at each other too often.

'You enjoy working at the Ministry, don't you?' he said. It was more a statement than a question.

'Yes, I do.'

'I guessed as much.'

'How so?'

'You seem, I don't know really, just different to everyone else.'

'Go on, Comrade Robinson, don't stop now!' she enthused, suppressing a smirk.

'Please, my name's Billy.'

'Nice to finally meet you, Billy. I'm Sonya.'

He nodded as if he already knew.

'Well, Sonya, you're actually cheery at work. I know everyone pretends to be. But with you it seems genuine. You're interested and you care,' he said, turning to her.

He caught her looking into his perceptive vivid green eyes, smiling coyly.

'You take that much notice of me?' she asked.

'I see you around,' he said, with a stifled grin.

He looked ahead at a group of children playing in the distance, one flying an orange-and-blood-red striped kite high in the sky, its tail of streamers flickering like a flame in the wind.

'You do disguise it well, I grant you, but I see through it. Certain mannerisms and body language. I can tell.'

'I'd better be more careful. Your thoughts, best to unthink,' she said.

'Please save that gobbledygook for work,' Billy pleaded. 'I prefer Oldspeak.'

She nodded.

'But what I can't understand is why? Why do you care? What makes you happy and hopeful? Just look around. We live in a largely barren world denuded of much of its flora, with many animals driven to mass extinction. We're always at war, always hungry and poor and live in dirt and decay. Worst of all we dare not speak our mind, living in incessant fear and under constant surveillance,' he said.

'Well, you can either be miserable and fake the happiness or try to make the best of it, Billy,' she offered but knew he didn't understand.

'Hey, look. There's some birdseed,' she said, pointing to a stall with a small selection of grain on display. It was a chance for her to lighten the mood. She purchased a pack of food for Hope. 'This little bag with last for months.'

When they got nearer to the children, Billy and Sonya stopped talking. As they continued walking, all but the boy flying the kite glared at them both until they were well past.

'You know, I only managed to get one cabbage today,' Sonya said, frowning and shaking her head.

'Do you see what I mean? One wretched cabbage. Please take one of mine,' he offered, holding the pale leafy lump in the palm of his right hand.

'Thank you, but I can't.'

'Here, I insist,' Billy said.

He pushed it into her bag as they approached the market exit.

'It doesn't feel right.'

'That's because we're only supposed to look after ourselves, not anyone else. No one does anything nice.'

'You're nice,' she said.

The clouds were growing larger and heavier, turning the sky a deep purply grey that cast a premature twilight.

'Thanks. You are too. Do you want to meet again?'

'I would like that.'

'It has to be somewhere, you know, discreet. I'll work something out and let you know,' he said.

'Definitely. I look forward to it.'

'You know to never use the internet or mobile phones, right?'

'Absolutely. Everyone knows they're just surveillance devices these days anyway,' she replied.

'Goodbye then.'

'Goodbye for now,' she said with a nod and a sideways glance.

They departed in different directions through the thinning crowd.

Light rain had started as Sonya walked home but all she could think about was Billy. It was the first time she had met someone who was interested in her the way he seemed to be. Exhilaration was an unfamiliar emotion and she was utterly enjoying it. *He is pleasant to the eye,* she admitted to herself, *and although he struggles with our circumstances, he does have a certain rebellious charm.*

By the time Sonya had entered the foyer of her apartment building and pressed the grubby little elevator button, she was soaking wet, an umbrella proving inadequate during such a downpour. But at least the lift door opened now after being broken for the past three months. Her nesting place was perched on level seven of Building 12 in a cluster of pigeon boxes that lined Fourth Street. She always kept her place tidy, swept the dark and dusty hallway outside her front door and cleaned the entry mats that formed sparse stepping stones between unseen neighbours.

Home consisted of two dimly lit rooms. Apart from a sofa and side table, the living area also contained what passed as a kitchenette on the far wall, a simple bench with a hotplate, a deeply scoured dulled stainless-steel sink and an old compact refrigerator that chugged noisily in the corner. Open floor plan they called it. The Telescreen on the wall above the little round rosewood dinner table would soon stop reporting production statistics and morph into the 1 p.m. news bulletin. Through a door to the left was a sparsely furnished bedroom with a small window that looked out onto the adjacent unit block.

Peeling off her wet clothes as she padded to the threshold of broken mosaic tiles that marked the entrance to a tight, beige-toned bathroom, she was careful not to walk on the jagged edges that had cut her feet on too many occasions. They would get fixed one day. She stepped under the shower and let the relaxing tepid water cascade over her head, reminiscing about the morning and Billy.

* * *

The clock glowed 1.34 p.m. across the room as Billy entered his apartment and dumped his groceries onto the kitchen bench, with the Telescreen humming in the background.

'Righto, what's for lunch?' he asked himself.

The answer was obvious. The Sunday meal was always cabbage casserole with some of that pink gelatinous stuff they called meat.

Today's unexpected and energising encounter at the market had him pondering into the evening. He had finally talked to Sonya. Many times he had tried to make it happen until by chance she was standing beside him. He was charmed not just by her beauty but by her manner and conversation, and for a moment his mind raced ahead to where their connection could lead. But he also had other pressing matters occupying his thoughts.

In the depth of night after the Telescreen had gone to sleep, Billy arose from his bed. In the cave-like darkness, he put on some clothes and a loose black raincoat, pulled its hood down over his head and felt his way to the front door. His mobile phone with its tracking application was left snug in the bedside drawer. The drizzling rain and moonless sky provided a perfect cover for his clandestine journey.

He skulked along streets and down lanes, keeping to the dull shadows away from the streetlamps. A night patrol forced him to press himself into the unlit crevice of a crumbly building facade until they had passed. Once he breached the outer limits of town, it was safe to use his little flashlight to guide him to the Proletariat area that all cities had. The domicile of the Proles, an underprivileged, uneducated and ragged working class that significantly outnumbered the rest of the populace. A place with hundreds of makeshift homes, mostly canvas tents, some little gnome-like dwellings and other substandard accommodation.

This is where Billy would meet a gang of like-minded individuals. Where a flicker of human spirit within the Outer Party, ignited by the spark of disenchantment, began to smoulder. There was only so much anguish a human being could endure whilst their basic needs remained unfulfilled. Too many decades of repression, squalor and struggle had created bubbling dissatisfaction. Gradually the twin tools of propaganda and fear began to lose their sharpness. Even the intoxicating buzz of triumph in the endless wars against alternating States had started to fade.

The group had begun to question whether there could be a better way of life, at first silently in only their minds, but gradually through whispered murmuring amongst each other. Of course, this was a crime that promised being sent to Area 15 for the criminally insane. But as time went by, some souls were so dispirited that fright had lost its potency. Was it a way out? Who cared if no one ever returned from Area 15?

'The west wind blows,' Billy announced quietly, as he crouched outside the entryway of a small dwelling.

'Welcome, brother,' came the reply.

A man Billy only knew as Adam ushered him inside and he found a place to sit amongst the other men cramped within.

'Are we almost ready to begin?' came a voice from the back of the room.

'Yes, brother, our strength will be in our numbers and our numbers are growing.'

'Can we rely on the Proles?' asked another.

The enormous challenge that the disillusioned and newly awakened minority had overcome was to replace the Proles deeply entrenched patriotism with social activism. Persistence, patience and provocation had yielded results.

'Yes, we have enough, many hundreds, and that will grow,' Adam answered. 'Tonight, we finalise our plans and ensure we have all the weapons and supplies that we need. We will be fighting with guerrilla tactics and terrorism. Creating anarchy and confusion will be the pillar of offence. Of course, anonymity through stealth is extremely challenging and requires caution and cunning. Masking your appearance, locating safe areas to meet and finding secure methods of communication are skills we all need to practice.'

Monday morning couldn't arrive fast enough for Sonya and the first thing she did when she got to work was check if Billy was there. Just seeing him was a relief, and she knew they had to be careful but he didn't even glance her way the entire day. Several more days passed without any sign of contact from him and Sonya was starting to think the whole thing was a dream. Mercifully work kept her busy and as she reviewed the monthly injury statistics report, she noticed the corner of a small brown square of folded paper poking out from under a file on her desk. She slipped the note into another file and left it there. After signing the report, she calmly lifted the file and opened it at her chest. Inside was the simple message: '*Meet for lunch at Central Park*'. Within seconds, she put the note into her pocket.

Time marched excruciatingly slow for the rest of the morning but the clock at last said 1 p.m., allowing her to venture out into the street for a short half hour. Although eager, she had the presence of mind to take a less direct route. She didn't want to make it look obvious she was on a mission to meet someone. That would risk attracting attention to herself as she headed towards the patch of scratchy grass under the dark green canopies of a dozen precious Oak Trees which formed the prized oasis called Central Park on Fifth Street. Vegetation was generally sparse, caused by pollution, overpopulation and climate change. Greenery of any kind struggled to exist and gardens were a rarity. Only thinly wooded forests survived with farms heavily reliant on technology to maximise harvest yields. It came as no surprise to Sonya that the park was well patronised but it was large enough to not be congested. Meandering down the middle pathway discreetly searching the faces, she finally found Billy sitting on the ground under the majestic spirally foliage of one of the sprawling Oaks. He must have come straight here. She casually walked towards him.

'Do you mind if I sit here, Comrade?' she asked.

'No, not at all, Comrade. Please do.'

'Looks like we might get some rain,' she said as she brushed aside some fallen acorns before planting herself on the yellowish grass.

'You might be right about the rain.'

There was silence whilst Sonya unpacked her blackberry jam sandwich. She subtly shuffled over a bit closer to him so they could talk quietly without being overheard.

'It's great to see you again,' she said before taking a bite.

'Thanks. I've been thinking about you a lot too.'

She smiled whilst observing some children in the distance kicking a ball around.

'You know inter-ministry relationships aren't allowed, don't you?' she asked.

'Of course.'

'That means we can never get permission to be a procreating partnership.'

'I know that too.'

'Well, I'm happy to be your work acquaintance anyway,' she said. 'It just makes it hard for us to get together that often, you know, whilst maintaining discretion.'

Billy bit his bottom lip and sighed. He held his tomato sandwich in front of his mouth.

'I've been to the Proletariat,' he said.

'You have?' She turned to him in awe. 'Really?'

'Yes.' He was looking at the grass, chewing as he spoke to muffle his words. 'We could meet there. You must travel carefully but once you're there it's safe. We can be ourselves. Not like here.'

'How? It's prohibited.'

'That's the problem. Too many things are prohibited. Leave it with me.'

After a further ten minutes of small talk, it was time to leave. In the palm of his hands, he scrunched up his lunch wrapping, got up, dusted the back of his coveralls, and a little folded piece of paper fell into Sonya's lap. She hastily slipped it into her pocket. He walked off towards the Ministry. A few minutes later she did the same. On the way back to work, she opened the note and quickly read it. It was instructions on how to get to the Proletariat.

Sonya had never experienced so many different emotions. The mixed brew of excitement, fear, infatuation and the lure of forbidden love was intoxicating. She was a little anxious about following Billy into the unknown. Her father had warned her not to trust anyone, retelling stories about how her grandfather got himself into trouble by confiding with too many people. But at the same time, she was compelled by an overwhelming curiosity and the need to be with Billy.

Every time she saw Billy at work her heart fluttered. Was tonight the night they would meet? The signal he would give was simple. He would just pass by her and say, 'there's a lot of patients today.' It would be three days before she heard his voice. Just like he had instructed, she made her way into the night, hoping not to get lost. As arranged, Billy was waiting for her near Adam's place but they didn't disturb him. Instead, they quietly weaved between the dotted canvas tents before pulling back the piece of tarpaulin masquerading as a door. Inside it was cosy and lit with an old oil lamp sitting on a small circular table. The only other piece of furniture was a little cupboard. Covering the waterproof sheeting on the floor were thick layers of fluffy multi-coloured blankets and several piles of plump cushions. Standing on the far side was a compact, warmth-providing wood stove with a pot of bubbling water on top.

'How lovely,' Sonya said as she sat down and snuggled into the cushions.

Billy had the largest smile. 'I'm glad you like.'

'It's wonderful! It feels so surreal.'

'Naughty but nice?' he added.

'Exactly.'

'Would you like some coffee?' he asked, holding up two empty mugs to her.

'Hmmm, yes please!'

'You're a bit of a rebel, coming out here with me, aren't you?' he said, grinning at her.

'I guess so.'

'I must tell you something,' he said. 'Coffee isn't the only thing brewing here.'

'What do you mean?'

'There is no easy way to say this but there is a rebellion being planned and I am part of it.'

Sonya's face contorted and her eyes widened. 'What?'

His serious tone continued as he tipped some coffee powder into the mugs. 'I'm part of a brotherhood of aggravated Outer Party members that are fed up with the way things are. We call ourselves The Union.'

She was still staring at him.

'Many of us disappeared in the early days when we weren't experienced enough to hide our thoughts, guard against tell-tale body language and to just know what was needed.'

'In the early days? How long has this been going on?' she asked.

He poured hot water into their mugs and handed her one.

'I've been involved for nearly a year but the group goes back longer than that. They risked their lives coming here. They also had to be careful of spies. It was highly dangerous – it still is, but now we have proven methods and trusty contacts working with us. Our numbers have grown steadily, especially since the Proles joined in,' he said.

'I can't believe it,' she said.

He slouched back on a cushion, blew on the hot beverage, and took a careful sip.

'It's true. We've sowed the seeds of revolution and after some careful propagating, we're about to harvest the bounty. This uprising will be unprecedented in more than a century and unlike any of the previous banal and impotent conflicts between the States. I have no doubt we're on the eve of an historic moment,' he said, looking directly into her transfixed eyes.

'When does it begin?' she finally asked.

'Soon. Maybe two weeks. We just need to confirm the final details with the Prole leadership.'

'If there was hope, it lay with the Proles,' Sonya murmured to herself.

'What was that you said?'

'Oh, it's just something my grandfather used to tell my father,' she replied.

'You've never mentioned your father. Is he alive?'

'Yes, his name is Brien. Although he hasn't been that well. Ever since the death of my mother a couple of years ago,' she said.

'I'm sorry to hear about your mother.'

'Thank you. She was a good woman. I was lucky to have her.'

He didn't speak, just leaned in and kissed her. A slight splash of coffee caused her to gasp and Billy let out the loudest laugh she had ever heard in her life. That night they lost their virginity to one another.

IV

So often it's the rats and fleas that alter the course of history. The swirl of a flag that sets off a battle that ends a dynasty. The disenfranchised together turn solo cries into a tumultuous chorus. The Proles were now motivated and active. Street demonstrations flooded into the city creating shock and confusion, with euphoric pronouncements that there was something beyond and better than Big Brother. Horrified on-lookers could only wonder how the participants imagined they would survive. Peaceful protesting was never tolerated by the Party and the Ministry of Love had always been rapidly deployed to squash insurgents with the ease of swatting annoying mosquitoes.

'You know we can't keep meeting here like this. It's getting too risky and I'm sure tighter curfews will soon be in place,' Billy said as he caressed Sonya under the thick canvas ceiling of their haven amongst the Proles.

Sonya tried to appear relaxed but her anxiety was beginning to show.

'I'm not entirely convinced about this business, Billy. I think it's too dangerous.'

'It is dangerous but I have to be part of it. We must try. Each injustice has become a domino, which, in isolation, looms over us. But lined up they become something else, a revelation about the fragility of the Party and the realisation that all it will take is one small knock to send the whole lot cascading, laying a path for us to follow, one domino at a time,' he replied.

She spoke softly as she lay against his chest. 'I understand the motivation and I'm not opposed to the idea, but how will you stay safe? Is the Ministry of Health safe?' she asked.

'Yes, it's at least of some benefit to the community. Speaking of community benefit, I'm going to be part of something really big soon.'

Her heart sank.

'It's best I don't say anymore but in case we don't see each other again, I want you to know that I love you,' he said, looking into her teary eyes.

'Oh, Billy, please don't do anything stupid,' she pleaded.

A tense silence followed. Sonya snuggled into his warm body and he put an arm around her shoulders. She closed her eyes and a single tear escaped down her flushed cheek.

* * *

Early setbacks only served to inspire The Union. Widespread destruction lit the flame of encouragement and created a firestorm of followers. The Union was surprised by the number of men who came out of the shadows in support of them. The arduous infiltration of the Ministry of Love and secondment of several of its employees significantly improved their chances of success. Determination flourished and methods grew in sophistication and effectiveness. With additional recruits, weapons, and targeted terrorism entering the fray, the scale of espionage strengthened and their networks began filtering throughout society.

'It's going better than we planned,' Billy said to Ethan, Cody and Jett, part of the Union hierarchy who were still able to meet at Adam's place, a now hazardous journey even under the cover of darkness. 'Those last two suicide bombs were a huge blow to the Ministry of Plenty.'

'And thousands of telescreens are being smashed every day by our masked rebels,' Adam said. 'As soon as Ministry of Love crews arrive to replace them, we smash them again!'

'Better still, we know they'll come, so we ambush them and let them choose to join us or die. Either way we get their weapons,' Cody said.

The insurgents were succeeding purely on the strength of numbers, and as they fell, just like a morphing Hydra they were replaced by even more. Small, localised battles and attacks on the government were isolated in their occurrence but tendrils of the same lethal root.

'So, is everything set for our next raid?' Ethan asked.

'Yes, we strike tomorrow morning,' Billy said. 'Cody and I are meeting up with the advance crew and with Darius alongside us, we should be okay.'

Darius was Adam's cousin, Party defector and member of the executive security team at the Ministry of Love.

'Here's to the destruction of the Inner Party Chancellery!' Adam said as they clinked glasses and raised a toast to bravery and good fortune.

Before the first rays of light cracked through the misty dawn, Billy and Cody had met up with the rest of the squad in the city. Darius entered the building using his unrestricted access whilst the others took up their positions. Billy was on level three in the Ministry of Health building just up the street from the Chancellery, Cody was in the small curio shop three doors along on the opposite side and the two other men were in a garbage collection shuttle in the street.

They all took cover when they saw Darius exit the building and rapidly flee southward. Billy checked his watch and followed the second hand tick its way towards the twelve. At exactly 9.30 a.m., an instantaneous orchestra of broken brick, splintering timber, cracking concrete, shattering glass and screaming people pierced the serenity of a fine Wednesday morning. The atmosphere was strewn with dust and debris and a siren started wailing. Angry flames and thick acrid smoke billowed through the ruptured orifices of the building.

Through the wreckage and ash, the surviving security guards and Inner Party members poured through the front door like fire-ants from a disturbed nest. They were easy pickings for the snipers. Cody took out the Director of Munitions and the Vice Director of the Ministry of Love before the Divisional Superintendent of the Ministry of Truth was felled by a shot from Billy. As Cody made his escape, Billy wasn't far behind but first, he helped the garbage truck men bundle two Inner Party hostages into the vehicle during the mayhem. Their operation was but one of many that marked a strategic escalation in the anarchy.

The co-ordinated widespread bombardment, chaos and disruption, coupled with the breach of government security, reverberated throughout society. The oligarchy had always maintained some distance from the unwashed masses by relying on the Outer Party but now this barrier, their protective cushion, was being eroded. Of course, the Inner Party who controlled the three State governments had arranged for two of them to be at war with each other at any one time in a continuous rotation for over a hundred years. But those conflicts were orchestrated by the Party for its own purposes. The revolution was different. Immense pressure was building within the Inner Party and creating extraordinary vulnerability and stress.

The foundations of civilisation were shaking, and the establishment was beginning to crumble. The revolutionaries had evolved. No longer a small group of disenfranchised individuals, they were now an organised network of resistance with resources that threatened the world's ruling elite. What was previously considered impossible was now happening – an unprecedented mass mutiny that jeopardised the Inner Party's control.

V

An emergency conclave of the Inner Party security council was being held in the war room deep in the bowels of the Ministry of Love. The elitist group sat solemnly in plush black leather chairs around the large, oval and highly polished ebony boardroom table, whispering amongst each other before the meeting started. The room was softly lit although a bright spot of light was directed at a gold-framed picture of Big Brother hanging on the wall at the far end of the room. Two young skinny waiters took drink orders and refreshed glasses as needed before being asked to leave. The chairman used his tobacco pipe to gently tap the table to signal the commencement of business.

'We're in trouble. All the traditional methods of restoring peace are failing us,' he said as the room broke into pockets of muttering. He continued to speak over them, 'The situation calls for drastic action. We cannot let this continue.'

'Should we nuke them?' came a voice from the other end of the table.

'Our nuclear arsenals are not an appropriate response to an insurgent populace. They aren't specifically targeted and create undesirable collateral damage and lingering toxicity,' the chairman replied.

'I agree. We have to be smart about this,' another suggested.

'Exactly,' the chairman responded. 'And that is why I have been speaking with the Inner Party's elite Advanced Curative Institute within the Ministry of Peace.' This was a secretive medical care facility for the exclusive benefit of Party members. 'They have biological agents which are expeditious and efficient and all round much more suitable.'

The chairman took hold of the toothpick resting in his Martini, placed the skewered olive it held into his mouth and munched on it before taking a sip.

'Has anyone heard of Banshee?'

Although alert and attentive his audience was deathly silent.

'No? Well, Banshee, put simply, is a biological weapon, named after the female spirit, whose wailing heralds the death of a family member. A fast and efficient virus that can be released into targeted populations to be absorbed by direct exposure or spread through contact with an infected victim. It attacks the central nervous system and multiple vital organs and bodily functions. Breathing is affected, immune responses become overwhelmed and neurological damage occurs simultaneously causing death within hours,' he announced.

He took off his spectacles, breathed on them and used the corner of his coat to polish the lenses. 'But there is another trait of Banshee that differentiates it from the rest. It is also clever. Although targeted mortality was one hundred per cent, it requires activation to become infectious and lethal. The agent causes death only after combining with the level of testosterone present in a mature male. It only kills grown men and only they can spread it.'

The meeting broke into several hushed conversations around the table.

The chairman went on to explain that women and children who contracted Banshee were unharmed, asymptomatic, and not infectious. Although old men were less affected, it was still enough to kill them. This characteristic of Banshee had been developed specifically to hit at the heart of an insurrection by targeting male aggression. Men were the main ringleaders, creating conflict and anger, generating belligerent violence and responsible for most of the combat. If the hostile male population could be removed, the devastated women and children left behind would unequivocally surrender themselves. After that, the areas would be repopulated with men dedicated to the Party and the restoration of peace and harmony.

****

Within days, the managers at the Ministry of Health had been briefed on the imminent deployment of Banshee and Sonya gave Billy the signal that she wanted to walk with him during their lunchtime break.

'I guess you've seen the huge increase in injured patients in the Ministry this week?' he asked as they walked around the block.

'Not to mention the casualties and Area 15 cases,' she replied.

'Have you seen the Telescreen news bulletins?'

'You mean the ones telling us of the small neighbourhood disturbances that are being successfully subdued?'

He nodded. 'Fake news. Just goes to show you that you can't trust anything they say. The Union is growing stronger every day.'

'Billy, one thing I do believe is that they have a new weapon and it's bad. Real bad. They told us about it yesterday afternoon at a departmental manager's meeting.'

He looked into her grave eyes. 'What is it?'

'It's a virus that kills men and only men. They are going to lockdown areas and release it into them to wipe out the rebels.'

'How effective did they say it is?'

'They were quite specific. It has a one hundred per cent mortality rate. Billy, you must get out of your place, now. Please, I'm begging you. Your area isn't safe anymore.'

'Where then?'

'Well, you can't go to my apartment – there's too many eyes. Go to my father's house. I've told him to expect you.'

Billy had to wait until his shift finished at six o'clock before it would be safe for him to leave the Ministry. By then it was too late to warn any of his friends from The Union. As he rushed towards his precinct, the border security closures were already being installed. Fortified walls of concrete and wire were being erected. There was no way he could get through even if it would do any good. It validated everything Sonya had told him.

The thought of running away and hiding repulsed him and he glared at the troopers as they strengthened the pillars, panels and fencing. Extreme measures were being taken to quarantine the inhabitants of the targeted release zones. This is where the virus would do its work. Sonya's warning and insistence were the only reasons he turned and headed for the sanctuary of her father's home on the western outskirts of the city. He needed to hurry. Without proper address identification, he would have to get there before the seven o'clock curfew.

With his overcoat collar stretched up around his neck and his cap pulled down to his eyes, Billy approached Brien's house with minutes to spare. It was a modest bungalow, tucked into a street of similarly designed dwellings. From the scattered flecks of peeling paint on the timber cladding, it appeared the home had at one time been emerald green with a crisp white trim. The windows were clouded with dirt and a few loose shingles dangled precariously over the porch. Billy scampered across the neat, cobbled path that dissected the front yard strewn with piles of discarded old broken furniture, bric-a-brac and junk. He tapped twice lightly on the heavy brown wooden door. It creaked open slightly and a hunched middle-aged man with greying temples and dark squinting eyes peered through. A chain jingled as the bolt was unlocked.

'You must be Billy. Hurry, inside with you,' Brien whispered.

Billy followed him into a small reception room and sat in the chair that Brien offered him. On a piece of paper, Brien gingerly scrawled a note and passed it to Billy.

'These old places only have one Telescreen. It's in the main living area at the back. In here you're okay, but don't talk too loudly. They may still hear you.'

VI

The deafening rumble of malicious drones across the sky reverberated to the ground and rattled Sonya's apartment building like a seismic aftershock. She held the kitchen bench while it passed. The Telescreen was echoing the sounds and showing the vision of warheads being dropped into the locked-down areas, the epicentres of the rebellion, unloading Banshee on the unsuspecting enemies of the State. She turned her head to divert her eyes but the voice on the Telescreen boomed triumphantly, *'Once delivered, the virus spreads effortlessly from man to man, silently and subtly seeping through the population, saturating the area and slaying the Big Brother hating traitors. There is no escape for them! All quarantined areas will remain closed until further notice!'*

Now the Telescreen was showing visions of disorientated, weak men unable to stand, dying within minutes of becoming idle. It was horrific, but the Party wanted everyone to see it. Their power, their victory; fear and order being restored.

Many men fell in the streets, others at home watched by helpless women. The entire locked-down areas became littered with rotting corpses that were piled outside awaiting collection. The sight of death became commonplace, horribly decomposed bodies providing a visually disturbing display of providence. The air was soaked with the unbearable and inescapable stench of decay. The dead could only be handled by women as men would die if they went near them, and every second or third night, special teams combed the thoroughfares gathering them up for transportation to Area 15.

The flame of resistance had been doused with Banshee and the conspirators consigned to history. Any hope of further fighting was futile, no effort was possible against a biological weapon of such devastating effectiveness. Within a short time, the dissidents were crushed and acknowledging absolute defeat. The revolt was over and as expected there were shocked and distressed people everywhere, like empty jars on a shelf, still with form but nothing left inside, crying out for salvation. The rats and fleas had fallen back into their place.

VII

Every Telescreen repeatedly blasted exhilarating announcements declaring Big Brother's complete success and proclaiming momentous celebrations. From the information being drilled into her, Sonya gathered she could at least expect to receive some extra rations, gain temporary access to various scarce culinary delicacies and that Billy was safe. It was hard to believe that everyone would also have a day of public vacation, something that had never happened.

She started to lose interest when the monotone voice began its spiel about rebuilding programs and the expansion of all government Ministries. The Ministry of Peace was particularly satisfied with the outcome. They confirmed a new war with one of the States, with complementary reports of monumental battles and euphoric victories. The perception of calm and routine had been restored and people felt reprieved as comforting contentment settled over them like a warm blanket on a winter's night. It was a relief to walk out the front door and be on her way to work because it meant leaving the Telescreen behind.

'Comrade Smith, could you please have a look at this?' Charles said as his wild bushy eyebrows twitched spasmodically. His trembling hand passed her the assessment file of a man who was currently waiting back at his workstation.

'What is it, Comrade?' Sonya glanced down at the file. She shook her head slowly from side to side. 'No. Really, that can't be right, can it?' She felt confused as she double-checked the results that didn't make sense. 'This man has Banshee?' She paused to think. 'But he is from NorThumbria.'

'That's right, outside the Thumbria quarantine zone! And guess what? There are at least three dozen more in the waiting area just like him but from all over Oceania. All of the men in the Ministry are exposed!' Charles said, looking startled and wide-eyed.

Sonya stared at his tense face in silence as her mind processed the information and realised its significance.

'Oh no, but how?' His eyes were already blood-streaked. 'Stay here, Comrade,' Sonya said as she hurried to the waiting area to see for herself.

She encountered the crowd of coughing men just as he had said, many with inflated pustules, some vomiting horribly smelling green bile, and all appearing dazed. When Sonya approached the less-affected patients, the swollen red veins in their eyes were obvious. Wandering around the room between the men in stunned bewilderment, she took more samples from a selection of them displaying a variety of symptoms and noted their details, particularly where they lived. She personally rushed the samples to the Tests Department to be analysed. Although it was good practice and made sense to recheck such surprising results, after what she had seen in the waiting room, there was no doubt in her mind what to expect.

The confirmation came as Sonya stood waiting for the outcome of the testing she ordered immediately. The analyst was unaccustomed to such behaviour but sensing Sonya's anxiety he rushed to validate the samples were all cases of Banshee. She also asked him to run some tests on her. Snatching the findings, she scampered in search of her immediate superior the District Supervisor. She found him in conference with the Inner Party Director of Supplies.

'Excuse me, Comrades, I'm sorry but I have something extremely urgent to discuss with you,' Sonya said. She interjected confidently and without hesitation. The men stopped talking and turned to stare at her with furrowed brows. 'Please, this cannot wait,' she added.

The Director gave them his leave and waved them away as they dashed to the Supervisor's office where she conveyed her message.

'You are right, Comrade Smith; this is extremely serious. And you are sure? You've double-checked everything?' he asked.

'Yes, Comrade Peabody. Triple checked. Quite sure,' Sonya replied.

The District Supervisor looked her in the eye and addressed her in a worried and urgent tone, 'Does anyone else know about this?'

This was the first time she had witnessed any emotion within him. Now Sonya was no longer guessing that there was a problem; she was certain. 'Only Comrade Nixon. Charles raised his suspicions with me,' she replied.

'Alright, keep it that way for now. I want you to prepare a report. Don't leave out anything and be ready to present it to a meeting this afternoon at fourteen-hundred hours,' he said.

Sonya nodded as they parted.

Sonya went back to her office to begin assembling her thoughts. She was certain this was going to be the single most significant event she would be involved in during her entire career at the Ministry. She couldn't help reflecting on how all this exposure to her superiors would benefit her position. But there was precious little time for such idle thinking. There were much more important matters to attend to.

Just then Charles appeared at her office door. He looked distressed and fatigued. 'Do you need any help?' he asked as Sonya noticed his shallow breathing.

'Thank you for asking, Comrade Nixon, but I think I can manage. Though please come in and take a seat for a moment,' Sonya said, offering him a chair. 'You must not tell anyone of your discovery for now. Not until I have prepared a full report and presented it to the Directors. Do you understand?' she said.

Charles nodded his head slightly.

'Are you feeling alright?' she asked.

'I'm afraid I'm a little nauseous and feeling faint,' Charles replied.

Sonya got up and went to him. She shook her head and sighed as she pulled open the front of his overalls to reveal a chest covered in pustules. 'I'm sorry, Charles.'

She called an assistant to put him on a gurney for conveying to the holding area before returning to her work.

Meanwhile, the District Supervisor had contacted the Managing Director of the Ministry of Health who convened an extraordinary meeting of all the heads of the Ministries. Sonya entered the stuffy room of men who were seated around a large boardroom table and noticed how many were coughing and taking comfort from sipping glasses of water.

As Sonya stood to address those gathered, she steadied her breathing and concentrated on speaking calmly. 'It is true that every effort was made to confine the deployment of Banshee within the designated locked-down enclaves. The Ministry of Peace saturated the areas and expected it to be transmitted from an infected man to another man. These were critical conditions for containment of the pathogen. However, we have proof that Banshee has mutated.'

She paused as her intently listening audience gasped in a collective 'What?'

'Banshee still only kills adult males but infected females are now also contagious and can pass on the virus with even a minimal exposure. Since the removal of the male victims and lifting of quarantines, women have been unknowingly spreading the disease. We have confirmed cases of it being contracted outside the application zones. We have no vaccine,' Sonya said as the meeting erupted into a collective of urgent husky whispers.

* * *

The wild and uncontrolled spread of Banshee was never supposed to happen. The Party that run the governments of the three super States had just managed to navigate the uncharted terrain of popular revolt. Now there was a devastating malady disseminating rapidly and killing men everywhere. Travelling Inner Party members had unknowingly infected other States. All the celebratory plans were abandoned, and rebuilding programs were thrown into disarray. Panic spread across the world as an antidote was desperately searched for.

Each government was hopelessly caught up in the swirling tornado of paranoia that traversed the globe, stumbling, and crumbling as days passed, searching for solutions that never came and searching for someone on whom to cast the blame. Within a short time, the Inner Party had lost control as each State government began suspecting one another of creating the unfolding disaster. Instead of working together as they had always done previously, each accused another of developing the mutation to render the other States vulnerable, take advantage of the global uprising and assume world domination. Trust disintegrated as tensions escalated. The situation became dismal and in the year 2040, the three desperate States took the unprecedented step of independently and simultaneously declaring war on each other.

VIII

After contracting Banshee and waiting two weeks since testing negative to the virus, Sonya sat with Billy drinking coffee at her father's house.

'Now that the quarantined areas are open, I need to go back to my place,' he said.

'It's safer for you here. Banshee is still running rampant there,' she said. She was clutching the mug with both hands. The coffee was hot and strong just how she liked it and the steam from the cup wafted in front of her face as she spoke. 'You have to keep away from everyone until we find out more about how to deal with this damn virus.'

'I'll be careful, Sonya. I need to go back to my apartment – my supplies are there, my identity papers, my life,' Billy said. He shuffled in his chair and looked over at Brien who came in and joined them gently placing a dainty plate of broken biscuits on his rickety old table.

'But Billy …'

'I hear what you're saying but I can't just sit here doing nothing. I've been hiding for weeks, waiting for a cure, an easy way out that may never come. I can't even work at the Ministry of Health because it's too dangerous. War is raging, real war between all three of the States this time, and if the Union can survive and infiltrate the military ranks, we can continue our fight for freedom. This is our best chance ever. I have to go,' he insisted.

Brien crunched on a piece of biscuit, letting the crumbs fall from his mouth onto the floor. He looked down at them for a moment and then took a sip from his cup.

So that was the reason he was so anxious to go back to his apartment. He wants to enlist, she thought. She knew once Billy had made up his mind it was hopeless to try and persuade him to do otherwise.

***

Later in the evening as the setting sun cast a pink streaky scum across the skyline, Billy set out towards his apartment block. Sporadic gunfire and explosions echoed through the streets. He crept from shadow to shadow, avoiding the skirmishes. Up ahead a battalion of Oceanic soldiers were defending a main road from an onslaught of invaders with rapid machine gun action. A grenade was tossed forward that erupted in a deafening boom and a cascade of scattered debris and dust. Although there had always been wars, they had been fought on faraway frontiers. Residents had never experienced such intense and bloody confrontations on their doorsteps.

The sky had darkened into a misty purple twilight as he entered his neighbourhood. Gunfire peppered the night air, and the streetlights that still worked came on. Down the road, a patrol was standing between him and his apartment building. A soldier caught sight of him and yelled at him to approach. He slowly walked towards them with his hands raised as he counted at least six guns trained on him.

'What are you doing here?'

'I live here. I'm just getting back late from work,' Billy said.

'Prove it!' barked the Sergeant.

Billy handed over the only piece of evidence he had, his employee card that he used to scan on entry to the Ministry, hoping the soldier wouldn't twig that he currently wasn't allowed to work there.

The soldier looked at the card and studied him carefully. 'Okay, get inside.'

Billy stepped over the rubble that had accumulated at the building entry and found the elevator out of order. He'd have to climb the six sets of stairs. The apartment was how he had left it on the day the area was barricaded. He fell backwards on the bed and rested.

In the morning he took two bags from the closet and threw them on his bed. He cast aside the larger of the two and opened the smaller backpack. He filled it with clothes and tossed in a container of toiletries. He pulled open the desk drawer and took out his identity papers, checked over them, then put them in an envelope and slid it into one of the pockets. He was ready to go to the recruitment office and become a soldier.

The level of destruction and suffering was far more intense and threatening than that experienced during last year's attempted revolution. Already barely tolerable living conditions were being reduced to struggling squalor and minimalist survival. People were just clinging to life by the thinnest threads of hope. Thundering blasts shook the ground and tempted already decaying buildings with collapse. The sky at night was brightly lit with flares of technicolour hurtling behind powerful warheads that flew into cities exploding in waves of fire and ruin, belching mushrooming clouds of toxic gas. Skull-piercing screams and volleys of gunfire filled the otherwise silent voids between the relentless bombardment. Satellites fell from the sky as all support systems and digital communication and data networks were destroyed. The all-too-recent stench of decay had returned, coupled with the smell of fear, anxiety and terror. The air was so dense with dust, destruction and death, its taste lingered in the mouth and clogged the chest.

Although the raging war was devastating, it was only one part of the double-barrelled peril assaulting the world. Banshee soon infiltrated the ranks and the soldiers fell to the ground, unable to rise. There was no escaping the silent epidemic. Even the Inner Party members with privileged access to their surreptitious Advanced Curative Institute were not safe. After the futility of sending men into the conflict became all too apparent, plans for additional deployments were abandoned. This only further agitated the already desperate

State governments, and the situation became frenzied and spiralled into madness. Warfare became completely focused on the use of long-distance nuclear weapons capable of mass destruction. It was as if they had decided losing meant leaving nothing for anyone.

IX

Sonya wasn't ready to face another eighteen-hour workday and yet she had no choice. She trudged through the icy wind towards one of the last standing bastions of society where her employment beckoned. When closer, she could see the long snaking trail of bandaged, hobbling, groaning and generally distressed men, women and children waiting to enter. The line moved so slowly that those queuing only had to shuffle along a step or two as she continued striding past them. Her clean, pale grey overalls embossed with the Ministry of Health sash of a black stripe with a red cross provided her with an unobstructed passage to the entrance.

The Ministry staff had tried valiantly to prepare themselves but struggled to cope with the highest magnitude of excruciating physical trauma and radiation poisoning they had ever seen. Arriving inside, Sonya was greeted by chaos and elbowed her way through the hectic and overcrowded reception hall, unintentionally pressing against a man's twisted arm, causing him to scream. She could barely hear the duty clerk providing her morning report. Although Sonya wasn't meant to, she stayed to assist with the triage of the mounting influx of patients.

Banshee was still ruthless. It only took a few hours to debilitate a previously fully fit adult male. The men around her were coughing and had obvious respiratory difficulty. They stumbled with blurry vision, swollen bright red eyes and dark, burnt-pink blotches that appeared all over their body. Later these blotches would morph into pustules that were soft and squishy but painless to touch. Once they ballooned to the size of a small bird's egg, they would burst and ooze a gelatinous, foul-smelling, yellow secretion. The final stages of the disease brought fatigue and delirium.

Sonya took control of the area, marshalling staff and yelling instructions over the cacophony of voices, clattering gurneys and moaning victims. 'Ignore patient identification and processing! Assess all patients here and get them into the Banshee Holding Section as soon as possible.'

This section was a newly created area where patients were doped with Deliciyum and stacked side by side on gurneys. There was nothing more to offer than illusionary comfort. Like an open vein, the Banshee victims flooded the Transportation Department and spilled into shuttles destined for Area 15, never to return.

'Do you hear that?' said a co-worker wheeling a gurney.

'Hear what, Comrade?' Sonya asked.

'That. That silence.' They both listened. Everyone in the Ministry's foyer could hear it now. The blasts had stopped. They rushed to the windows and looked outside. Dazed women were leaving their hiding spots and starting to wander the streets like bewildered zombies.

'The war is likely coming to an end,' she told them. 'There's probably still some women in the army but I fear we are running out of men able to fight.'

Many nodded as they knew she was right.

Within months there would be no men left alive. Anywhere.

Sonya plonked herself down on one of the long cool metal benches in the reception area and leaned back with her hands resting on top of her weary head as she stared through the window at the jittery rekindling of activity in the street. The meandering river of victims queuing out front had begun to dry up and now just an intermittent trickle of injury cases and men with Banshee arrived. Sonya's attention was drawn to a young soldier in uniform, pushing his way through the front entry doors and staggering inside. It was Billy.

'Hello, Sonya.' He coughed as she approached and she put her arm around his shoulders. 'It's not good.'

'Dear God! Billy, what happened?' Sonya gasped.

He didn't speak but she could see he was nursing a crudely bandaged arm, bloody cuts to his face and torn clothing exposing angry purple bruises as she guided him into the core of the building. The arm didn't look too bad. She was much more concerned about the ravaging menace of Banshee. Her gaze focused on the whites of his eyes, which were crossed with red lightning. He had difficulty drawing breath. They looked at each other and both silently understood it was hopeless. He blinked, trying to focus through his blurry eyes.

'What happened?'

He answered her through the rapid onset of hazy disorientation and dizziness. She laid him on a gurney and tried to make him as comfortable as possible. Tears spilled down her face as she nursed him through the last moments of his life.

During 2041 the world was becalmed. This ceasefire was different to those before. There were no announcements or broadcasts, no celebrations or rejoicing, just eerie silence. The quiet and stillness felt queer, after the continual barrage that pounded like a relentless throbbing headache. No more soldiers stomping, no more screaming or crying, no birds twittering overhead; nothing apart from an occasional breeze rustling through dried leaves and a dead branch snapping with a crack and falling to the ground with a thud.

As Sonya prepared for the day ahead, she could easily have started humming to herself, blissfully unaware of the dire predicament being confronted. At least the weather was fine with a pure blue cloudless sky that invited you to swim in it, and not a wisp of wind. Stepping out into such a beautiful summer's day, how could anything be wrong? The feelings conjured this morning belied what had happened and ignored the future.

With no functioning government, it became necessary for women with leadership aspirations to step forward urgently and form a crisis executive assembly called the Sisterhood. It was comprised of thirty members, ten from each of the defunct Super States. Although none were accustomed to governing, they all held supervisory roles within the now-defunct Outer Party. Being one of the more senior and ambitious employees of the Ministry of Health, Sonya had assumed the mantle of Managing Director and was immediately accepted as a member of the Sisterhood when she volunteered her services. Sonya was about to participate in the Sisterhood's first convention.

They met in one of the few remaining buildings with mild damage that previously accommodated part of the Ministry of Transport but had been repurposed into the Sisterhood's new headquarters.

'Hello, comrades,' Sonya said, trying to smile at everyone as she entered the room.

The polished tinted glass windows of the grand executive suite taking up the top floor had great views over the crumbling landscape for miles around. Those present waited for the last of the group to arrive and take their places. Sitting at the head of the opulent parquet table, Charlotte, the elected Chairwoman, opened the meeting. She was tall and pencil-thin and wore her light auburn hair in a tightly cropped style that complimented her hazel eyes and pale, slightly freckled complexion. She was also the daughter of the late Inner Party's District Governor and had recently lost her partner who took her own life at the age of 30, leaving Charlotte with many unanswered questions.

'Welcome, my friends, and thank you for your attendance.'

The delegates acknowledged her greeting with a nod.

'Our challenges are mammoth. This is no exaggeration. We have been left with an unrecognisable civilisation. The Great War of 2040 has left us with no adult males. Actually, let's not call it great anymore. Let our first resolution be to rename it the Insane War of 2040.'

They all agreed.

'Our earth has also been severely damaged. There is potent global soil contamination that has almost obliterated our already scarce vegetation.' She scanned the faces in the room and all were gripped by her words.

Although peaceful, after the air had cleared, the world was left desolate and largely infertile, its surface covered in large areas of barren grey dirt and divested of a lot of its previously fragmented nature. All infrastructure suffered extensive destruction, most houses and buildings withered like crumpled skeletons stripped of flesh, and plants were clothed in wrinkly brown leaves. Once great cities had been pummelled into small towns.

One of the younger members, called Jacinta, spoke next, 'We do have access to the emergency seed stores in the frozen underground vaults of old EurAsia. They won't be needing them, having been annihilated along with Eastasia. But we will have to be careful where and how they are used.'

'What of livestock?' asked a middle-aged woman with flowing grey curls.

The animal kingdom, long since dethroned, now consists only of cows, pigs, hens and a few species of fish.

'Domestic herds have been decimated and will take years to recover, and the oceans are awash with pollution and poison. All water must be boiled before drinking,' Jacinta replied.

'What's the status of the Food Manufacturing Facilities?' Sonya asked.

Jan told the meeting that for many years, a vast amount of food for human consumption was based neither on plants nor animals, but rather on unicellular life. A yellowish froth, a churning primordial soup of bubbling bacteria, taken from the soil. Then multiplied in a laboratory using hydrogen extracted from water electrolysed by solar power, as its energy source. When the froth's siphoned through a web of pipes and sprayed onto heated rollers it turned into a rich golden flour. In its raw state it could be used as the basis for a variety of edible products. The bacteria were also modified at the molecular level to create the specific proteins needed for manufactured substitutes of such things as meat, milk, eggs, even lauric acid or palm oil, and the long-chain omega-3 fatty acids found in fish. The carbohydrates that remain after the proteins and fats have been extracted were also usable.

'Well, they mostly don't exist anymore or if they still do are badly damaged, I'm afraid to say,' Jacinta said.

'I am sure you will agree, sisters. This is painting a dire predicament. Our most urgent priority is the food supply. We need to secure and nurture what we have left and develop ways and means of maximising future yields if we're to avoid famine. Following this is the need to control population growth. We must limit the number of mouths to feed. Fortunately, this won't be a problem for at least twelve months as it will take that long for the older boys to reach adolescence,' Charlotte said.

The Sisterhood focused on what could be implemented straight away. Strict rationing was applied to the small supply of agricultural product available to slow down its consumption. The meeting agreed that intense soil analysis and crop propagation be undertaken urgently. Seeds would be rapidly tested. All current measures were designed to provide more time but consideration also needed to be given to how and when to replace and rebuild the manufactured food facilities. Before adjourning the meeting, the women resolved to reconvene in a few days to give themselves time to consider their options and come up with some possible longer-term solutions.

XI

Although struggling to keep dry from the rain blowing in under her flailing umbrella, Sonya was grateful. Rain was needed. It was cleansing and the world needed a wash, and besides, she would be at work in a few minutes anyway. The Ministry kept her busy. It was a distraction but being at the frontline of unfolding tragedy was also confronting and a constant reminder of the weighty burden of Sisterhood business. Sonya had hardly left her office in the past few days, buried in fat reports that were piled upon her desk and wrestling to study them as they screamed of society's continual degradation. Starvation was rampant. Walking skeletons were filling the streets and she had never seen such a plague of emaciated living dead in the Assessing Department. Conflict was beginning to raise its ugly head yet again as primitive survival instincts provoked fighting over food.

Exhausted after many hours at work, Sonya was relieved to enter her little apartment, kick off her shoes and put the kettle on to boil some water as she still had some coffee. She instinctively looked at the Telescreen before realising that it was always black and silent now. No one was watching anymore. Her little finch, Hope, was twittering excitedly in anticipation of being let out of his cage for a fly around the room as was customary at this time of the evening. She lifted the door and freed him. He flew to the bedroom, landed on the windowsill and paused, confused by the fresh air flowing through his feathers. By the time she had remembered the open window, he was gone. As the bird flit away, Sonya prayed that, somehow, Hope would survive.

The next morning Sonya got out of bed and stared out the window, searching for Hope for far too long. She had to hurry or else she would be late for today's meeting of the Sisterhood. After some updates on stock levels and supplies of basic food produce the agenda promptly turned to finding answers.

'We don't have many options but plenty of obstacles to overcome. Choices and time are running out, sisters, and it's causing widespread despair and suffering,' Charlotte said.

A few members of the Sisterhood were keen on the idea of creating specially designed facilities for the purpose of shoring up the food supply. It was Susan who coined the phrase 'Production Farms' and the name stuck. The idea was to locate these farms in pockets of land where soil testing had shown minimal contamination with the highest levels of potential productiveness and start intensively cultivating them.

New manufactured food facilities would also be included within the farms to replace the destroyed ones. The hydrogen pathway used in cultivating bacteria into human sustenance was developed over many years and is a well-established process being ten times more efficient than photosynthesis. Also, whilst only parts of plants are consumed, bacteria flour is entirely eaten, which increased productive efficiency many times. And because it's brewed in giant vats, the land efficiency is twenty thousand times greater. All farming except for fruit and vegetables is done by ferming: brewing microbes through precision fermentation and multiplying certain micro-organisms to produce particular proteins and would need to be restarted as soon as possible.

'You know, we've also got to consider that Banshee could still be around and will kill the boys as they mature,' Susan added.

'The Production Farm concept could have a number of benefits,' Charlotte said as she rubbed her chin with her hand musing over the possibilities. She had a way of drawing in her taut cheeks and pursing her lips when she stopped to think, which accentuated her gaunt face. 'If we enclose the farms, it will prevent desperate attacks and produce being stolen, and if we include self-contained facilities, all the boys could be relocated to live inside them. They would be quarantined from Banshee as they grow older and then they could work the farms and focus on food production.'

'We will have to get the crops underway first and build around them, and we'll still need women working the farms for a little while until the boys can take over,' Jacinta added.

'Yes, Jacinta, but the boys are still young enough to stay unaffected by Banshee,' Sonya said.

'For now, or so we think,' Charlotte said. 'Some of the older ones could be at risk quite soon.'

'It would be cruel and unjust to lock all the boys away if they are immune. They could live in the community at least until they turn, say, twelve years old,' Sonya said.

The other women around the table were all nodding their heads and mumbling.

'Do you really think that's a good idea, Sonya? Wouldn't it be unfair, not to mention extremely difficult, to continuously round up all boys in the community as they turned twelve years old and send them into the farms after they've experienced over a decade of normal life? It would cause never-ending distress to mothers and sons as the dreaded separation first approached and then arrived. Wouldn't it be better if they were completely raised in the farms?' Charlotte said.

The women had become stony-faced and silent.

'We could introduce the boys to agriculture and manufactured food processing as part of their education so that they would be ready to carry out this vital work as soon as they matured and could relieve women from the burden,' Charlotte added.

'Banshee could also mutate and start to affect the younger boys,' Jacinta said.

'That's unlikely,' Sonya said.

'It's mutated before.' Charlotte dipped her head whilst raising her brow.

The concept of marshalling and corralling males into safe inescapable compounds called Production Farms was discussed at length. It carried numerous other advantages that the Sisterhood also considered important.

As well as addressing the priority of safeguarding and maximising crop production and keeping the boys sheltered whilst they grew into a ready-made full-time workforce, the farms would provide the means to limit population growth. By having males separated from society, a population boom could be avoided reducing pressure on the already strained food supply.

Another member also raised the topic of male aggression and arrogance in leadership roles being responsible for a history of wars and conflict. It was noted that the previously powerful Inner Party was controlled by men and governed by a patriarchal constitution.

'They had not only been at war for at least a hundred years but had thrown the world into chaos,' Jacinta mentioned.

'I find it hard to believe they could have been so incredibly stupid and selfish to not only use biological weapons which were extremely dangerous and not thoroughly tested but to do so without understanding or contemplating the probable outcomes was foolish. To launch attacks on each other without enough concern for the ultimate consequences was utterly irresponsible,' Charlotte said.

The Sisterhood reached the consensus that ultimately the Insane War was proof that men could not be trusted.

'It could be that the Production Farm concept is a convenient and feasible method of achieving our long-term goals and allow us to plan a society of our choice,' Charlotte said.

Flushed with a cold sweat, Sonya could barely believe what she was hearing.

'This is a crazy idea!' she said. 'They will be prisoners, working as slaves. What about human freedom? What about their civil rights?'

Sonya was standing gesticulating with her hands and flapping her arms in frustration.

'Order! Order!' Charlotte commanded, rising from her chair.

'How can we even consider this?' Sonya added.

A couple of other women were shuffling in their seats and muttering their support.

'Please, Sonya. Everyone! We have to think clearly without emotion.'

'We are in dire unprecedented times. We have very few choices and have to move quickly,' another member contributed.

'We have to at least seriously consider this,' Charlotte added.

Sonya drooped, shaking her head, and sat back down, dejected.

'How could we get them all into the Production Farms?' another asked.

'I don't think it will be difficult. Women are still scarred by the catastrophic effects of war, famine and Banshee, and will be relieved that we have an answer for them,' Susan said.

'That would be the case I'm sure,' Charlotte said. 'Quarantining for safety, concentrating on food production and avoiding a population explosion are surely persuasive arguments. Besides, if we make it policy, they will have no choice but to comply.'

'Yes, but when our situation is brought under control and if we find Banshee has been eradicated, would we release them?' Sonya asked.

'Let's just take it one step at a time and not get ahead of ourselves,' Charlotte replied.

Sonya pursed her lips and frowned.

'Keeping men in the Production Farms as a form of mandatory birth control on society is one thing but what about procreation?' Sonya pleaded. 'There will come a time when we do need more children.'

Mild-mannered, Ministry of Science ex-employee, Monica cleared her throat then said, 'We can rely on artificially assisted reproduction and sex selection. The old Inner Party's Advanced Curative Institute had perfected these methods to control the balance of males and females for decades. It's one of the only areas of medical intervention that they actively encouraged, on a need-to-know-only basis of course. When the Sisterhood considers it appropriate, women could elect to have a female embryo implanted. Male babies can be produced inside the farms.'

Sonya was beyond flabbergasted. She looked around the table and most of the women were deep in silent thought, processing all that had been said.

'We certainly have a lot to consider. Let's take a lunch break,' Charlotte suggested.

All the women had a good understanding of what was being proposed and why. It had been an intense morning and there was much to mull over. There were so many profound decisions to be made, rendered more stressful by urgency and the lack of alternatives. The meeting adjourned for the members to consider the information over a luncheon of roast pork and greens with berry glaze crackling, accompanied by bottles of 2022 Domaine de la Romanee Conti Burgundy. The Sisterhood still had some perks.

About an hour later, the conference resumed and after considerable conversation and debate, several momentous decisions were made, much to the chagrin of Sonya and a few of her vetoed allies.

Charlotte closed the historic meeting by summarising the conclusions drawn by a vote of the majority. 'We hereby agree that our highest priorities are the protection of our boys from Banshee, a guaranteed food supply and control of population growth. We also believe in removing the possibility of future male aggression that has led us to the point of near human extinction.'

'Hear! Hear!' the Sisterhood chorused.

Sonya wondered just how much they were motivated by revenge.

Charlotte paused dramatically to acknowledge the affirmation before proceeding. 'By necessity then, and I emphasise that with little choice, we have decreed that for the foreseeable future society needs to remain wholly comprised of adult females and their daughters. Unconfined reproduction will be by artificially assisted female embryo implantation when we deem it permissible, based on the availability of sustenance. All boys will be moved into Production Farms as soon as they are constructed and all male births will take place in the farms.'

In a forlorn, almost inaudible mutter, Sonya whispered to herself, 'This isn't the world that Billy fought and died for.'

As Charlotte slowly sat down, she wobbled slightly as if buckling under the weight on her shoulders whilst contemplating the enormity of what she had just announced. A hush engulfed the room for several minutes. A landmark resolution had been made to effectively remove males from society and from participation in the reproduction of humans. They would spend their whole lives in farms, devoted entirely to making food.

Susan finally interrupted the solemn silence and said, 'It may not be forever. The situation could always be reviewed someday.'

Although it was a thoughtful sentiment and offered a glimmer of hope to those few that were horrified by the repercussions of their collective decisions, Sonya held doubts that such overarching arrangements would ever be unwound by these women.

'Yes, quite true,' Charlotte concluded. 'But for now, they will be strictly managed for the well-being of everyone. Good afternoon, sisters, stay safe until we convene next week,' she said as the gathering broke up.

As Sonya dashed home, she initially began to regret not resigning from the Sisterhood as soon as their immoral vote was cast. But no, as a member she would at least be involved in their future decisions and try to influence their direction in a way she felt was right. And besides, it was important not to give up hope. Piles of dead leaves crackled and crunched under her feet. A gust of wind lifted a handful of them and they swirled around and around in front of her. Sonya stopped and watched as the mini tornado of dancing foliage playfully imitated life before falling back to the ground. Childhood memories drifted in and out of her mind. As a small girl on her way to school with her mother, she would often shuffle her way through autumn's crispy cast-offs. She could only recall parts of her youth. Not much at all, just moments in time. Sometimes dramatic, sometimes mundane, but never forgotten.

Continuing to walk in the dimming nightfall and whistling breeze, she thought of something her grandfather, Winston, often said when she was a small child. It was a reoccurring memory, lodged in her wandering mind. A simple phrase:

'Blessed are the meek, for they shall inherit the earth.'

She couldn't really remember in what circumstances she had heard him say this, only that at some point, he did. Neither had she ever understood the significance of his observation. However, during the height of the revolution, it struck her that her grandfather might have been referring to the Proles. That context being relevant to his lifetime. But now Sonya realised that his wisdom had reached further than he could have possibly comprehended. The power struggle, a race that ran throughout centuries of human history, had finally crossed the line. The patriarchy had been brushed aside, like a crumb feebly clinging to a lip, replaced comprehensively by matriarchy but at what cost?

XII

'FOOD FOR ALL!' the billboards shouted across the towns. Electric shuttles cruised the cleared streets, flyers flooded every corner and door-to-door announcements from the Sisterhood broadcast that the construction of food Production Farms was about to commence. It promised salvation, a flicker of faith in the future amongst plummeting supplies of meat, crops and grain. Sites across the State were selected according to the quality of their soil and where vast acreages could accommodate dormitories and factories in addition to the arable farmland. They got the cultivation underway immediately and huge armies of women participated in the building works and within a year they began operating.

Courtney, a short and rotund woman of about fifty years of age, dressed in khaki overalls, came out from her office to greet the shuttle carrying the Sisterhood. Her dark hair streaked with grey was tied in a tight bun and her wide grin left no doubt that she was exceedingly proud to be the supervisor demonstrating one of the first of the newly minted facilities today. As they disembarked, the women gaped in awe at the fortress-like complex enclosed by high concrete walls and impenetrable gates, and Charlotte was particularly impressed with the robust twin portcullis's guarding the secure entrance. Lofty sentinel towers were placed strategically around the lengthy perimeter. Sonya wondered how the other women could not notice the resemblance to prisons of old as they proceeded through the cold, stony archway. As it happened, many surviving prisons had been repurposed into new facilities.

'Welcome, sisters. As you will see, beyond the administration office we are entering, which is used for management and information storage, each of our farms is split into two main compounds by internal fences and controlled gateways. One contains our childhood facilities and the other houses the mature wing. A separate but connected complex contains the farm and all the agricultural processing and handling services,' Courtney said as she led the way.

The childhood compound comprised of three sections called the Birth, Nursery and Basic Education departments.

'It's rather simple,' she continued. 'The Birth Department was where male babies are born.'

'A clinic?' asked Monica.

'Yes, if you like, and a laboratory. It's responsible for the creation of the embryos and for the delivery and care of infant males. Women will be employed as surrogates or "Birthers" for our male embryos. We should be ready to start up within six months,' Courtney said, pointing a fat stubby finger at the glass porthole in the door. Through it, they could see the isolated workshop where the male embryos would be developed. Further along, they walked down a corridor that serviced several birthing suites on both sides and the post-natal maternity wards.

'Now we'll go to the Nursery Department,' Courtney said.

Once weaned, male babies would need to be removed from the care of the Birther who would then be free to receive further embryo implantation as required. The infants would be placed in the Nursery Department to be raised by full-time nursing staff until the age of five. These brown brick buildings were merely large grids of sleeping dormitories and classrooms.

'A preschool,' Charlotte said.

'Yes, and after that they transfer into the Basic Education Department, or boarding school, where they will stay until around age seventeen. During this time, they receive education in reading and writing and participate in a variety of recreational pursuits. More importantly, they learn how to work the fields, everything about seeds, plants, propagation, water, fertiliser, cultivating, harvesting, procurement, packaging and shipment,' Courtney said.

Thus far, the Sisterhood were delighted, complimenting Courtney and metaphorically patting each other on the back for a job well done. Even Sonya wasn't too dismayed with the concept of clinics, nurseries and boarding schools. Then they went through the gate into the mature wing.

'This area will house all the adolescent and adult men,' Charlotte said. 'Obviously, the living quarters will be vacant for at least a couple of years. It will come online over time as the boys mature.'

There were many more barbed wire and surveillance lookouts that caused Sonya to frown. The general living facilities provided in both the childhood and mature wing compounds were similar and featured sleeping dormitories, meal distribution centres, hygiene and ablutions blocks, a laundry, and several different activity areas.

Can you imagine if this was it? Sonya thought as her touring group mingled in the central courtyard. *Caged like animals.* She had fought hard for the inclusion of a hair and grooming parlour and some semblance of recreational facilities. Without her lobbying, there would be no library or music and hardly any hobbies provided for.

'Should we go on to have a look at the Agricultural Section, or would you like to take a short break?' Courtney asked.

They decided to continue into the core of the facility, the main reason for its existence. Beyond the machine sheds and spacious warehouses were vast fenced fields planted with rows and rows of lush green crops being earnestly tended by a flock of women. The boys would gradually take over these duties as they grew older. There was also a factory full of vats incubating bacteria, a laboratory to generate its proliferation and machinery required to process and develop it into flour and other edible products.

'You've done an excellent job, Courtney. You and your whole construction team deserve hearty congratulations. Our boys, and eventually men, will be exceedingly happy here and more than content to contribute to feeding our nation. On behalf of the Sisterhood, thank you very much,' Charlotte said, leading to a spontaneous burst of applause. Only Sonya didn't clap; instead, she looked around in disgust that they could be so pleased with this. *Nothing more than prisoners and slaves.*

***

By 2043 all the initial Production Farms were ready to be occupied and it was time to implement the next part of the Sisterhood's plan: the global conscription of every boy. It all hinged on the familiar and time-honoured method of propaganda and fear. A new broadcast emblazoned throughout society claimed that female Banshee carriers could put maturing boys at risk. The Production Farms were promoted as safe havens whilst they tried to develop a possible vaccine, providing everything from birth to schooling, to sustenance and farm work to maintain and maximise the precarious food supply.

The Sisterhood even coined a slogan to support the cause:

'SERVITUDE IS FREEDOM!'

Although the boys had to live and work in the farms, they were free of the virus.

The irony was not lost on Sonya, who shook her head in amazement when it was discussed at the last Sisterhood meeting. The combination of these motives made the seismic shift in demographics a relatively straightforward and trouble-free process.

***

A bright, inquisitive, eleven-year-old lad named Chad was preparing to leave his mother and sisters and go on the adventure of his life.

'You may be ready to go, Chad, but I'm having a hard time letting you,' his mother said.

'Oh, Mum, I'll be okay,' he said with the twisted grin of an embarrassed son on the cusp of adolescence. Chad was overflowing with youthful excitement and enthusiasm and couldn't stop talking about the move.

His mother, like any other, wanted to see her son kept safe. She knew it meant consigning him to the local Production Farm without delay but it was still one of the hardest things she would ever have to do and she couldn't help worrying.

'It's only for a while anyway, until there's a vaccine,' she told him.

'That's right. I'll see you soon,' he said.

He brought nothing with him to the Production Farm apart from his first name and the clothes he wore and even those were exchanged for a new sleeveless, pale grey tunic that was handed out to each arrival.

XIII

Over the last couple of years, Sonya had overseen the transformation of her Ministry into the renamed Health Department. Rather than just providing the usual medical assessment, rudimentary first aid and pain relief, under her leadership, the staff had developed a greater appreciation of care for their patients and introduced a system of ongoing case management and follow-up. Although the mysterious Area 15 being underground and fortified had also survived, there was now a greater emphasis on medical training and surgical intervention.

She also continued to hold her position on the board of the Sisterhood that had expanded its membership but now only met once a month with an agenda that was typically mundane. With no more war, no more Telescreens, no more surveillance or oppressive police and minimal technology but an ever-improving living standard, calm and peace had descended over society. Some of the older male youths in the Production Farms had moved into the mature wing Agricultural and Bacteria Fermentation Service and the burgeoning food supply had greatly improved, creating an atmosphere of hope and optimism amongst the women and a spirit of co-operation and rejuvenation.

The Sisterhood were holding their July meeting in the old but refurbished Ministry of Truth building, where a hundred or more workers once toiled under dull light. The whole place had since been brightened by the installation of several large windows, allowing an abundance of natural light to flow through and giving it an airy atmosphere. Sonya took a deep breath as she sat down on the squishy chair. She adored the smell of the large oval Eastern Red Cedar table. She was seated three along from Charlotte, who was still in charge and gave her customary greeting.

'Welcome, sisters, please take your places. We're about to get started.' She waited momentarily for quiet. 'Can I please have someone second the reading of the minutes from our last meeting?'

Sonya looked around the room at all the familiar faces. Many smiled back at her.

'I will,' Susan said.

'Thank you, Susan.'

'We have one carried-over item. Sisterhood elections. We need to vote on whether we open the council up to popular election or do we continue to restrict membership to only those who are nominated by an existing member and accepted by the majority,' Charlotte announced. 'Can we please have a show of hands of those who vote for popular election? Four in favour. Now a show of hand of those who vote for continuing restricted membership. Thank you. The latter is confirmed by the majority.'

'We're also still receiving plenty of applications from the mothers of some of the boys in the farms, asking if they can see their sons,' Susan said.

'Our policy hasn't changed,' Charlotte said. 'No visitation rights. It will only complicate the situation. Issue replies reaffirming our response.'

The meeting carried on routinely until they got to other business.

'Although we're all grateful for the progress that has been made so far and how we've been able to successfully navigate our way through an exhausting and challenging time, it doesn't mean things are perfect.' She paused to shuffle some papers in front of her. 'There has been a suggestion that perhaps some men may not need to be confined to the Production Farms.'

Sonya looked up at her, startled, as she absorbed the clearly audible gasps around the table. *Finally, they have seen reason,* she thought. She had always been a strong advocate for relaxing the strict confinement of the draconian farms and finally she felt a glimmer of hope that they were starting to come around to her way of thinking. After everything that had passed, every tough choice exercised and all within recent memory, she couldn't understand what had changed their mind but she was hopeful. There was a buzz around the room that hadn't been felt for a long while.

'Suki, would you like to explain further, please?' said Charlotte, stepping aside to let her address the meeting.

Suki stood to accept the invitation. She was the youngest board member, having replaced her mother Monica, who died last year. Suki was determined and strong-willed but was clearly feeling nervous as she began.

'Thank you, Charlotte. I have been speaking to dozens of our constituents and hearing a lot of discussion amongst many women about whether it would be possible for a small proportion of men to live with us, outside of the farms,' she said.

The group were still trying to comprehend the concept as Suki cast her electric blue eyes around the table, observing the sparks of confusion, before looking at Charlotte for reassurance.

'The idea has some merit, but also some risk. All opinions are welcome here, so please continue,' Charlotte said.

Suki smiled. 'Thank you. Obviously, our priority has always been to maintain the integrity of the food supply and population control. So, of course, it's essential that most men remain within the Production Farms. It's hard to deny that the decision to impound the boys has been proven to be a wise one. But now that the situation is reasonably under control, we are amidst a rebuilding boom. There is much to be done in fixing our broken housing and infrastructure, and we need help,' Suki explained. 'My question to you all is, would it be feasible to carefully select particular men for purposes other than food production?' she asked the group.

Sonya was getting more enthused by the minute and could hardly believe what she was hearing.

'It would have to be strictly controlled,' said Jacinta from her corner of the table as the others around her mumbled in agreement.

'Absolutely. Therein lies the risk. Each aspect needs careful thought and management,' Suki said.

'What sort of help are we actually talking about?' Jacinta asked.

'There are a couple of possibilities,' Suki began. 'Firstly, domestic service – for example, housekeeping duties and assistance with cleaning, cooking, that sort of thing. Secondly, they could be a big help in building and repair work as well as all forms of manual labour. That's something we all need,' she emphasised in a condescending tone, although no one took offence. 'There is also another more personal function they could fulfil. Many of my friends, associates and constituents have also complained about the absence of heterosexual intercourse,' she added. There was a mixture of reactions from the women around the table.

Kitty, a frail elderly woman who had not fared that well during the famine and had a habit of pontificating, was a little anxious and said, 'We must not allow men to start breeding. That would cause a shift in the whole dynamics of the structure we have established and could destroy everything we have achieved so far. Unrestrained reproduction and allowing male children to be born into the community would lead to uncontrolled population growth and could ultimately ruin the Production Farms and overwhelm the food supply.'

'Yes, this we know,' Charlotte added.

Sonya had been sitting quietly, absorbing all the discussion and considering everyone's comments and she was becoming increasingly disheartened. They still wanted men as slaves but just doing different types of work for them.

Suki spoke slowly as she chose her words carefully. 'They would have to be sterilised. I mean the only way we could do this would be to allow sterilised males back into society.'

The women nodded. The penny dropped and so did Sonya's jaw. The men would still be slaves without the right to procreate. *Of course, this makes sense. They haven't changed their thinking at all,* she confessed in her thoughts. She had reached boiling point and couldn't contain her anger any longer.

'There must be another way. Surely, this is a travesty of human justice,' Sonya said.

'The meeting acknowledges and records your concern, Sonya,' Charlotte responded. 'But, sisters, I must stress that we can't afford to jeopardise our exclusive population control or risk exposing ourselves to the cognition of men that led us to the Insane War. There is no other way forward. We should move to a vote as to whether we feel the idea should be researched and further how it could be implemented,' she added.

'All those in favour.'

Everyone in the room, including Sonya, raised their hands.

'It is unanimous,' Charlotte said with a surprised glare. 'Can I call for volunteers to form the steering committee to report back to us?'

Sonya was the first to enthusiastically raise her hand, along with Suki and Lara.

'Are you sure, Sonya?' Charlotte asked.

'Yes, absolutely. I am totally committed to it,' Sonya replied.

'I'm not quite sure I understand. A minute ago, you didn't seem convinced it was even a good idea. Have you changed your mind?'

'Yes. I figure that getting some men out of the farms is better than none at all,' Sonya said.

Charlotte nodded slowly and although she was only half convinced, she said, 'Okay then, the three volunteers are hereby appointed.'

Sonya also understood that being involved was the best way of keeping herself informed of developments and ensuring her influence on the outcomes; the same as why she had not given up her position in the Sisterhood. She was a strong believer in 'keeping your friends close and your enemies closer'.

The taskforce of herself, Suki and Lara started constructing the policies for quality assessment and quantity control, as well as co-ordinating a plan for implementation. It would be necessary to introduce selection criteria, and special education and training, as well as organise a system of distribution and placement of the men into the homes of women who could benefit from the arrangement. There was a lot to do but Sonya relished a challenge and if this was going to happen, she damn well wanted to have her say in how it did.

XIV

The little sub-committee of just Sonya, Suki and Lara ploughed into their new project with determination and gusto and by early 2049, they had created two new classes of men called 'Domestics' and 'Recreationals', or 'Doms' and 'Recs' for short. Doms would undertake household domestic services and the Recs would provide women with recreational sex. All other men dubbed 'Producers' would continue to live in the Production Farms as normal.

The integration of men into society was an epic shift in the paradigm of the original plan and took months of meticulous planning and rigorous management and nearly three years of co-ordinating and building the systems and infrastructure required. Because Sonya had taken the lead in crafting the policies and procedures, and in recognition of her indefatigable effort and considerable talent in successfully implementing the Sisterhood's agenda, Sonya was made the first Chief Administrator of the Doms and Recs Program.

✳ ✳ ✳

After six years of Basic Training in the Production Farm, Chad now found himself standing amongst an assembly waiting to be called into one of the adjacent examination rooms. Instead of going straight into the Agricultural Section at age seventeen, the youths were sent to the Assessment Department for evaluation as potential Doms and Recs. Chad's dark black hair and intense brown eyes reflected his wise, inquisitive temperament, complementing his friendly and obliging manner. Although his rugged good looks and penchant for physical training had elicited peer group ridicule, Chad remained unfazed and was now tall and muscular and liked feeling strong.

His name was called, and he was greeted by a stern-faced woman with a crinkly brow, dressed in a white suit complete with a white apron and gloves. The nurse told him to lie on a narrow bench which was about waist high and covered with a thin white sheet. There were all kinds of charts on the wall and bits of equipment that he didn't understand, and he kept asking questions that were left unanswered. Instead, she poked, prodded and probed him and recorded the results in a file. Following many days of health, strength, endurance and fortitude testing, he underwent a series of psychological analyses.

Placid, deep-thinking individuals with cooperative and helpful dispositions and strong physiques were ideally suited to becoming Domestics as they would adapt well to working in the domain of household services. They needed to be sufficiently docile and affable to participate in a female-dominated society, performing duties such as cleaning, washing, cooking, serving guests and running personal errands, as well as attending to repairs and property maintenance and working in the construction industry.

Only the most charismatic and attractive males with charm and highly sociable personalities were nominated for the classification of Recreational. They were also required to be inherently good-natured, appropriately composed and emotionally competent. Their place in the household required them to have superior physical appeal and be attentive to personal hygiene and grooming.

With assessments concluded and selections finalised, Chad was directed to join the group designated as Doms. They were told to gather anything they wished to take and ushered into a section within the Education Department that none of them had ever seen before. Through a frosted glass door, they entered their new segregated dormitory. Each of them moved through the rows of bunk beds and claimed one by putting their bags down on it. This would be their new home for the next year. Fuelled by teenage exuberance and growing anticipation, Chad and his fellow fledgling recruits stayed up late into the night talking about what it all might mean.

After their morning exercise regime, the apprentice Doms were guided into their classroom and asked to take a seat. Chad, Kane and Steve, good mates already, chose desks towards the back of the room. Chad thought their teacher looked old as she sat at the front of the class and although she was glaring at them whilst waiting for their attention, her vacant stare betrayed her total disinterest in what she was doing. Before the Insane War, her long-since-dead husband had been a member of the Inner Party and she had never participated in paid employment. Theirs was a life of privilege and luxury and so how she missed it, often reminiscing about what no longer existed. As she stared ahead, her vacant eyes glazed over and she began to daydream. Before her, the table was beautifully spread with a creamy lace cloth that featured incredibly detailed embroidered patterns of wildflower blossoms. The gently flickering flames in the open hearth danced off the silverware and glinted in the glassware. The red wine was poured and the meal served as she traded glances with her husband sitting opposite, his mischievous grin signalling their later passionate lovemaking on the rug that was warming in front of the fire.

Her mind gradually returned to the classroom. 'Alright, let's begin. My name is Ms Kate,' she announced over the noisy chatter. 'Before I outline the semester, are there any questions anyone would like to ask?'

Chad hesitantly raised his hand.

'Yes, ah, Chad, isn't it?' Kate said, looking at the chart of faces with names on her desk.

'What are Doms and Recs?' Chad asked. There were many stories and wild rumours circulating the dormitory and he couldn't contain his mushrooming curiosity.

'What a great question, Chad! And not entirely unexpected. However, that is what we're here to learn. Suffice to say, for all of you, it will be your life's work, your purpose and a big benefit is you won't have to live in a Production Farm,' Ms Kate replied.

This set off another round of frenzied chatter amongst the lads and although it wasn't even nearly a good enough answer for them, it was all she was prepared to say at this stage.

Returning to her script, she resumed describing what they could expect to learn from their time with her.

'Your mornings will be devoted to a regimen of physical exercises, just like the taste you had this morning,' she said. The programs were designed to create habitual attention to fitness. 'Two hours of tutorials will follow, focussing on improving life skills needed in adulthood. And after lunch, the afternoon is yours to spend as leisure time,' she added. 'Games, art, reading, music, the choice is yours.'

The boys looked chuffed. It all sounded pretty darn good to them.

'Okay, let's get started with our refresher on reading and writing,' she said.

They frowned a little.

XV

Three weeks later, Chad lined up with the other Doms at the laboratory in the Birthing Department to receive their last course of Banshee vaccine, a trial serum developed by the Health Department just in case the virus was still lurking.

'You don't like getting these shots, do you?' Chad asked Steve, who was standing behind him.

'No, I don't! And I'm not looking forward to this one either considering how much it hurt last time,' Steve complained.

'It did a little, I guess,' Chad said.

'My arm ached all day!' Steve protested.

Chad just shrugged and pursed his lips. 'Come on, it's not that bad!'

One of his other friends was determined to skip his turn and tried to confuse the nurse by changing positions in the queue and holding his shoulder to feign his discomfort from the pretend needle. The nurse was wise to the ruse and brought him to the front and with some gentle persuasion managed to give him a jab, amongst much laughter and cheering from his mates.

With patched right arms, the lads congregated in the leisure area for afternoon games. Chad sat opposite Steve, studying a chess board in front of a bunch of observers.

'What do you make of all that stuff about Doms in class this morning?' Steve asked.

'Bishop takes Knight,' Chad said as he swiped Steve's black horse.

'I know, it makes you feel lucky and kind of special to have been selected, doesn't it?'

'Our job seems interesting, that's for sure,' Kane said, looking over Chad's left shoulder and offering him a hint.

'Hey, no helping!' Steve said. They all laughed.

'It sounds okay. I'm not scared of farm work but hopefully, it'll be better living outside these walls,' Chad said.

***

During the months that followed, the Doms learnt their trade. They were kept busy developing skills in housekeeping, cooking, gardening and building and maintenance, including elementary carpentry, plumbing and electrical. Meanwhile, the Recs' understanding of anatomical functionality would be taken to a new level, one that only Recs were privy to. They had to learn the mechanics and theory of recreational intercourse, mastering the skill of pleasuring and satisfying women. Nothing at all to do with reproduction. Both Doms and Recs were indoctrinated with the principle that procreation could only be achieved through artificially created embryo implantation.

Chad's class was progressing well. No longer raw recruits, they were developing rapidly and becoming mature individuals. During the final week of their education, Ms Kate covered the challenging topic of sterilisation of Recs and Doms, or 'processing' as it was called. The explanation was kept deliberately vague. They were just told how important it was for them to be 'processed' with a simple and relatively painless procedure because it helped them in their jobs and to assimilate with women. No mention was made that the procedure was to remove their ability to reproduce as they had no awareness of natural conception or fertility, having been schooled only in the laboratory-assisted pregnancy that was now society's norm.

Since long before the Insane War, the only form of sterilisation known was castration, and so during the early formulation of the Dom and Rec policies, it was to be applied to both. But Sonya started searching through any surviving medical archives she could find. They were few and far between, and anything she did find was in poor condition. She eventually stumbled across a reference to an operation not heard of for decades. It was a much more subtle form of male sterilisation called vasectomy. The texts described it as a relatively non-invasive procedure that was totally effective and permanent.

Sonya had fought to have the technique universally adopted but after meeting severe resistance, had to be content with convincing the Sisterhood it was at least appropriate for Recs. She persuasively argued that they didn't require such a radical intervention having been assessed with appropriate personalities and superior intelligence, insisting instead that a simple vasectomy would suffice. There was even concern that further emasculation would unnecessarily compromise their function and performance capabilities as they would need testosterone if they were to fulfil their primary purpose. In the end, Sonya convinced the committee that a swift snip of the vas deferens was the best option.

At least for the Recs, Sonya had no chance of changing the Sisterhood's or Charlotte's determination that those selected as Doms were to be sent to the Domestic Processing Department for gelding. The emasculation policy not only ensured that no unlawful breeding could take place but it also diluted their libido, which supported the requirement that Doms not engage in any sexual activity. Furthermore, producing almost negligible testosterone had the added benefit of curtailing the arousal of any innate aggressive mannerisms or anti-social behaviour that might develop post-Assessment, something that was considered unlikely to be a problem for Recs due to their selection process. It also provided a most convenient way of distinguishing Doms from Recs and provide inescapable identification of either.

Processing was the final stage of the certification of Recs and Doms and during 2049 the first batch who had reached eighteen years of age were being neutered and released into the community. Chad would have to wait until next year.

XVI

'We're just about ready to launch the Female Procreation Program,' Charlotte said.

Women were about to be given the option of having a daughter. Hopeful mothers would have their eggs harvested in the Implantation Clinics to be fertilised by a 'male genetic material donor' that the woman selected from the Production Farm with her preferred characteristics. A successfully formed female embryo was then implanted.

'How are the Health Department maternity wards coming along, Sonya?' Jacinta asked.

'They are making good progress. There are some waiting on the arrival of equipment but they should be finalised within the next few months,' Sonya said.

'Great work again. Thanks, Sonya,' Charlotte conceded whilst not looking up.

As soon as the Doms and Recs Program was implemented, each member of the Sisterhood were provided with one complimentary Dom. Sonya was busier than ever with a hectic career so she was thankful to get some home help, and it was at least a start in saving some of the poor wretched souls from a life in the Production Farms. She was given Jock, a strong, tanned young man with tightly cropped blonde hair and impeccable manners.

'Hello, Jock, pleased to meet you,' said Sonya, looking directly into his mottled hazel eyes.

'Likewise, Ms Sonya,' said Jock, with a perfect smile.

'Please, it's Sonya from now on, okay?'

'Certainly, Sonya,' he responded.

He carried her bag for her on the shuttle homeward as they talked about themselves and got to know each other. When they arrived, Sonya, being so used to living on her own, felt a little awkward as she showed him around her house and to his quarters.

'Thank you, Sonya. This place is wonderful. A real credit to you,' Jock said.

'I'm glad you like it. It's difficult to know what to expect.'

'It's perfect.'

It took some time to adjust to the idea of having a male living in her house; however, Jock's easy manner and excellent training would soon quell any concerns she held. Within a week he had organised the household routine, attended to the leaky faucets, patched the hole in the kitchen wall and had started to work on the annoying drainage issues in the front yard.

PART II

2050 – 2065

XVII

'Come along lads, don't dawdle,' said Marcey, who had the job of escorting the Doms from their dormitories. She was carefully balancing an armful of files as she led the group across the sunny courtyard. The stragglers skipped to catch up as Chad's eyes darted from side to side. None of his friends seemed to show any concern but his stomach was squirming with butterflies.

As they approached the plain clay brick building, the words 'Processing Department' stood boldly printed above the large red entry doors in front of them. After they entered, Marcey told them they would have to wait until the clerk came back to take them through. As she plonked the files down onto the counter with a thud, her pager beeped and she reached down to turn it off.

'Please, stay here. I won't be long,' Marcey turned and went back out the front door.

Chad could not wait patiently and his curiosity and growing angst compelled him to start wandering around this mysterious and windowless place. First, he spotted his file sitting on top of the pile so he took it with him.

'I'm going to have a look around. Don't say anything to anyone, okay, boys?' Chad said as he exited the reception area and entered a narrow corridor. He followed a sign showing the way to the 'Processing Suites' and cautiously approached the door at the far end then opened it slightly to check what lay beyond before venturing forward. It was another long and narrow passageway of dull grey light with several doors off each side. Each door on the left was marked 'Domestic Processing' and those on the right as 'Recreational Processing'.

Just then the door at the far end of the hallway opened and a woman appeared. She wore a flowing white gown, a white apron tied around the middle and soft white shoes. A small cap covered her hair and a pair of thin gloves protected her upheld hands. But what intrigued Chad was the thin mask disguising her face. He nervously watched her approach and as beads of cold sweat accumulated on his forehead, he noticed a little badge that said 'Doctor Moonie' pinned to the chest of her uniform.

'What are you doing here?' she asked in a muffled voice.

'I just have to deliver this file to reception but I'm afraid I'm a bit lost,' Chad said, thinking quickly.

'Keep going back that way and turn left,' she said, indicating with a nod.

'Okay, thank you very much,' Chad said, smiling nervously as she walked past and disappeared into another room.

He continued a little further before stopping at one of the doors labelled 'Recreational Processing' and carefully pushed it slightly ajar to peer inside with cautious round eyes. There was a huge open-plan room full of surgical tables and medical equipment. Several people dressed like the doctor were huddled around someone lying on a table who was mostly obscured by a white sheet. To the right, Chad could see another five surgical tables lined up and on each someone lying silently. They were also covered in their own white sheet up to their neck with square holes that exposed their groin.

As he let the door close quietly, he was feeling more uneasy, although across the hall a door marked 'Domestic Processing' was calling to him. He dreaded to look but couldn't resist. The room inside looked pretty much the same as the other one with guys lying on rows of surgical tables, except here they were asleep and devices around the tables made loud beeping and whirring sounds. Doctors were fussing about and all Chad could hear was the muffled chatter from behind their masks made worse by the noisy machines. At first, the doctors that were operating at the nearest table had their backs towards, Chad obscuring his view. Then as he was about to leave, one of them moved to one side and placed a severed clump of bloody flesh into a metal tray. Chad held his breath for a few seconds and felt faint. With a racing pulse and feeling sweaty he retreated to the corridor feeling confused and nauseous.

'Whatever this processing business is, it doesn't look good,' he said to himself in a gasping whisper. *And having that cut off would hardly be painless. I'm going to have to find a way of avoiding this horrible thing and then be careful to keep it secret from everyone else so that it never ever happens to me,* he thought.

* * *

Meanwhile, Marcey had returned to the reception area to hand over the group to the clerk but they had already gone. She walked to the counter and said, 'Sorry about that. I was called away. Was everything okay with the last batch?'

'Yes, no problem at all. I found all of their files you left on my desk.'

'Great work. Thanks,' Marcey said and walked back out.

* * *

Pushing on further down the corridor through two swing doors, Chad entered an unattended area. A small sign said 'Dom Discharge Station'. Chad had come to where Doms were sent after they had sufficiently recovered in the post-operative ward.

On the desk, he could see piles of stationery arranged neatly next to a computer terminal. On the left side, there was a basket labelled 'INPUT', which was full of files, on the right side was another basket labelled 'DISCHARGED', also containing a stack of files.

Chad opened the Personal File he was still carrying and looked at the paper on top marked 'Domestic Processing Form'. The first part of the front page was already filled in, but the section at the bottom was blank. By copying from one of the other completed files, he drew the word 'PROCESSED' in black ink so it looked like the stamped ones and filled in the empty sections with the date, a code and an authorisation. Then he placed his file with the form inside amongst the others in the input basket.

As he was about to leave the Discharge Station, the clerk came towards him, trying carefully not to spill the large full glass of water she was carrying. 'Hello, are you here for discharge?' she said.

'Yes,' said Chad, confidently.

'What's your name and Dorm number?'

'It's Chad, Dorm 314, Ms.'

She walked over to her desk and carefully put the glass down before swivelling her chair around and sitting in it.

She flicked through the files in the input basket, 'Ah, yes. Here you are.' She opened the file and she briefly skimmed the first page of the form and signed the second. She said, 'It's normal to feel a little residual pain but it won't be for long.'

He nodded.

She marked his form with a 'DISCHARGE' stamp, then signed it.

'Okay, that's all done. If you're feeling alright you can make your way back to your dorm,' she said and waved him on.

Another Dom entered the Discharge Station and gave her his details. She glanced at Chad's file sitting on the top of the Discharge basket and scratched her head momentarily before putting the next one on top of it.

Chad exited into the courtyard, stood and took a deep breath of fresh air before hurriedly striding back to his dormitory. He would have to lie low there for two or three days until his roomies started to come back and then the real challenge of concealing his missed processing would begin.

XVIII

It hadn't taken long for Jock to find a small close-knit group of Doms in town to socialise with. They were in a similar situation to himself, having been given Wednesday afternoons as free time to spend at their leisure. Although not necessary, women were encouraged to give Doms some time off and Jock had become more than just a reliable Domestic, he had become Sonya's faithful friend. The trusted local Doms were all around the same age and had been working in their respective households for more than a year. They spent most of their time together talking whilst playing cards in an abandoned shed behind an old factory.

'Does anyone know how to play poker?' Jeremy asked, addressing the group one balmy afternoon. Most shrugged and shook their heads.

'Is it another card game?' Saheeb asked.

'Yes, it is. I found an ancient book at home with the instructions and I taught myself how to play. It sounds more fun than what we've been playing,' Jeremy said.

'If you say so,' Felix said. 'I'm keen.'

They all agreed to try it. Jeremy ran through the rules and they started to play. It went that well that they ended up in a full afternoon marathon.

The following Wednesday, the poker game started as soon as they met.

'I want to tell you guys about how we can make this much more interesting,' Jeremy said.

'More interesting, how's that?' Jock asked.

'By wagering money on the game that is collected by the winner of each round,' Jeremy said. 'You all get paid allowances, don't you?'

'We have a bit of cash,' Jock replied.

'Not a lot though,' Felix said.

'We don't need a lot,' Jeremy said.

'But isn't that … gambling?' Isaac asked, with a furtive glance around the room and towards the open door as if someone might overhear him.

'So what?' Jeremy said.

'Well, it's illegal, for one thing,' Soon Lee said.

'No one will know about it unless one of us tells someone,' Jeremy reasoned.

They played a few hands for practice with Jeremy explaining the changes along the way. They all picked up the idea quickly and their own little poker club was formed. It being a clandestine activity that had to be kept hidden only amplified its appeal. Soon after, Jeremy introduced the group to another one of his favourite hobbies, making illicit moonshine. He had set himself up a little distillery to make a potent, clear spirit resembling Gin.

The thrill of the game, the secrecy and his early winnings led to Jock's dependency on gambling. Many of the other men in the group were also showing subtle signs of addiction but when Jock started losing, he disguised his anguish by over-indulging in his other vice, getting drunk on Jeremy's booze.

'Good grief, look at the state of you!' Sonya exclaimed as Jock staggered in the back door. Sonya hurriedly jumped up and grabbed hold of Jock's arm, and guided him to a chair. Fortunately for Jock, Sonya was more interested in remediation than judgement.

'This is getting ridiculous,' Sonya said as Jock folded his arms on the table in front of him and let his head slump forward onto them. 'You're going to have to stop this, Jock,' she added. 'If you don't, you're going to get yourself into serious trouble.'

Jock groaned and lifted his head a little. His face looked gaunt and colourless.

'Quick, into the bathroom. You're going to be sick,' Sonya said. She helped him drag himself into the shower. Jock's foul vomit mixed with the water swirling around his feet before disappearing down the drain hole. After he was cleaned up, she put him to bed where he immediately started snoring loudly.

'What am I going to do with you?' Sonya asked herself. 'One thing's for sure, I'm locking up all the alcohol.'

The difficulty was that by morning Jock was always fine and back to his usual self, and he couldn't understand what all the fuss was about. Sonya had a hard time convincing him that there was any problem at all.

XIX

Sonya gazed at the calendar on her desk.

'The tenth of January 2050,' she said to herself. She found it hard to believe that next month she would turn 30 years old. Sitting in her favourite linen chair by the window soaking up the warm rays of sunshine spilling across her lap, she blew on her hot cup of tea and watched the steam wafting away. After a few sips, she resumed the painstaking task of creating the little hand-written invitations to her party that she would soon deliver. It was a quaint, old, almost-forgotten tradition that had come back into vogue. As she placed each piece in a pile to one side, she thought some more about the guest list. She knew all the friends from the neighbourhood would come. Some like Tabitha, Sally and Nicola had already turned 30 and commemorated their birthdays with Sonya. It was an exciting time to be able to celebrate, something that had been disallowed during their childhood.

Then there was her friend they called 'Mad Mandy', who was always rather serious and intense. She held aspirations of changing the world but her ego was easily bruised by those that questioned her views and perhaps that's why she would often lie on the ground and stare into the black and blue twilight and dream of other places. Mandy's ideas fascinated Sonya and they often discussed her ambition to travel. Not just visiting nearby towns but leaving the planet in search of extra-terrestrials. Mandy swore the universe was harbouring more intelligent life forms than just women on Earth.

She would also invite her fellow employees at the Health Department including her best friend Connie who worked in reception and had been invited to join the Sisterhood a year after Sonya. Connie was a few months younger than Sonya and was of slight build and average height with long wavy brown hair and translucent green eyes. Sonya would also be obliged to invite all the other members of the Sisterhood. Even Charlotte. Although Sonya could get along with most people, she really struggled to like Charlotte.

As the replies started rolling in, preparations were well underway. A crudely carved timber banner displaying 'Happy 30th' hung over the front entry gate to greet guests. It contrasted with the brightly coloured decorations that adorned the front porch. Sonya filled the house with streamers and garlands and put red ones in every room, her favourite colour. The decorations spilled into the backyard where Jock had done an admirable job of getting it ready for the party. A string of homemade, multi-coloured lights festooned the perimeter and a large wooden dance floor was positioned in one corner with a space for the musicians to set up close by.

Sonya had promised herself a sleep-in on her birthday but she was so excited she woke even earlier than usual. It hadn't rained for two weeks and although she liked the rain, she was hoping that it wouldn't spoil her party. As the attendees arrived, Sonya welcomed them at the door and showed them inside. It was great to see so many of her former patients as well as several neighbours from surrounding streets joining the festivities. One elderly woman who had known Sonya's mother attended as well as the woman she had bought birdseed from before the Insane War. Sonya formed long-term friendships in the most unlikely of circumstances and possessed the rare knack of staying in contact with consequential strangers. Those people that you only meet through a brief isolated encounter. A midwife who had helped Sonya set up and train the first maternity ward staff also stopped by, although was on standby for an expectant mother nearing labour.

Wine flowed freely, complementing the chatter and laughter. Sonya's oldest friends told stories that made her blush, much to everyone's amusement. After a few drinks, even Jock contributed witty anecdotes he had gathered over the past year whilst living with her.

With an important announcement, Jacinta stood and chimed on a glass to gain everyone's undivided attention. 'Thank you, all. Charlotte, who would have loved to have been here with us tonight, sends her deepest apologies for not being able to attend and has asked me to pass on her congratulations to Sonya. She also wanted me to let you know that the Sisterhood is awarding Sonya the "Star of Honour" for her work with the Health Department.' This created enthusiastic applause and whistles. The shocked expression that smacked Sonya's face gradually faded into one of humble gratitude.

'Everyone, please charge your glasses,' Jacinta said. 'A toast to the birthday girl, Sonya!'

Later they all gathered around to watch Sonya open her presents. A 30th birthday was a milestone that marked true adulthood and she received a variety of gifts to treasure for the rest of her life. Most were handcrafted keepsakes. She admired the exquisite matching pair of long-extinct elephants ornately carved from primeval pearlescent ivory. Next, she unwrapped a set of perfectly preserved lavender-scented candles, made extra special because the luxurious-smelling plant had not been around for more than a decade.

Connie helped Sonya bring out the salads for people to help themselves, whilst Jock, although looking a little unsteady on his feet, was nearby tending the spit roast suckling pig, an extremely expensive and rare treat. The incredibly talented string quartet played all of Sonya's favourite music throughout the evening. After the meal concluded, a deliciously tempting dessert made its way out to the table whilst the musicians accompanied everyone in a stirring rendition of 'Happy Birthday', which finished with three hearty cheers led by a clearly very drunk Jock.

The smudge of clouds that blotted the misty sky during the day had floated away and left behind a bejewelled black sky. With the sun at rest, the bonfire was lit and the yard glowed in the afterburn of the shimmering golden blaze. Everyone took a turn at toasting little marshmallow-type treats and Sonya had the crowd rolling in fits of laughter as she withdrew her long fine pointed stick from the fire only to reveal a smoking clump of charcoaled ooze time and time again.

Singing along with a guitar carried on late into the evening but by now the party was over and Sonya was left with just her best friend Connie as they huddled around the dying campfire.

'I'm having real problems with Jock,' Sonya confided.

'Really, what's happened?'

'He's drinking too much. I'm worried he's becoming an alcoholic.'

'Oh no! That's not good.'

'I know. And I really like him but I'm running out of ideas on what to do about it. Sometimes he can barely function, let alone do any work. I keep a bucket on my desk under the leaky ceiling when it rains.'

Connie was shaking her head.

'It's not only the roof. I've got a list of things. The front porch has holes and looks like it could fall down, the back door is almost off its hinges, the yard needs work and not to forget the dodgy plumbing. I could go on and on.'

'If you can't bring yourself to get rid of Jock, get another Dom.'

'Oh, I don't know.'

'Yes, you should. Treat yourself for your birthday. While you're at it, why not a Rec as well?'

'Nah, that doesn't really interest me. I'm too busy with work and I like my hobbies. Too much reading, gardening and knitting, I guess.'

'Well, at least think about another Dom. It sounds like you've got no choice. You need help, Sonya.'

Sonya shrugged. 'Maybe.'

'I tell you what. I'm going to the auctions next week. Come with me. I'll pick you up and we'll go together. Just come and have a look.'

'Okay. I suppose so.'

'Good, I could do with the company,' Connie said as she stood up. 'Anyway, it's getting late so I better get going. But I'll see you next week, okay?'

'Thanks, Connie. See you next week.'

Sonya knew it had been a perfect birthday. The fire was merely a burnt mound of simmering red charcoals expelling gentle wisps of thin grey smoke into the still night. The house was still again.

A silver kettle lashed with smoky black stains was gently bubbling over the coals and Sonya drained the last amount of the hot water into her cup of tea. She strolled into the house and saw Jock passed out face down on his bed, snoring. She went in and put a blanket over him before continuing up to her bedroom. Staring out of the window at the freckles of starlight in the clear dark night, Sonya was deep in thought again as she cradled the warm brew in her lap.

Throughout the Insane War, her father had cowered from the fighting. Brien was frail and often ill and wanted no part of it. He was frightened. Not like brave Billy, darling Billy. Her mind wandered back to the time when she lost him. She remembered as if it were yesterday; every detail was sharp even after ten years. When he arrived at the Ministry of Health on that fateful day, she had met him in the reception area.

'*Hello, Sonya,*' he coughed as she approached. '*It looks like we might get some rain,*' he'd said. She mildly huffed at the memory.

'*What happened to you?*' she'd asked as she checked his bandaged arm and searched for the tell-tale signs of Banshee. He didn't say anything but once inside the Assessment Department, her anguish had turned to despair as she quickly realised he was beyond saving. She felt pain. A pain unlike she had ever known. During her whole life, she had been afflicted with the uncommon malady of unrestrained emotion. Nobody back then shed tears over death but she had to momentarily turn away and compose herself.

He blinked, trying to focus through his watery eyes. She had pressed him again, '*What happened?*'

She could still feel his heaving chest and hear his weak spluttering voice as he managed to spit out the miserable story.

'Our platoon was doing reconnaissance in the suburbs when we were ambushed. I escaped to your father's house. It was bad.' He paused and drew a long raspy breath. *'The bombs, going off everywhere. Loud. Very scary. Your father was terrified and hiding under the dining table when one hit the roof. It fell in on top of him. He's dead Sonya, I'm sorry, I ...'*

She wiped his eyes as he rested mid-sentence. He took a sip of the water she held to his quivering lips before continuing.

'I tried to get him out but a beam crashed onto my arm. It was hopeless. You know he had Banshee.' He briefly looked at her with despairing eyes before closing them.

Billy had managed to drag himself from the rubble, wrap his arm with torn strips of bedsheet and stagger towards the Ministry to find her. After struggling to make the hazardous journey, he eventually hobbled up the front stairs of the building, one slow step at a time.

'I'm sorry,' she said solemnly. *'I wish there was...'* Her voice trailed off as she adjusted the bandage on his arm. He nodded in defeat as she placed her arm around his waist and guided him to a nearby gurney. He gingerly got up onto it and laid down. Sonya looked at his face. He looked peaceful as she wheeled the gurney into the Banshee patients' area alongside all the others waiting for transportation. She stayed and held his hand for almost an hour.

He died there aged 23, during the Insane War of 2040.

Sonya's dreamy trance ended with the ghostly vision of Billy's beautiful face.

XX

The book of life was about to turn the page for the graduating Doms who were to venture beyond the walls of the farm. They packed their meagre collection of personal possessions into small knapsacks as they prepared to leave. Chad wouldn't call himself nervous, just cautious, maybe wise beyond his years, but today his mouth was dry and his stomach curdling. After all, he was harbouring a secret that none of the others knew. He had no appetite and had only taken a couple of mouthfuls of breakfast unlike the rest of his friends who were boisterous and jittery with excitement and youthful enthusiasm.

One at a time, they approached a desk where the supervisor checked their details and thumbed through their file making sure it included a copy of their identity documents and certification before handing it to them and letting them board the electric shuttle.

Chad swallowed hard when his name was called and stepped forward.

The clerk checked over the file before saying, 'All good. Next!'

Chad said 'thank you' as he headed towards the small shuttle that would take them to the Marygold Auctions, the most prestigious auction house in town. Chad recalled the lesson where they had been told about the sales system. Prior to then, his thoughts were like a jumbled jigsaw puzzle being assembled with the auctions being the last piece.

***

Sonya was busily preparing herself to leave for the auction house after waking from a dreamless sleep. Up early and a fast breakfast meant she was dressed, ready to go and waiting for Connie to arrive.

'Jock, I'm leaving soon!' Sonya called from the bottom of the stairs.

'Okay. Have a nice day,' Jock said as he staggered halfway down the staircase and stood, waiting for a reply.

Sonya looked at him with a worried frown. 'Have you been drinking, Jock?' she asked.

'Maybe just the one.'

'We agreed, none before dinner,' she said.

'Won't happen again, Sonya.'

A knock at the door caught her attention. Connie was here at last.

'Hi, Sonya, are you ready?'

'Let's go,' Sonya replied as she pulled the door closed behind her.

The shuttle arrived and Sonya and Connie travelled to the imposing stone building that housed the weekly auctions. As they entered through the grand doors fit for a giant, they were greeted by a marble-floored auditorium and confronted with rows and rows of seating that faced towards an elevated stage. The voluminous hall was filled with hundreds of women all trying to be heard over one another and Sonya led the way to some vacant chairs, six rows from the front. A woman in a neat uniform with a little hat and trim pinafore was moving through the aisles, calling out 'Programs! Snacks! Get your programs here!'

As she got nearer, Connie waved her over and paid across ten Earthlets with her identity card. Connie offered Sonya some salted kale chips from the packet she just opened but she wasn't interested. She was too absorbed in the little booklet that outlined the timing of the auction and provided a brief description of each man on today's schedule.

The room was abuzz with loud babbling chatter swirling around the theatre and resonating off Connie who was bouncing about in her seat. As Sonya cast her eyes over the multitudes of women, she found the prospect of competing with them quite intimidating, even though she realised that not everyone was there to bid. Most of the women in attendance were not in the market to acquire a Rec or Dom but merely there for entertainment.

The auctioneer stood on a platform behind a rostrum with a microphone, tapping a small wooden gavel to gain everyone's attention. She asked for quiet and announced that they would be starting soon. The first parade of young men filed out and stood in a row across the middle of the stage. They were all dressed in the customary light grey sleeveless tunics that all males wore, although theirs looked fresh and new. Sonya cast her eyes down the line. She fixed on a youth whose uncommon appearance immediately drew her interest. Although they were all broad-shouldered and brawny, he was exceptionally tall and had thick black wavy hair with dark, innocent and beguiling eyes.

'I guess he looks okay,' Sonya said, pointing him out to Connie.

'Yeah, he does. But then again, they all do.'

'Remember, I am just here to look,' Sonya said.

Connie nodded.

The auctioneer signalled for the first in line to step forward. A muscular youth with fair hair and vivid green eyes. He looked straight ahead as the auctioneer introduced him to the crowd in a loud clear voice. 'This is Byron, our first Class A Recreational today. A good sturdy example that would make a great addition to any home. All Class As have distinguished themselves in training and are considered prime Rec specimens. They also come with a full twelve-month guarantee instead of the standard six.' The auctioneer adjusted her microphone. 'He is fresh from training and is almost nineteen years old. Do I have an opening bid please?' The bidding commenced slowly but soon gathered pace before ending with the fall of the auctioneer's hammer at 2300 Earthlets and applause from the audience. Byron left the stage. Another two men in the line-up were similarly dealt with.

Then a slightly older male next in the row came to the front. 'Now, sisters, this is Jason. Recently traded, he is twenty-two years old with a few years of experience. He is so good at property maintenance and manual dexterity that he could have easily been a Domestic. Jason is a talented and practised Rec with glowing references available. Perfect for someone looking for a knowledgeable Rec with the benefit of being very handy and capable of some home repairs. Do I have an opening bid please?'

The room fell silent. Traded Recs did not have the popularity of newly trained ones. Gossip circulated that it was more difficult for them to adapt to the mannerisms and requirements of a new household after being exposed to another, where expectations, styles and practices were often different. There was also risk attached to why he had been traded, although there could be many reasons that didn't reflect poorly on him at all. A bid came from the back of the room of only one thousand Earthlets.

'Come on, sisters, Jason has a certificate of guarantee that his previous owner did not have any issues with him and that they had died of natural causes,' the auctioneer said.

The auctioneer begrudgingly accepted it as the opening bid, then had difficulty raising another until eventually a couple of bids followed in lots of one hundred, then tens, until the hammer finally fell at what everyone conceded was a 'bargain'.

'Next, we have Brady, a highly desirable Dom. No need for me to say too much really. A fine example as you can see,' announced the auctioneer, casting her eyes around the hall for an opening bid. After Brady sold for nearly three thousand Earthlets, the youth with the thick black hair and dark eyes stepped forward.

'Our next young man is Chad, another prime Dom,' declared the auctioneer.

Chad gulped but his throat was dry. He looked out into the sea of women but could see nothing, blinded by a hazy blur of colour.

'Chad is fresh from training and a little younger than the average Dom, having just turned eighteen, but that's certainly not an issue.

Not only is Chad an intelligent and placid individual but he is also a fitness enthusiast with the biceps to prove it! An obliging personality with a highly commended certificate in construction work. He is a very capable young Dom and ideal for a range of situations from the small close-knit household to an extended family.'

Sonya shifted in her seat as she admired the young man. He looked so nervous. Maybe they could help each other.

'Can we start the bidding at say, two thousand Earthlets?' the auctioneer suggested with a gesture of raised hands.

Sonya's pulse quickened as the first bid was promptly placed. There were at least five women currently proffering. The price had already jumped to 2900 Earthlets and Sonya was in awe of the flurry of hands. The woman to her right, four rows in front, currently held the highest offer.

'Do I hear three thousand anywhere?' said the auctioneer, scanning the crowd.

A bid came from a few rows in front of Sonya. 'Three thousand!'

'Three thousand I have,' the auctioneer said.

'Hey, isn't that Charlotte?' Connie said.

Sonya leaned forward to have better look. 'I believe it is.'

Sonya raised her hand and in a bold, elevated voice, said, 'Three thousand one hundred!'

'Thirty-one hundred! Fresh bidder! Can I see three thousand two hundred?'

'Three thousand two hundred!' Charlotte said.

'We have three thousand two hundred, is there anymore?'

'This is crazy, you can get a Rec for that,' Connie whispered to Sonya, screwing up her face in confusion.

Sonya held her breath as she stared at the back of Charlotte's head, which was not too far in front of her. Just as the auctioneer was about to tap her hammer for the third and final time, Sonya yelled out a bid of thirty-three hundred.

'Sonya, really, do you know what you're doing?' Connie asked incredulously. 'Thirty-five hundred,' came Charlotte's counterbid.

Sonya wasn't listening, transfixed by the auctioneer.

'Four thousand!' Sonya shouted in a confident voice. She was determined to win Chad and save him from Charlotte. However, Charlotte came back after an extended pause with forty-one hundred.

Sonya called out, 'Four thousand, five hundred and fifty!'

This created a noisy muttering amongst the audience.

'That's way too much,' Connie insisted.

'Forty-five hundred and fifty, once,' announced the auctioneer. 'Going twice. Are there any more bids?'

Sonya held her breath and scanned the room.

Charlotte was shaking her head in defeat.

'If you're all done, all silent, third and final call. Sold!'

'Why so much? Why this one when there are plenty of others?' Connie asked.

'You know I don't like losing, especially to Charlotte. And I guess I just got carried away in the excitement of the moment! Anyway, like you said, I need help and so does my neglected house,' Sonya answered.

As the next Dom on the stage moved forward, Sonya and Connie stood and headed towards the rear of the hall where they found a door to the settlements and collection area. The sales assistant, a spotty, fresh-faced girl in her late teens, was seated behind a counter, tapping at the screen in front of her, and when she had finished with the buyer of Brady, Sonya approached. They could see Chad inquisitively glancing around, standing patiently at the back of the room. Sonya gave the woman her name and other details.

'Here are Chad's registration papers,' said the sales assistant, not looking up from her screen and placing a thin vanilla folder on the desk. 'Please sign here,' she said, holding a tablet and light-scribe in front of Sonya. After Sonya scanned her identity card for payment, the salesgirl signalled Chad to come forward.

The pimply girl looked up and said, 'Okay, your payment has gone through.' She made a note and continued. 'Should he have any issues, you can return him for a full refund of your purchase price or exchange him for another one within six months. Just make sure you keep all his documentation.' Another form was signed. 'Of course, that's very unlikely,' she added.

'That's good, thank you very much. You've been most helpful,' Sonya said.

'Okay then. Thank you for your business.'

The sales assistant lifted a section of the counter to allow Chad to pass through and carrying only his knapsack, he made his way over to Sonya.

'Hello, Chad. I'm Sonya and this is Connie.'

Chad nodded and with a friendly smile reached out to shake her hand. 'Pleased to meet you.' Her hand felt soft and smooth and was small enough to fit snugly inside his.

'He seems lovely,' Connie said to Sonya as they walked out into the bright sunshine of a fine autumn morning. Then she waved them goodbye as she went to catch her shuttle home.

XXI

Chad was trying hard not to let his nervous energy betray his outward expression of composed calmness as he sat silent but fidgety in the shuttle travelling to his new life. Had it not been for his extensive tuition and many months spent mentally preparing, the whole experience would have easily overwhelmed him. But until today it had all been theory; nothing more than a faraway mythical adventure read to children at bedtime. Now it was really happening and he was about to put everything he had learnt into practice. He knew he was ready and knew what was expected of him.

As they sat together, it didn't take long for Chad to start talking. All Sonya had to do was ask him what it was like growing up on the farm and from then she could hardly get a word in. He spoke for almost the entire journey about his childhood activities and how the farm was a happy place full of friends, fun and education. He eventually took a breath and began to take in his surroundings.

Sonya sensed his youthful optimism and could tell he looked forward to the future as much as she. He was a testament to how humans could survive and thrive since the dark times of the Insane War. It was fascinating for her to hear openly and honestly from a young man who was a manifestation of the system that she had a large part in creating.

As the shuttle scooted along and Chad gazed out of the window, he felt freedom. Of course, he knew he wasn't free. But to be looking around without seeing high concrete walls in any direction was surreal and beyond what he had ever imagined and there was one other aspect so far that Chad had rapidly become aware of. He had been accustomed to living only with males; however, in this part of the world, men were scarce.

The ride would only last a few minutes but there was so much to see. The busy shuttle station, the bustling streets and businesses and the soaring apartment blocks. Then as they headed out of town over a bridge that was suspended above a wide river, Chad felt giddy as he peered down into the fast-flowing water far below. In the distance, there were brown flat fields covered in dusty dirt and the occasional dot of greenery. The skeletons of long-since-dead trees were scattered throughout the landscape. Although the grey, barren background was typically banal, Chad soaked up every detail. Now on the other side, they moved swiftly through avenues of crowded dwellings. He observed the houses up ahead were more sparsely situated on larger plots of greener land and when the shuttle came to the next stop, Sonya announced it was time to alight.

They walked down the road and turned the corner. Chad constantly blinked and shook his head, mesmerised by the houses peppered with women and girls caught up in their daily activities. As they approached a pretty, little house which was the colour of faded violets, Chad could hear loud, raucous screaming and laughter echoing towards him. It was a group of little girls playing in the front yard. A colourful spotted ball came bouncing towards him being followed by one of the girls. Instinctively, he started playing with her, kicking the ball away, making her chase him for it. Sonya watched on and his exuberance made her smile. The small girl in pursuit giggled and another girl standing in the yard yelled for him to score a goal. He booted the ball and it cleared the fence and flew straight into the open front door of the house, which resulted in a tremendous crashing sound. The girls all gasped and turned around in horror.

Their mother came storming outside holding the ball in one hand

and a piece of broken stone in the other. Her face was screwed up in a frightful scowl. The ball had knocked a mottled grey marble statue of an angel from its pedestal in the hallway, causing it to smash to the ground. It was suffering a chipped arm and a broken head. Sonya apologised profusely to her neighbour and offered to have it repaired. By this time, the girls had scampered away and Chad was standing sullenly looking at the ground. Sonya was trying to reassure him under her breath, that everything would be fine and for him not to worry. As they walked away, they looked at each other and Chad gritted his teeth and mocked a worried face as Sonya rolled her eyes, then they both fell into fits of suppressed tittering.

They continued along until they came upon a substantial two-storey 1850s twin-gabled Gothic manor set back from the road on more than an acre of land. After the Insane War, there were many houses abandoned due to their owner's displacement or death. When it was discovered that Sonya's apartment building was at risk of collapse, she left in search of a new home by walking through the outskirts of the city that had been pummelled into a condensed town. After only a few days, she found the emptied place she now called her own. Although it had many broken windows and needed a thorough clean-up, it had escaped major structural damage.

Sonya swung open the gate on the white picket fence and led the way along the grey-pebbled path, then up three steps onto the wide-front verandah. The well-presented house made Chad feel instantly welcome. Before Sonya reached to unlock the front door, it was opened from within by Jock. He stood, staring at them in surprise for a few moments and then watched them as they entered the inviting grand marbled entry. Chad gazed upon the impressive ornately carved timber staircase that soared towards the second floor in a sweeping curve.

'Hello, Sonya. Welcome back. Did you have a good trip?' Jock asked, still looking confused.

'Yes, thank you, Jock,' Sonya replied, pleased to see he had sobered up.

Jock closed the door after they were inside and followed them into the parlour.

'Jock, this is Chad,' Sonya announced. 'He is my new Dom.'

'Oh, I see. What a surprise. I am pleased to meet you, Chad,' Jock said.

'Yes, I wasn't sure what to expect at the auction but I'm sure you'll make Chad feel welcome and work together.'

Jock smiled. 'Of course.'

Chad had also assumed that he would be the only man in the house and felt a little intimidated even though he towered over Jock as he returned the greeting and shook hands. Jock had a strong grip. He was only about a year older than Chad but his demeanour was serious and cool.

'Jock is my other Dom, Chad,' Sonya said.

Chad acknowledged her comment with a nod.

'You must be worn out after such a big day,' Jock said.

'Yes, I am, and extremely parched,' Sonya declared.

'Would you like drinks brought in?' Jock asked.

'That would be wonderful, thanks, Jock,' Sonya replied, collapsing into the thickly padded sofa. She invited Chad to sit in the armchair opposite.

'So, there are only two Doms living here with you? No Recs, Ms Sonya?' Chad asked.

'Yes, that's right. But, please, it's just Sonya from now on,' she replied.

Jock came back in, carrying a drinks tray, balancing some goblets and a jug of juice. He filled the glasses and handed them around before strolling over to the window, looking out into the front yard.

'If you don't mind, Sonya, I'd like to finish mending the front gate hinges,' Jock said.

'Sure, go right ahead, Jock,' she said.

'Nice to meet you and welcome to the house, Chad,' Jock said as he left the room.

The two sat sipping their drinks. As Sonya talked about the house, Chad surveyed his surroundings and became immersed in their details. The parlour was spacious and filled with light streaming in through a wide bay window draped with floral patterned curtains. Plump and luxurious sofas and armchairs were positioned around a knee-high shiny oval rosewood table. A few smaller tables of similar design were positioned around the room adorned with ornaments of all shapes and sizes and one had a cut crystal vase sitting on it full of artificial flowers created from the memory of a bygone era. The crackled grey marble mantle that framed the fireplace was topped with pictures, a glass paperweight and some candles above a firebox, which looked ready to be lit. Behind him, he saw a wall of exquisitely carved timber bookcases crammed with books, most of which looked ancient and some positively tattered.

'I guess you are anxious to explore, Chad, and have a look around your new home,' Sonya said.

'Yes, Ms Sonya,' Chad said. 'Very much so. I have been dreaming of this day for what feels like my whole life.'

Sonya looked him in the eye momentarily as if studying him. It was a profound statement, utterly genuine, the pure truth.

'It makes me so happy to hear you say that. I can't tell you how glad I am to welcome you, Chad, and I hope you'll be very comfortable here.'

'From what I've heard so far, I couldn't be happier!'

'Well, if you're worried about anything or have any problems, I want you to promise me that you will tell me straight away. Don't hesitate. Okay?'

'Yes, Ms Sonya,' Chad said.

'Please, just Sonya.'

'Okay, Sonya.'

'Now, let's go and find Jock,' she said.

Out at the front gate, Jock looked up at them. 'Yes, Sonya,' Jock said.

'When you're finished here, please show Chad where the guest room is and take him on a tour around the place. Give him a run down on everything before dinner.'

'No problem. I'm just about done here.'

'Thanks, Jock,' Sonya said as she left them to it.

'Come on, Chad, follow me,' Jock said, as he set off leading the way back into the house.

Jock ascended the stairs and Chad was lagging, distracted by the homely warmth and comfort enveloping him. From the top landing, Jock called to him.

'Sorry,' Chad said as he bound up the steps two at a time.

Jock pushed the solid dark timber bedroom door open and let Chad step inside. 'Okay. This is your room.'

It had pastel blue walls with a colourful patterned square mat covering most of the thick planks of dark hardwood flooring. Under a window against the far side sat a large bed with clean, puffy pillows and a quilt. Opposite was a wall of closet space. A picture hanging above the bed caught Chad's eye and he leaned over to have a closer look. It was a hand-painted landscape with a forest of green trees with broad canopies and lush undergrowth. He stood staring at it, his eyes trying to absorb every detail almost as if reading a book.

'Sonya painted that. She's quite good, isn't she?' Jock said.

Chad nodded.

'It's from before the Insane War, you know, when there were trees everywhere. Sonya has told me all about it,' he added.

'I'm afraid I don't know much about the world back then,' Chad said.

'Nah, none of us do. I think it sounds too good to be true. Apparently, there were plants of all descriptions everywhere, from the smallest of weeds to the tallest of trees. And all different animals and even birds that could fly,' Jock said.

Chad stared at him, nodding.

'Yeah, I know. Amazing, right? The best part, and this is really going to be hard for you to believe, was that there was so much more food to eat. So many different types of vegetables,' he said, bobbing his head vigorously to emphasise his remarks. Chad could sense Jock's feigned enthusiasm, almost sarcasm, that masked his morbid disillusionment. It contrasted vividly with Chad's own overwhelming appreciation of life. 'You'll have to ask Sonya to tell you all about it one day,' Jock added.

'I will,' Chad said.

'And she will love telling you. She loves talking about it.'

'The room is very nice,' Chad said.

'You can leave your bag here,' Jock said before they continued down the hallway.

They passed a bathroom and a spare bedroom.

'Is there a gymnasium or any exercise equipment around?' Chad asked.

Jock shook his head from side to side. 'No, that's not something we've ever bothered with. If you really wanted to, maybe we could find some space somewhere.'

'Could go in the spare bedroom,' Chad said.

'And this is Sonya's room,' Jock said.

Chad lingered in the doorway for a moment, confounded by the stunning décor.

'You can go in.'

Positioned directly in the middle was a plump double bed covered with a duck egg blue quilt and at least half a dozen various-sized cushions laid against the rich oak headboard. Next to it was a small dressing table with two drawers and sitting on top an oval mirror. In the far corner near a window framed in luxurious floral velvet drapes was a petite ochre writing desk. It displayed an ancient set of writing implements.

'You can only come in here to change the linen or for cleaning the room,' Jock explained.

'Obviously, yes, I know the drill,' Chad said. He ventured into the walk-in closet and brushed his hand along the hanging outfits.

'Yes, I guess you do. I think you'll fit in here quite well,' Jock said.

Chad looked at the view outside the window. 'Yes, I'm sure I will. Where is your bedroom?'

'Oh, well, I use the one downstairs. There's no room for you down there, so you're up here.'

'Do you think you'll move upstairs now that I am here?'

'Why? No need for that,' said Jock with a shrug.

They descended the highly polished timber staircase at a leisurely pace and wandered through the house as Chad familiarised himself with the layout. Moving through a short corridor, they entered the service areas at the back of the house. A chopping board on the kitchen bench was piled with finely diced carrots and a pot of water on the stove held peeled potatoes. A bunch of half-prepared mixed greens had been left sitting near the sink.

'I'll have to get back to getting the dinner ready soon but first, I'll give you a short tour of my quarters,' Jock said. He signalled for Chad to follow him.

They ducked their heads under a low archway that led into a narrow passage with several doorways. Jock opened them one at a time. Down one side was a bathroom with a shower and toilet, a laundry utility room where an old washing machine was chugging along to itself in the corner and a small living room containing a compact sofa, two easy chairs and a walnut cabinet. Down the end of the hall, they stepped through a door to the expansive backyard of the property. A clothes rack sat sunning on the veranda drying a light grey sleeveless tunic and some female underwear.

They passed an empty room as they returned down the opposite side of the hall before Jock opened his bedroom door for Chad to peer inside. It was just big enough for a tidy single bed and a small bedside table that supported a tall, skinny, black lamp. On the left wall, several tunics hung on pegs. Chad wasn't surprised by the humble, albeit practical, accommodation.

'Well, that's it. Not much to it but it's home,' Jock said as they returned to the kitchen. 'Now, I really do have to get dinner ready.'

'I should freshen up first. I reek a bit,' Chad said, looking down at the dark rings of perspiration under his arms.

'Use the bathroom upstairs. You'll find clean tunics in your bedroom so put the one you're wearing in the laundry basket,' Jock said.

When Chad came back downstairs, Jock was in the dining room setting the table.

'Ah, there you are,' Jock said.

The dining room was large and ostentatious and built during a time when extended families made a special effort to gather at mealtimes. The cedar dining table with bold carved legs could accommodate twelve people comfortably and probably did long ago when it was owned by members of the Inner Party.

'Do you need any help in here?' Chad asked.

'No, it's all good, thanks. Why don't you go and relax? Join Sonya in the parlour for a pre-dinner drink,' Jock replied.

Sonya was sitting in a soft leather armchair, next to the fireplace that was now filled with dancing flames. A beam of moonlight illuminated the window behind her.

'Hello, Chad. Please, come in,' Sonya said as she got up and pulled the curtains together, making the room even cosier. 'Would you like a drink?'

'Yes, please.'

'Do you drink wine?'

'I haven't tried it.'

'Silly me, of course you haven't. Well, I have a bottle of one of my favourite whites open so I'll pour you a small glass.'

'Okay, thanks.'

She handed it to him before sitting back down. With the chunky cut glass goblet in hand, he settled in amongst the soft cushions on the sofa opposite and took a sip.

'What do you think?' she asked.

'It's good, thank you.'

'You're welcome. It's nice to sit and take a break before dinner, seeing it's been such an eventful day. Don't you agree?'

'Yes, I am feeling a little overwhelmed by it all,' Chad said.

'You'll be okay,' she continued. 'I'm certain you won't have any trouble getting used to our routine. You'll see, it won't take long before you'll feel you've always been here.'

'Thanks,' he said.

'Although there is something I should mention to you about Jock,' she said, shifting in her chair whilst looking at Chad with a serious expression.

Chad maintained her eye contact.

'Jock tends to drink too much wine and suffers from its effect. And when I say too much, I mean way too much. So, you'll need to be careful not to do the same. Moderation is the key to taking alcohol. And I'll need you to keep an eye on him for me. He may require our help,' she said as she got up and walked to the fireplace and gave the embers a little poke.

Chad nodded confidently. 'I understand, of course.'

She sat back down and took a sip from her glass.

A little later, Sonya and Chad were raucously laughing when Jock appeared in the parlour. He stood, silently observing for a few moments before clearing his throat. 'Dinner is ready.'

'Thank you, Jock,' she said, drying her eyes with the edge of her hand.

The gleaming silverware was perfectly positioned on the large cream tablecloth. Sonya had found the cutlery set in a sealed embossed metal box in the basement shortly after moving in. Each piece carried an insignia, a shield with two ancient birds of prey on either side. The house also contained records describing a viticultural estate called Falcon Crest that had occupied hundreds of acres in the district over a century ago. In between the knives and forks, Jock placed a pale blue porcelain bowl and plate and a fresh, bleached napkin in front of three of the chairs. To the right of the dishes stood two polished crystal goblets that sparkled under the light of a delicate chandelier.

One for wine, the other for water. Jock pulled Sonya's chair out for her at the head of the table and directed Chad to her right.

Large bowls of green bean and lentil salad, carrots and potato mash were in the middle of the table where all could reach. After Jock poured the water for everyone, he put the jug next to the wine decanter on the table and sat down opposite Chad. Sonya poured wine into each of their glasses because Jock was allowed one with dinner.

Chad and Sonya had been chatting and laughing incessantly during the entire meal, excited by the momentous day and probably a little affected by the alcohol. Jock sat soberly but accepted Chad's offer to help clean up, whilst Sonya retired to the parlour to do some more reading. The men carried armfuls of used dinnerware to the kitchen.

'So, you've been here for about a year, is that right?' said Chad, taking the opportunity to start the conversation.

'Yeah, that's right.'

'You must have been one of the first batches to be released then.'

'Yep, I was, the first. I was twelve when I went into the farm after both my parents died during the Insane War.'

'Sorry to hear that,' Chad said.

'Thanks, but there were plenty of us orphans.'

Chad nodded.

'What about you?' Jock asked.

'My father died of Banshee, of course, but Mum is still alive. Well, as far as I know, that is.'

'And this is your first position fresh from Dom training,' Jock said.

'Sure is. Sonya seems nice,' Chad said.

'Yeah, she is nice enough,' Jock said as he rinsed the plates before filling the sink with hot water.

'What else can you tell me about her?' Chad asked.

'I'll wash, you wipe,' Jock said, handing him a towel before continuing. 'I think she is genuinely a good woman. She's been good to me. I think we work well together and I'm sure you will fit in too.'

'Thanks. I hope so.'

'Don't get me wrong. Although she is friendly, she does command respect,' Jock said. 'What she says goes. She likes efficiency and order and if something isn't right, she'll let you know very quickly. Not in a demeaning way but just so you know it's got to be fixed. She likes things to go to plan.'

Chad was absorbing the information like a dry sponge soaking up water. Dom training had taught him that knowledge was the foundation of all relationships and fostered respect and ultimately his assimilation. Whilst they spoke, Chad was also reading Jock, and he sensed an underlying tension that he couldn't quite yet understand. Jock seemed friendly but occasionally guarded.

'I think deep down, Sonya has dreams of going back the way it used to be in the old days – "a better world", as she calls it,' Jock said.

'And what do you think?' Chad asked as he finished drying the last of the dishes.

'We have to get by with what we've got. There's no point trying to change it.'

He was no philosopher, that was for sure, and dreamy notions didn't appeal to his pragmatic view of life. Whereas Chad admired youthful quirky eccentricities, Jock shunned anything of a playful nature.

Jock sat silently, thinking and swirling the water in his glass before taking the last gulp. Chad said goodnight to him and Sonya before retiring to his room for the evening. Although he'd begun to sense contentment, today's adrenalin was still pulsating through him and as he mounted the staircase two steps at a time, he was thinking how difficult it would be to get to sleep tonight.

He could hardly believe it; the first night in his new home, in his new bedroom. A shudder escaped as he closed the door behind him and he stood, gazing around, trying to take it all in. Sitting on the bed, he emptied the contents of the tan canvas knapsack he'd brought from the farm. It wasn't much but it was all that he owned – an old, familiar and slightly ragged tunic that he wore to bed, a spare tunic that he had only worn a dozen times since new, a few old books, a pack of worn but usable playing cards and a thin reference manual that all Doms received upon graduation.

He opened one of the closets and found a place to hang his spare tunic amongst the three new ones that Jock had put there for him. He tossed the one he was wearing over the end of the bed and slipped into his sleeping tunic. It felt comfortable and reassuring. A token from his former days and a life left behind, but also a reminder of how far he had travelled. He crept into the springy bed and slid under the thick blankets. He started to read one of his books under the pale golden glow of the bedside lamp but didn't finish the first page before falling asleep.

XXII

Chad ran a circuit through the neighbourhood early every morning. He couldn't help but stop about halfway on a crest and admire the view with a quiver of delight for all the choices to come, each of them laden with discoveries. The landscape stretched before him, rising and falling like waves on a gentle ocean dotted with restored homesteads set amongst sparse and precious trees and gardens.

He'd just got back sweaty and panting when Jock came over to him.

'Morning, Chad. I'm just about to start shifting some soil in the front yard. Care to help?'

'Sure, but can I just finish my exercises first? They only take me about half an hour or so,' Chad said.

'Okay. But why do you do all those sit-ups and crunches and what not?' Jock asked.

'It's to keep fit and strong, Jock. Something that was drilled into us back in the farm. Don't you remember? You should try it.'

With severely reduced testosterone it was easy for Doms to lose muscle tone and those that took to exercise fared better.

'No thanks. Don't need it. Chores keep me active enough,' Jock responded, leaving Chad to it.

A little later Chad was pushing a wheelbarrow whilst Jock was shovelling mounds of freshly delivered sanitised earth around the garden. Chad relished the opportunity to get his hands dirty and build comradery. In the afternoon Chad challenged Jock to a game of ping-pong and he was agreeable once they found some spare time.

'Would you like to serve?' Chad said. As he handed over the small orange ball, he could clearly detect the smell of alcohol on Jock's breath.

'Which Production Farm did you come from?' Jock asked, tapping the first ball over the net with a delicate flick of his wrist.

'South Sector Side Three,' Chad answered.

Click clack, click clack, the ball bounced from one side to the other.

'Ah, that explains why I never saw you around. I'm from North Sector Side Two.'

'Yeah. I guess they'd be pretty much the same though. All farms have an identical setup,' Chad said as he slammed the ball across the table, causing it to bounce out of Jock's reach.

Jock shook his head.

'Did you play much handball?' Chad asked, with a fast serve.

'A bit. I was interested when I was younger but then Dom training started.'

Click clack, click clack.

'What did you think about being selected as a Dom?' Chad asked.

'I didn't mind. I wasn't that keen on farm work. Domestic chores at least got you out of the farm and it seemed pretty cool at the time,' Jock replied.

Jock missed the ball. 'You're good at this.'

Click clack, click clack.

'And now?' Chad asked.

The ball whizzed over the net and past Jock.

'It's okay, I guess. Can't complain about how it's turned out. You?'

'Oh, me – I think it's great. Couldn't have worked out better.'

'Looks like you're winning,' Jock said.

Jock's insincere smile gave Chad an uneasy feeling. It was as if Jock was reluctantly accepting him, whilst harbouring a festering resentment. It was hard to pinpoint, and it was still early days, but

Chad was starting to think Jock's excessive drinking might have something to do with his emerging depression and dissatisfaction with life.

After dinner on Saturday night, they all moved to the cosy parlour to partake in their first weekly Gin Rummy contest, a card game Sonya had suggested. A small circular table was positioned in the centre of the room. Chad shuffled the cards as Jock tended the fireplace and coaxed the flames into roaring rhythmic dancing. The score was kept on a little bit of paper. In a wink, three hours had gone by. Chad enjoyed himself and found Sonya's company incredibly good fun but Jock's disinterest in the game and increasing isolation from the conversation became more obvious as the night wore on. Eventually, he told them he was tired and stomped off to his bed.

The following morning Chad awoke bursting with vitality and ran more than ten kilometres in faster than usual time. He still felt euphoric when he got back and stood at the kitchen sink gulping a glass of water. Bunches of dark purply grey, grape-like clouds advancing rapidly towards the house accompanied by distant but looming thunder heralded an approaching storm from the north. He gazed out the window as the rain began to fall in sporadic spits.

Chad spotted Jock in the yard hauling a barrow load of firewood towards the woodshed when the bullets of rain began to pelt down. He was saturated as he pushed on through the boggy ground that was being whipped up by the torrential downpour. The front wheel caught in a wet hollow and tipped the barrow over, taking Jock with it. Covered in thick mud, he scurried to the back door and Chad heard him call out to him.

'What happened to you?' Chad asked, cracking a wide smile at the sight of Jock swaying in the doorway, looking a complete mess. He was obviously somewhat inebriated.

'Throw me a towel, will ya? I can't come inside like this,' Jock said, ignoring the question. He peeled off his tunic that clung to his skin like a wet, soggy magnet and tossed it on the ground.

Chad ran and grabbed a towel from the bathroom while Jock vigorously wiped his feet on the doormat. As Chad handed him the towel, he floundered as the terrifying memories of the Domestic Processing Suites flashed through his mind, fiercer than the glowing silver lightning that was currently shattering the grey sky.

He stood gazing with vacant eyes as the visions of clinking medical instruments, masked faces, rows of tables set with patients and little bloody trays flooded his head with horror. The reoccurring nightmares that had faded over time were now shiny and new again. It was a stark reminder that he wasn't like Jock, a Dom, at all, and that he truly needed to keep that reality to himself.

'Come on, will you?' Jock said as he grabbed the towel from Chad in frustration and began mopping himself with it.

Chad snapped back to the present with a jerk of his head.

'Sorry. I ...'

Jock walked off to his bedroom shaking his head and grumbling to himself.

XXIII

'Why don't you come for a run with me this morning before breakfast?' Chad asked.

Sonya looked at him across the table slightly bemused. 'Me?'

'Yeah. Come on, it'll be fun and good for you. We don't have to go fast.'

'Well, okay, but I won't be able to go too far.'

'That's fine. Get ready and let's go.'

They set off on Chad's daily circuit, periodically slowing to a walk to allow Sonya to catch her breath. When it started to lightly rain, they headed back home.

They stood in the kitchen, trying to brush the water from their wet clothes.

'Would you like to come with me every morning?' Chad asked.

'Do you really want me tagging along?'

'Yes, I enjoy your company,' he said. He couldn't help noticing how her soaked shirt clung to her heaving chest and how cute her dangly damp hair looked as it cascaded down each side of her face.

'In that case, yes, I would like to,' Sonya said. 'Here, let me help you out of that wet tunic.' She took a step towards him with outstretched arms.

'Ah, no thank you, that's quite alright. I'll have a quick shower in Jock's bathroom,' Chad said as he made a swift exit.

Sonya smiled to herself. *The wonders of Dom training.*

XXIV

'The weekend can't come fast enough,' Sonya said to her colleagues busily preparing for the Health Department's annual quality control review. The normally long working days had extended into late evening for the past two weeks as they dealt with an unusually large volume of patients and the newly created and heavily patronised maternity wards. Although located at the head office, as Managing Director, Sonya was overseeing the review of every one of the dozens of Health Department branches in the State.

Every procedure within the organisation had to be tested, making sure they were documented correctly and the level of hygiene throughout the workplace would be scrutinised. But, of course, there were always areas for improvement, everything from incorrectly stored chemicals, to a shelf full of stained beakers and a missed Petri dish full of incubating bacteria left on one of the rear work benches. The experience would culminate in a one-hundred-page report of recommendations each Health Department would have to work through.

The break from work that Sonya had been craving had finally arrived. The breeze had eased, and it was a warm afternoon with storm clouds brewing in the distance. Sonya had just stepped from a relaxing hot bath and was brushing her shoulder-length blonde hair with long sweeping strokes when a noise coming from outside stole her attention. She looked through the window. It was Chad helping Jock in the yard. A large slice of earth had slid towards the house during the last torrential rainstorm and was causing problems with mud accumulating around the door. It had been a frustrating problem they had been trying to ignore for some time. Now that Chad was available to assist, they were finally getting around to fixing it by erecting a retaining wall and positioning large boulders along the edge to reinforce it. Sonya watched Chad intensely, observing his muscular legs striding towards the rock pile and his bulging biceps as he heaved heavy stones and dropped them into place. As the sweat dripped from his forehead, he raised his tunic and used it to wipe his face, briefly exposing his loins. Her hair had mostly dried as she placed the brush on her desk.

She couldn't stop staring at him. *This is just crazy,* she thought. *He's a Dom for goodness' sake. Put it out of your mind. Even if relationships with Doms weren't forbidden, he wouldn't know how to respond. It wouldn't be fair on either of us.*

As she went to move away, he glanced up and saw her at the window. Chad smiled and raised his arm and waved to her. Her heart was racing and so was her mind. She was sensing intense physical attraction and her thoughts were scrambled. *I mean, he just can't,* she thought. She would have to suppress her feelings and cast off her infatuation. She smiled and waved back before he returned to his work.

XXV

'Fifty-one, fifty-two, fifty-three,' Chad said, counting his push-ups on the floor of the gymnasium as Sonya entered. He paused and rolled over onto his back with a heaving chest, catching his breath.

'Chad, I was wondering,' Sonya said. 'Have you ever thought about visiting your mother?'

Chad sat up. 'Yes, I have. But I didn't think it would be appropriate to ever mention it.'

'On the contrary – I think it's a good idea and I'm sure she would appreciate seeing you. Do you remember the address?' Sonya asked.

'Yes, I do. She may not still be there though.'

'We can only try and find her. I'm happy to take you. Maybe tomorrow?'

They caught the shuttle to the suburbs on the far side of town and walked a couple of streets amongst rows of small cottages. As they approached Chad's childhood home, he hesitated.

'What if she doesn't want to see me?' he asked. 'She never visited me.'

Sonya frowned. 'She couldn't, Chad. No one's allowed to visit the farms.'

They walked up to the plain brown door on the little house and knocked. A small girl quite a few years younger than Chad answered.

'Hello, can I help you?' she asked.

'We're looking for Kay, does she still live here?' Sonya asked.

'Mum! Someone's at the door,' the girl shouted.

A lean, middle-aged woman with long, whitened hair came to the door dressed in the customary pair of brown overalls. As soon as she saw Chad, her face morphed into a quivering mess of cries and tears.

'Mum, it's me, Chad,' he said, advancing towards her. 'And this is Sonya.'

'Chad. You mean my brother?' said the small girl.

Kay took hold of him and led them into the front room. She sat next to him, speechless, staring into his eyes. Finally, she said, 'I can't believe it. You look great. You have no idea the number of times I tried to see you in the farm. They wouldn't let me anywhere near you.' She started to sob again.

'I know, Mum. I'm so sorry. No one knew it would be like that.'

'But you're out now. You must be …'

'I'm a Dom.'

She nodded. 'Are you happy and well?'

'Yes, very much so. Sonya is wonderful. I'm so grateful for the lovely home she has given me.'

Kay turned to look at Sonya and mouthed, 'Thank you. Thank you.'

'Come and say hello to your sisters. Well, your other two, anyway,' Kay said, putting her arm around his shoulders as they walked down the hall.

Sonya trailed a little behind, admiring the reunion with swelling gratification. She couldn't be happier for Chad.

XXVI

Chad and Sonya were about to set off on their morning run when Sonya asked him if he would like to go for a walk instead to see the local park that had recently been replanted as part of their community's huge effort towards greening the landscape. The days were getting warmer and apparently, the saplings were now a spectacle to behold. He readily agreed. They strolled side by side under the cloudless silky blue sky. Chad listened as Sonya talked. She was in a reflective mood. She often was these days, her mind flicking through memories like the pages of a much-loved book.

Her childhood home had been a small timber cottage crammed on a tight plot of land in an over-crowded area. The place no longer existed, having been destroyed by a mortar shell. Sonya's father was a quiet man who had kept to himself and didn't cause trouble. He didn't want to follow in his father's footsteps, perhaps being scared by his fabled stories. Sonya's childhood was tough. She remembered that her parents, especially her mother Jane, always seemed tired. Food was scarce, and she was forever hungry. It habitually felt like it was going to rain but often never did. She was briefly reminded of her father's old book that she had found amongst the rubble that was once her family home. It was the only precious item she managed to salvage from the wreckage. The sacred keepsake still sat pride of place in the centre of her bookshelf at home. It held such enormous sentimental value, that she could never bear to read it. Every time she tried to open it, she was overwhelmed with emotion. Her eyes welled now just telling Chad about it.

She could hardly remember her grandfather, Winston, who had lived for 86 years. The vague details she knew about him were mostly conveyed through the fading memories of her father. Winston did not have an easy life; in fact, it was a desperate struggle. He was what her father called a 'non-conformist' and something of a rebel. His behaviour was frowned upon by the government and had led to some sort of brush with the law in 1984. He eventually settled down, met her grandmother and they had one child together – her father Brien, known back in the day as 60791 Smith B. Sonya had scarcely any information about her grandmother apart from her father's description that she was a kind and hardworking woman who did the best with what meagre resources she had, and that her name was Mary.

Chad and Sonya approached the entrance to the park; the grass was fresh and there was a central path lined with rows of thin-trunked fig trees no more than two metres tall. There was a vendor selling sweets from a small cart and they purchased some. Sonya spotted a vacant bench seat and steered them towards it to rest and take sips from their water bottle.

They started walking again and in the distance, they could hear noisy little girls as they followed a winding path that led them through some advanced bushes. They came out into a child's playground full of girls running and climbing and swinging on various bits of equipment. They watched on for a moment, then a girl on a swing asked, 'Will you push me?'

Chad obliged and began pushing the girls on all four swings at once, making them go higher and higher with fits of screaming and laughter. He looked back at Sonya and she was smiling at him, shaking her head, and saying, 'Not too high! not too high!'

When he noticed a football match being played on the adjacent field, he just had to join in. As he was being chased by a dozen excited, jostling girls trying to stop him from scoring a goal, Sonya came to realise how good he was with children. She wasn't going to bother having any daughters, but now she was thinking that Chad would shine in the role of a child carer. It made her really start to feel that having a daughter or two was a wonderful idea. She was sure he would be thrilled if she had one. Just then he tripped and fell but quickly got back up, sporting a grazed knee. He wandered back to Sonya like a soldier wounded in battle with a comic frown to make her laugh.

When they got home, she told him to put his foot up on a kitchen chair so she could look at his knee. Her pulse quickened as she tenderly dabbed the scratch with a dampened handkerchief and cleaned some marks from his thigh with some vigorous rubbing. His skin tingled at her touch, and he knew she felt it too as they both looked into each other's mischievous eyes. He was so frustrated, wanting to caress her and be close to her, to be intimate with her as he knew he could, just like a Rec could, but realising that for him it was impossible.

If I tell her, she could send me to Area 15, he imagined. As thoughts of defeated desire clouded his mind, she leaned in and kissed him Then he kissed her back, much to her surprise.

When they moved apart, he said, 'I'm sorry. It's just that I like you a lot.'

She grinned and thought, *For a Dom, that is so cute.*

'It's okay. I like you too,' she said and then gave his knee another dab. When he feigned terrible pain, she said with a wry smile, 'Oh, I think you'll live.'

XXVII

Jock was in the gymnasium mopping the floor when Chad walked in, chatting with Sonya. As Jock finished up, he wondered why the two of them were gradually spending more of their days with each other and what they could possibly be talking about all the time. He felt very lonely, and if he cared to admit it, a bit jealous of their unusually close bond. Chad thanked Jock as he left with his mop and bucket. An uneasy tension between them lingered in the air then dissipated like smoke from a smouldering pile of ashes that could reignite with the slightest provocation.

Sonya had come to watch Chad in the gym on several occasions to admire his routine and he had suggested that she should train with him so he could help her maintain her fitness. After completing their exercises, they sat next to each other on the floor, panting and sweaty.

'Would you mind running a bath for me, please, Chad?' she asked.

'Of course not. I'll go up now.'

'Thanks.'

He wiped his brow with a towel and threw it around his shoulders before heading upstairs. She could hear the shower running and the bath filling. When she entered the bathroom wrapped only in her towel, he was in a fresh tunic and turning the bath taps off. She closed the door behind her.

'There you go, it's all prepared. You have impeccable timing,' he said. He headed towards the door as she tested the water, giving it a swish with her hand.

'While you're here, would you be a saint and wash my back for me?' she asked.

He turned his head back to look at her and said, 'Sure, okay.'

She had her back to him as she let the towel fall to the floor before carefully stepping into the bath and sinking into the warm water. 'There's an exfoliating sponge over there on the vanity.'

As he gently scrubbed her soapy back all over, he observed her naked femininity, distorted through the shimmering water. He marvelled at her vulnerability and the display of confidence she had in him.

When the job was done, he handed her the sponge.

'Thank you,' she said as she laid back against the edge of the bath.

'I'll leave you to it,' he said as he left, closing the door behind him.

He sat in his bedroom and heard the bath being drained and her walk to her bedroom. With Jock still cleaning downstairs, Chad felt an insatiable desire to go to her, to see her, to smell her. Her door was open and she was sitting at her dressing table, combing her wet hair.

'Here, let me do that,' he said, coming up behind her.

She was a little startled but didn't flinch.

'Thank you.'

As he took each handful of her long blonde hair, he ran the brush through it with slow lengthy strokes. Then as he was about to take another handful, he instead let his hand slip down the front of her shirt and caress her chest. She closed her eyes. He dropped the brush and used both hands to gently knead her breasts, panting at the back of her neck before kissing it.

She stood and turned to him. 'But you're a Dom, you know that it's …' Her quiet voice trailed off.

His arms fell to his sides and he gulped heavily. Could he trust her? *She trusts me, I'm sure,* he thought.

'But I'm not,' he said at last.

'Not what?' she said, staring at him.

'A Dom.'

Her eyes momentarily glanced downward.

'You mean you're a Rec?' She heaved a loud gasp. 'How, though?' There was a pause. 'Don't worry, I think that's wonderful news. You have no idea how relieved I am, but how?'

'No, I don't mean that. I wasn't processed as a Dom or a Rec. I missed out on it altogether.'

'What? Is that even possible?'

'Well, yes, I dodged it. When we went to do it, I snuck off and saw what they do to Doms, so I changed my file to look like I'd been processed and then they discharged me.'

Sonya stepped backwards and sat heavily on the bed, her eyes still transfixed on his.

'Oh my gosh, that's incredible. I'm actually happy for you – for us,' she said.

'I'm glad too.'

'Why didn't you tell me earlier?' Chad shuffled closer towards her. 'I was scared, worried that you might send me to Area 15. I had to be sure I could trust you.'

Sonya stood, threw her arms around him and gave him the tightest of hugs as they fell on the bed kissing. Before matters went further, Sonya broke the embrace and sat up to face him.

'This does present us with another consideration though,' she said.

Although still lying on his back, his brow furrowed in query.

'Well, not being processed means that you're fertile.'

His quizzical expression didn't change.

'It means we can conceive a child naturally if we want to, without me going to the Implantation Clinic. I can have children with you instead,' she explained.

'Really? I don't understand. That's hard to believe.'

'I know but trust me it's true. Of course, this must be our secret. And there is one other possible complication,' she said.

'Oh no, and what's that?'

'If we do have a baby, it could be a boy. We could have a son.'

Chad sat up abruptly with his mouth agape and eyes widened almost comically.

Everyone knew women were only allowed to give birth to daughters through embryo implantation at the clinic. It was impossible to have a boy outside of the Production Farms. If a son were discovered there would be no avoiding an investigation into the circumstances of his birth and no doubt that he would be removed from them and be sent along with Chad to Area 15.

Chad turned pale.

'Are you sure?' he asked.

'Yes, without clinical intervention the baby could be either a boy or a girl.'

'Oh my gosh, I see.'

'There's a bit to think about, isn't there?' she said, gently stroking his forehead.

* * *

They were both unusually quiet over lunch, something Jock immediately noticed. He took the opportunity to mention the upcoming roof repairs but no one was interested. After Chad helped Jock clean the kitchen. Jock went on to do the laundry, whilst Chad said he would tidy upstairs. Sonya followed him up to her bedroom.

'Having a baby is a huge risk,' she said.

He nodded.

'But I've been thinking about having children. And if we're careful it could be wonderful. I could easily take care of the Health Department records with my unrestricted access to the system.'

'What if it's a boy?' he asked.

'We'll disguise him as a girl for as long as we can and then we'll eventually figure something out later. What do you think?'

'I trust you and I'm in your hands, but I'm game if you are.'

'I am. It's what I've always wanted. It's as if fate has delivered us each other. I've always hated the way the Sisterhood treat men.'

'You are a bit of a rebel, aren't you?' Chad said.

'That's not the first time I've been called that.'

They laughed together and embraced. As they kissed, they landed on the bed and spent about an hour there.

XXVIII

The one thing Sonya would change, if she allowed herself to, would be to exchange Jock for another Dom. She could hear his distorted singing coming down the pathway first. Then the scuffing at the entry as he tried to find the keyhole with his unfocused eyes and fumbling fingers. She opened the door to find him once more, senseless and incoherent. With little warning, he fell over on the front porch, creating a bloody gash on his forehead. She called Chad to help her. It would take weeks for the wound to heal and even longer for the red stain on the floorboards to fade.

Others would have given up on Jock by now but Sonya wasn't going to. She knew he was a good man worth saving but he was cunning and continuously found ways of frustrating her attempts to drag him from the whirlpool of his addictions. After she prevented him from accessing the alcohol at home, he merely switched to buying Jeremy's Gin and snuck it in with him.

In a further vain bid to curtail his gambling, she stopped paying his allowance; however, the thought of missing his beloved poker afternoon loomed towards him like a gathering dust storm on the horizon. The first time he stole money it was from Sonya. Her unattended wallet was just too much of a temptation. It was just a matter of taking an amount that wouldn't be noticed. Once on this slippery slope, Jock would regularly steal from her. It was something he became exceptionally good at. His habit required constant feeding and frustration bred desperation when he couldn't get enough. Jock had taken to thieving around the neighbourhood and reports were filtering back to Sonya that money and items were going missing in the area; something so rare that no one could remember it ever happening for decades.

***

Chad finished getting the gardening done on his own. He went through the back door, straight into the bathroom and glanced at the mirror, then took a second look and grimaced. He grabbed a fresh tunic from the laundry and jumped in the shower. He went upstairs to Sonya's bedroom door and gently tapped it twice with his knuckles. Sonya invited him in.

'We have to be careful.'

'Don't worry, Jock's passed out drunk for the evening.'

As he came towards her, he pulled his tunic over his head and cast it aside. There was a moment of lingering silence as they stood, looking at one another. She turned her back to him and lifted her cascading fair hair so he could unclasp the delicate yet heavily bejewelled necklace she was wearing that dangled at her chest. Drawing it from her, he kissed her neck then placed the chain on the desk with a clunk. She pulled down the front zipper of her overalls and slowly pushed them off her smooth shoulders one at a time. The overalls fell to the floor. She kicked them off and hopped under the bedcovers with Chad close behind.

XXIX

The bright sunlight streaming through the bedroom window woke Sonya and made her blink several times. Sitting up in bed, she was consumed by a sudden wave of nausea. Her belly felt full and bloated. A soothing hot shower provided some relief but she only managed to swallow half her breakfast and a kale smoothie. She went to say goodbye to Chad who she knew would be in the gym. He smiled and waved in between the strain of pulling a bar of weights from above his head, up and down across the back of his sweaty shoulders.

She arrived at the Health Department feeling tired but attributed it to her late nights with Chad. A sigh escaped when she sat down in front of her computer. Then she was sick. Regurgitated pungent, pale green oatmeal splattered her desk. Two of her closest co-workers immediately came to her aid as she wiped her mouth and hastily attempted to clean up the bile-like mess. It took all of Sonya's considerable talent of persuasion to convince them to stop fawning over her. Even though she told them she felt better and dismissed it as merely an upset stomach, she sat and worried and found it hard to concentrate. All she did was fumble around at her desk pretending to be busy.

By lunchtime, she had got no work done and her colleagues encouraged her to take the rest of the day off. Finally conceding it was a good idea, Sonya left and decided a stroll in the fresh air would clear her head. As usual, the street was a blur of bustling pedestrians. Throngs of women were hurrying along between businesses and dodging others busily chatting in huddled groups. Many were dragging small girls behind them, whilst older sisters were still at school. There were also a few men on missions striding speedily with their heads down without stopping on their way to wherever they needed to be.

A bit further down the road from her office, there used to be a lovely park where she would occasionally sit and eat lunch with Billy on the grass under a shady oak tree. There were lines of bench seats there now but they were standing on dry ground and set amongst rows of barren tree trunks. A few small saplings were also trying to establish themselves. Sonya headed towards it as she attempted to collect her thoughts. Brief bouts of queasiness had been coming and going for the last few days but this was the first time she had physically been sick. After taking a sip of water at the drinking fountain, she sat on a nearby bench to watch the world pass by. The lively little girls, who were climbing on the playground equipment in front of her, provided a welcome distraction and before long it was time to go home.

Morning nausea continued to plague her for days and when her menses hadn't arrived when it was supposed to, Sonya suspected she might be pregnant but brushed it off as a symptom of overwork and needing some rest. When it didn't arrive the following week, it preoccupied her every waking moment.

Pregnancy tests were available for women who had been to the Implantation Clinic to check the success of their procedure. During her lunch break the following day she took the stairs to the materials depot on the third floor of the Health Department. The staff didn't even record Sonya's presence as she took a tester from the inventory and secreted it in her pocket. As soon as she got home that afternoon, she went straight to the bathroom, opened the box and took out the little stick. Her hand was shaking as she anxiously waited for her urine to provide the answer. The wait was excruciating, although it was only thirty seconds of watching the little blank results panel on the tester. Slowly, the two small blue lines materialised, confirming her suspicion. She clutched her stomach and felt giddy. The simultaneous combination of overwhelming joy and contrasting fear made her feel so light-headed she had to grab the vanity to stop herself from collapsing onto the floor. She checked it again; the proof was in her hand. As she sat on her bed she muttered, 'Now to tell Chad.'

'There is something I need to tell you,' Sonya said, finding him alone in the kitchen. 'Where's Jock?'

Chad looked at her and pointed to the backyard with his head.

Without hesitating, she said, 'I'm pregnant.'

He grabbed hold of her hand and looked into her eyes. 'Congratulations! That's wonderful news,' he said, in a low voice. As they wrapped their arms tightly around each other, she closed her eyes, feeling the grainy material of his tunic.

'It's early days, still about seven months to go,' she said. 'I've already updated my files at the Health Department showing my visit to the Implantation Clinic.'

'Okay, do we tell Jock?' he asked.

'Yes, of course.'

'What if it's a boy?'

'We can't trust him enough to tell him that,' she answered. 'Just like everyone else, he mustn't find out. But let's not fret too much about that yet. We might have a daughter anyway.'

'Okay,' he said, slowly nodding his head. 'When do we tell him?'

'Now is as good a time as any. I'll go get him and we'll meet you in the parlour.'

Jock was making a poor effort of sweeping the path to the back door. He sat the broom against the wall as he followed her into the house. When they got to the parlour, Chad was already pouring some drinks.

'I've got some news, Jock,' she said, taking a seat opposite him.

'What news?' he asked.

'I've been to the Implantation Clinic and I'm expecting my first child,' she said with a wide grin. Jock got up and went over to offer his congratulations with a kiss on the cheek and a warm, but not too tight, hug. Chad was handing out glasses containing small doses of sparkling wine and Jock realised that Chad already knew. He stepped forward, and took the glass Chad was offering.

'I didn't even know you were thinking of having a daughter. You've never mentioned it. When did you go to the clinic?' Jock said, still fuming as he sat down next to her.

'Oh, I went a couple of months ago. It's not customary to announce anything until the pregnancy is confirmed,' she said.

'A toast to Sonya and her baby,' Chad said as he raised his glass high in the air.

'Here's to a happy and healthy daughter,' Sonya added.

For a moment, Sonya thought she sensed Jock's malevolent scowl.

XXX

All babies were meant to be born within the maternity ward at the Health Department and Sonya had dutifully registered her imminent delivery with them, even though she had no intention of going there. Through obvious necessity, she was going to give birth at home with the assistance of Chad. His support was unwavering and she was impressed with how well he absorbed the information she gave him and faced the daunting yet exciting unknown with courage.

She was also blessed with an uneventful pregnancy and felt fine most of the time. Apart from the usual twinges and tiredness, her main grievances were intense mood swings and episodes of doubt. Sometimes she would be brimming with optimism that her baby would arrive and everything would be wonderful. At other times she would be overwhelmed by anxiety, dreading how she would cope with the birth of a son, especially as Jock's condition had only worsened as the birth loomed.

Often at night, she would wake in a cold sweat, soaking wet and trembling fiercely. In the quiet darkness, she could feel her chest pounding and hear her lungs sucking in huge gasps of air. But this time, within seconds of sitting up in bed, she was struck across the body with searing pain that made her keel over in agony. She couldn't move for a few seconds but managed to reach over and switch on the bedside lamp. Under the dim yellow light, she peeled back the thin blankets and looked down to see two bright red spots on her nightdress that looked like little beady eyes staring up at her. Horrified, she felt her stomach. Nothing was out of place and as she rubbed it, the pain subsided. She searched around feverishly to see if there was any new blood to be found. To her relief there was none. She laid back down and closed her eyes as her heartbeat returned to normal and she fell into a deep sleep.

No matter how challenging things became, Sonya knew that she had to give up second-guessing herself and just get on with it. Her destiny was mapped and she had to follow it. No, embrace it.

* * *

In the early stillness of pre-dawn came the gradual onset of labour. Sonya's baby was on its way. As planned, Chad asked Jock to go on an errand that would take him into the next town and require him to stay there at least overnight.

As the hours passed, Sonya's contractions were regular and not as excruciating as she had feared. She was in good spirits, coping well and sitting on her bed when suddenly, a violent spasm of pain struck her and she fell on the floor, screaming. Chad ran to her and picked her up and laid her back on the bed. Sonya had fallen on her swollen front and a crippling ache was coursing through her entire body. Pinkish fluid spilled from between her splayed legs. She cried out in a terrifying yell that was accompanied by uncontrolled whimpering.

Chad started to panic as he mopped her brow. 'Do you want me to go and get some help?'

'No! No! You mustn't!' Sonya begged, weeping and gasping deeply.

'I have to!' Chad exclaimed as he darted from the room.

Chad was scampering fast down the hall when he heard Sonya shriek. 'The baby is coming! The baby is coming!'

He returned in a flash.

Sonya was lying on her back with her knees up and Chad could see the top of a small hairy head swathed in birthing mucous, squeezing its way into existence. Between breaths, Sonya pushed. One more deep breath, a hard push, and as she howled like a Banshee her baby was delivered into Chad's waiting arms. Amidst loud wailing, Chad cut the cord and clamped it just as she had taught him. He wrapped the baby in a towel and placed it on Sonya's heaving chest.

'Well, tell me.' She gasped.

Chad gazed into Sonya's eyes, took a deep breath, and replied, 'It's a boy.'

Sonya stared at Chad agape in disbelief, even though there was no reason to doubt his word. She had felt it all along but checking for herself was proof, just as pinching yourself proves you're not dreaming. She reached down, opened the towel and stared silently at the tiny, squirming, noisy boy. She took a few seconds to absorb the moment she had been contemplating for months. She covered him up and put him to her breast.

'What will we call him?' Chad asked as he listened to the contented suckling.

'I've given this a lot of thought,' Sonya said, looking down at her baby. 'What do you think of calling him Sam? That's short for Samuel.' She paused. 'And also Samantha.'

Chad's face lit up with a beaming smile.

'A name for a boy to be raised as a girl,' Sonya said.

'That's perfect. You think of everything.'

'And when he gets older, well, we'll worry about that in about thirteen years' time,' Sonya responded drearily as she laid back against the pillow.

* * *

The squeaky wheels of the shopping cart could be heard all the way up the street as Jock dragged it behind him. He was greeted by Chad as he held the front gate open for him and there on the porch stood Sonya holding her swaddled newborn.

'Well, I'll be darned,' Jock said as he dropped a sack of seed on the ground.

Chad parked the cart.

'When was she born?' Jock asked.

'Yesterday afternoon, a week early. She couldn't wait any longer!' Sonya replied as he came over for a closer look at the sleeping infant.

'What are you going to call her?' Jock asked.

'Sam, short for Samantha,' Chad replied.

'That's a lovely name. It suits her.'

Chad helped Jock carry the supplies inside whilst Sonya sat on the porch in the sun with Sam.

XXXI

Down in the backyard, through the surviving Sycamore trees with their broad rounded emerald crowns and just beyond a large muddy green, waist-deep dam stood the disused caretakers cottage. Sonya studied it as she approached its facade. The faded lilac-coloured front door directly in the middle of the quaint little house was straddled by a wide, badly weathered gable. It had a small porch and although the timber exterior was covered in peeling brown paint, the structure looked solid enough.

Chad came up behind her as she gazed ahead at it.

'What are you doing down here?' he asked.

She was deep in thought and rubbing her chin. 'I'm thinking with a little bit of a tidy up, this place would be perfect for Jock,' she replied.

'For Jock?'

'Yes. We could get him out of the house without getting rid of him altogether.'

'He is more of a hindrance than a help, that's for sure.'

'Yes, unfortunately, he's not improving and is more of a risk to us now than ever.'

'And it'll give us some more space and privacy,' Chad said, winking and giving her a quick pat. She raised her eyebrows at him.

They stepped inside and although they had to carve their way through dozens of ghostly spider webs as they navigated through the grimy dust, the house was sound. They peered into the front reception room before continuing down the hall. To the left was a bedroom and an old but functional kitchen on the right, with a bathroom and laundry further towards the back. Although it was small, it was adequate for one person. The interior was a grubby yellowed white but it just needed a new coat of paint and a good clean. It also had a generous-sized covered veranda that overlooked the large oval pond towards the main house.

Chad helped Jock with the cleaning and painting and a week later, the cottage was ready. There wasn't a lot of packing to do as Jock only had a few clothes and personal possessions. Chad helped him carry the few heavier bits of furniture that Sonya donated, and noticed how calmly Jock had accepted the move, knowing that he had no choice. The relocation was complete within an hour. The home décor was modest with scant regard for ornaments and curios. Jock didn't care for such things anyway and was too preoccupied with the weight of his baggage to notice as he struggled inside with it and dumped it on the floor.

XXXII

After Sam woke from his lunchtime nap, Chad took him into the backyard to play with a ball. For an almost two-year-old, young Sam had a strong kick and a keen aim. Sonya came out from the kitchen, carrying a sandwich and glass of juice. She walked carefully, minding her step as she was heavily pregnant with their second child. *The second one's always easier*, so she'd been told. It was certainly comforting to know that her adulteration of Sam's birth records at the Health Department had gone undetected. Even Chad knew what to expect this time around.

* * *

It was another Wednesday evening. Sonya checked the clock on the bedside table. It was the time of the week she had grown to dread the most. Jock would be home shortly from his afternoon leave, staggering into the backyard in his usual state of severe inebriation. It was best to catch Jock as he came around the side of the house before he attempted to fumble his way down the back on his own. With the help of Chad, the situation was at least manageable. When they heard muttering and the familiar crunching of footsteps on the gravel, Chad walked around to meet Jock. The moon was winking at him between passing clouds. The first thing Chad always said to Jock was 'don't talk' as he steered him inside to his bed.

'What are we to do?' Chad asked as he walked back into the kitchen and saw Sonya on a chair rubbing her ballooned belly.

'Every time we try to help him, he works against us,' Sonya said.

'Putting him in the cottage keeps him away from us and Sam but he's worse than ever,' Chad said.

They ascended the stairs and checked on their son as they passed and went into their bedroom. The strain was starting to surface, soon to seep through the seam of their sealed secrets.

'I've even tried to stop him taking off on Wednesday afternoons but he sneaks out anyway, and not just Wednesdays,' Sonya said.

'We can't lock him up, can we?' Chad asked.

'Not really and even if we could, for how long?' Sonya said.

She liked Jock and she hated witnessing his spiralling decay.

'At least we have each other,' she said. As he followed her into the bedroom she disrobed. He closed the door behind him, slipped off his tunic, and climbed into bed with her.

***

It was a huge relief that the birth of her second child was quick and effortless and without any issues. Sonya and Chad were the proud parents of a new daughter they named Beth, and three-year-old Sam had a little sister. She was a big healthy girl with tiny sprigs of blonde hair. Having a daughter was a lot less complicated and Beth slipped into the household with only the usual disruption caused by any newborn.

XXXIII

Distant muttering gave way to guttural groans and crunching gravel on another Wednesday night. Sonya lay awake as usual, waiting for Jock to come noisily blundering across the yard heading for the cottage. Chad was finishing up in the bathroom, so she got up from her chair in the nursery and went downstairs to make some herbal tea. When she opened the curtain and peered out of the kitchen window, Jock looked more disorientated and drunk than ever. He conversed incoherently with himself as he bumbled along barely in control of his faculties. The dappled moonlight shining from behind the gently rustling leaves and dangling florets of a Sycamore tree lit her frustration as he staggered left and right. She sighed. Although on a meandering course, Jock was heading in the direction of the pond. His swaying motion caused his head to bob around like a cork in the ocean.

She held her breath as he stumbled at the pond's edge and fell face-first with a splash. A few bubbles escaped from around his head as he lay motionless and unable to free himself from the grip of the water. Sonya ran to the door, yelling out to Chad on her way. It felt like she'd run for hours across the hard cold ground with her nightdress hitched up but scarcely a minute had passed. She quickly grabbed a handful of Jock's hair and lifted his head out of the water. She gasped in horror at his soggy, blue-tinged face that had a jarring, peaceful expression.

Chad came running to the back door and she called him down to the pond. She was struggling to drag Jock from the water when

Chad arrived to help her lay him on the mossy edge. Jock was taking shallow sporadic gurgling breaths so she pushed down on his stomach. After he belched a gut full of fluid and began coughing and spluttering, they rolled him onto his side. Once he gained a semblance of consciousness, they carried him into the house and dressed him in a clean tunic before laying him on the sofa. He would have to sleep there tonight where Sonya would keep a watch over him.

The next morning Chad came downstairs and followed the loud snoring that was calling from the parlour. He found Sonya awakening in a chair and Jock still in deep slumber.

'We'll have to get a fence installed around that section of the pond,' Sonya said to Chad as she stretched and yawned.

Chad frowned, slowly nodding his head.

XXXIV

The Production Farms had been operating successfully for nearly fourteen years. The eldest of the Producers were now approaching 30 years of age and some still held onto the fading childhood memories of the world that existed before the Insane War. With life offering nothing but eating, sleeping, a few hobbies and mostly just farm work every day, some were starting to suffer from their confinement with gnawing frustration and mental fatigue.

'Why are we locked up here forever? I know we produce food but they could still let us out sometimes, couldn't they?' one of the men named Jacob, with flame-coloured hair and fire in his belly, asked a small group working in the noisy woodshed on a balmy afternoon. 'We know men are different to women but why are they in control?'

The clanging of hammers and sound of sawing in the background made it a little difficult to hear him.

'We're the ones that are working so aren't we just as important?' he continued.

Many around him were nodding their heads and grumbling in agreement. Output was kept at capacity with regularly scheduled maintenance but no farms ever closed. There were no holidays for the Producers. The work was physically demanding, constant and unyielding, with only a small amount of mundane leisure time.

'Aren't you guys sick of whittling timber, wood-working and

candle making?' Jacob asked. 'Even cards, chess and ping-pong have their limits!'

'Yeah, we've all wondered what it would be like to live outside these walls. I'm sure it would be better than being stuck in here,' said another by the name of Nick.

'That's right. Doms and Recs get out, why don't we?' Jacob said.

'It doesn't seem fair but what can we do about it?' asked a gangly teenager.

'Do you think we could escape?' Jacob whispered, glancing around to make sure he hadn't been overheard by any staff. Everyone looked at him in silence. 'We could you know. It's possible.'

'How? There's no way out,' Nick said, shaking his head.

There was only one exit from the farm but it was protected by sentries and there was also a portcullis in the medieval style to get through first, which created a cavity between it and the actual door. Neither was opened at the same time, making it a difficult path to freedom.

'Nah, not through the gate,' Jacob continued. 'Over the wall.'

'But the walls are so high,' Nick opined.

'We could build a ladder. Look at the amount of timber we have around here,' Jacob said, furtively pointing to it with his finger.

The seed of escape was sown and with a little further discussion and planning, it began to germinate into a growing, breathing, mission. The lads were careful, organising their plans in secret was invigorating and just talking in whispers about it recharged their vigour. Over two months, the group of plotters began assembling a ladder using some of the recycled timber that was provided for carving and kept it hidden under one of the woodworking sheds. Although only about 30 guys were directly involved with the undertaking, rumours had spread throughout the farm and a lot of the men were aware that something was happening. Most were eagerly observing from the sidelines, hoping for their success.

When the day of their attempt at breaking out arrived, Jacob led the way. A dozen fit lads carried the ladder swiftly across the yard and threw it up against the northern wall in a matter of seconds. One by one the hopeful escapees smiled and waved as they climbed, cheered on by the scattered groups of men admiring their courage and tenacity.

The farm staff were caught completely unaware. Guards came running from the watch towers on either side of the ladder. Jacob was almost to the top as the women approached. Only two more steps. He was ready for a fight and withdrew a blade from a secreted pocket sewn into his tunic. Just as he was about to set foot on the parapet, a guard made a desperate lunge at the ladder. A struggle erupted and Jacob took a swipe with his knife but the improvised escape route was pushed from the wall. The audience of onlookers gasped, some yelled. The ladder flew back through the air, taking its occupants with it, landing with a thud on the ground and breaking into a few pieces. Most of the men got up and dusted themselves off, feeling the humiliation of unavoidable defeat. However, one man with a cracked spine lay motionless, whilst another sat up dazed, holding his bleeding forehead.

Naive overconfidence intensified the deeply felt disappointment in the overly ambitious and fruitless project. During the years that the farms had been operating, there had never been a reported escape attempt. The frustration of wasted time and effort and the sudden cruel loss of hopes and dreams were too much to bear. The fuel of anger ignited a firestorm of blazing fury that had never burnt within the farms.

The incensed young men charged at the gate, yelling, waving planks and brandishing tools. Smoke rose from the windows of several dorms before flames flared whilst feeding on the outside air. More men filed into the courtyard upon hearing the commotion but they could scarcely see through the thick, black, choking smoke that billowed towards them. Their eyes stung and it was hard to breathe. A mass riot was underway. The farm staff could not have been more surprised had a green alien disembarked from a spaceship to greet them in perfect English. The small hostile group of deflated escapees were joined by a growing contingent whipped into hysteria, now sharing the disenchantment.

The siege escalated when the insurgents dragged several administration assistants from their office. The women screamed as the guys cheered. The treatment of the women became more violent as they struggled for freedom. The enraged men held blades at the hostages' throats and forced them to kneel in front of one of the smoking dormitories.

'Back off or they die!' yelled Jacob.

The guards withdrew into the towers. The rioters waved their fists in the air and momentarily rejoiced.

'Now what do we do?' Nick asked.

Jacob looked at him and said, 'this is what,' then shouted towards the tower. 'We want to speak to the Farm Administrator!'

A short time later, she arrived at the top of the parapet, looking down at the men in the courtyard.

'What do you want?' she asked.

'We want better conditions for the men in farms. Less work, more leisure.' A chorus of hooting came from the crowd. 'And we want the freedom to come and go as we please. Any man that wants to leave must be allowed to. Is that too much to ask?' Jacob responded.

'We need time to consider your demands,' said the Farm Administrator before turning and walking away.

'We can wait,' Jacob said.

The standoff continued overnight and into the next day. Early reports of the riot spread from farm staff to their families and then throughout the community. There was growing fear that other farms could suffer the same fate.

***

The Sisterhood's six-member security committee hastily convened a meeting that morning at Charlotte's house to address the crisis and discuss the men's demands.

'I don't think we should even be negotiating with them,' said Madison, the Head of Law and Order.

Sonya shook her head ever so slightly at her whilst suppressing a sigh. 'We could offer to establish some sort of staged release of men back into society,' she said.

'We've been over this before and the majority of us don't want it. We decided there was little benefit in going down that path and on the contrary, it would just create more problems,' Charlotte said.

'Okay, could we at least try a type of temporary leave or allow breaks from the farms for the men? Perhaps set up a new program, like we did for Doms and Recs,' Sonya asked.

'I don't like it, too complicated,' Charlotte said.

'I agree,' Susan said.

No one supported Sonya's suggestion.

'I'm afraid the proposal is not acceptable, Sonya,' Charlotte said. 'And we should probably shut down the Dom and Rec Program until we get this situation brought under control.'

'Has anyone got any better ideas?' Charlotte asked.

'I do,' Madison said.

***

Under the fading light of nightfall, back at the farm, the men were getting restless. They hadn't seen the Administrator since they announced their demands. Jacob was becoming suspicious. The staff were either waiting to see if the situation would resolve itself, or they were organising some sort of countermeasure. Jacob decided that a few should try to go over the wall again using the hurriedly repaired ladder. A large group of the protestors started charging at the gate, yelling that if they weren't let out the hostages would start dying. This created a diversion for Jacob's gang to get over the wall quickly and quietly behind one of the warehouses.

The men helped Jacob lift the ladder up after the last had scaled the parapet and swung it over their heads to place it against the outside wall. Just as they climbed down and scattered into the darkening landscape beyond the farm, loud bangs caused them to stop abruptly and look behind for a moment before they continued to run.

The armed reinforcements had finally arrived. The weapons had been retrieved from the secure isolated vaults that hadn't been accessed for decades. The women with guns entered the farm's front gate under flood light and demanded that the hostages be released. When they refused, warning shots were discharged into the sky with little effect as the men didn't understand.

Without waiting, the guards opened fire on those at the front. The targets dropped in pools of blood. After a dozen bodies fell, their comrades paused and became quiet. They leant down to check on the fallen few who were lying on the ground in mounds, like volcanoes oozing molten red lava and flooding the dry dirt around them. Realising they were dead, the rioters scurried away to their dormitories and the hostages ran. As soon as the last of the men dispersed, the farm staff moved in under guard to remove the corpses and begin the long process of cleaning up.

In the full conclave that followed, the Sisterhood were debriefing the aftermath within their recently refurbished headquarters. Sonya and the other council executives sat in a row across the front facing the rest of the members assembled in the great hall with its perimeter of towering sandstone columns and lofty cathedral-like roof.

'Welcome, sisters. We have a lot of issues to address today so let's get straight to business,' Chairwoman Charlotte said.

The gathering gradually fell silent as she gained their attention.

'Firstly, Production Farm security. Madison, would you like to report?'

'We don't condone the use of firearms but from what we have recently experienced, it seems clear that we need to establish armouries within the farms,' Madison said.

Armed security personnel were to be trained and stationed as full-time occupations, although they would remain discreet to perpetuate the perception that the farms were not prisons but merely places of employment where the Producers carried out their duties and contribution to society.

'And the Doms and Recs Program, has it been restarted?' Charlotte asked.

'Yes, it has,' Sonya confirmed.

'Now what about the men that escaped?' Susan asked.

'Those found in the vicinity of the farms were shot. A few that made it to the nearby town were reported to security patrols by residents and disposed of. None of them survived,' Madison said.

'Okay. What about the ringleaders still in the farm?' Charlotte asked.

'They've all been rounded up and confined to a secured storeroom,' Madison said.

'What's to become of them?' one of the members asked.

'I think we should make an example of them. A public hanging in the farm courtyard should be enough of a warning against trying anything like that again,' Charlotte said.

'That's wrong. I believe we would be making the situation worse. The men are already angry so I fail to see what that sort of spectacle would achieve,' Sonya pleaded.

'I have to agree with Sonya. I think they should be sent to Area 15. That's standard procedure for this type of thing,' said another.

The rest of the women concurred whilst Charlotte seethed.

'Are there any other suggestions in relation to preventing future insurrection?' Madison asked.

'One solution could be to convert them all into Doms. The emasculation modification has been proven to reduce aggression and invoke a calmer and more passive personality,' someone suggested.

'Again, I think that is totally unnecessary, and I'm speaking as the architect and Chief Administrator of the Recs and Doms Program,' Sonya said.

'Why?' Charlotte asked.

Sonya thought, *because these men might lead free lives one day*, but said, 'Because it would make them less productive and capable of intense agricultural labour.' She sat further upright in her chair and leaned forward with her arms folded on the table in front of her. 'There is also the risk that we leave ourselves exposed to something like Banshee, should it arise and threaten the continuation of human life.'

She wasn't convincing enough and disagreement continued amongst the women. There were obvious ways they could take action to insure against such a possibility and they had already started the process.

'Besides, it would be seen as a punishment and Doms should not be portrayed as being punished,' Sonya added. 'Why don't we try providing the men with more stimulation within the farms?' she continued.

'More entertainment?' Susan asked.

'Well, yes, entertainment. Perhaps more sport or some elementary contests,' Sonya said.

'What about football?' Madison suggested.

'That would require too much space,' Charlotte said.

'Bowls might be okay. That's compact,' Sonya said. 'It can be played in teams and provide a bit of competition.'

'Wouldn't it be too sedentary?' someone asked.

'Well, it might be. Perhaps we could also introduce boxing matches,' Susan said.

A comprehensive training regime was hastily introduced throughout the farms. Boxing would provide an outlet for the more aggressive individuals, relieve tedium and provide entertainment for spectators.

Sonya breathed a sigh of relief.

XXXV

Connie had organised to take some of the kids from Sam's class at school to the river for a swim. It was hard to say no to a determined five, going on six-year-old with a vivacious appetite for fun. Both Beth and Sam often swam in the backyard pond, and sometimes went to the river with their parents. Although a little cautious, Sonya agreed to let Sam go with Connie and the group of girls and she watched them trot off in their swimming costumes to wait for the shuttle that would take them into town and drop them a short distance from the water.

A chilly breeze had whipped up by the time Sonya arrived to take Sam home in the afternoon. As she approached, she was a little startled to see a few naked girls come running up from the river. She anxiously searched for Sam and found him with Connie who was helping a couple of shivering girls get dried and dressed.

'Oh, hi, Sonya,' Connie said. 'I was just about to get Sam out of her wet togs and into some dry ones. Most of the girls ditched their bathers but Sam wasn't keen.' Connie smiled at Sam. 'Insisted her swimmer shorts were new and wanted to wear them.' Connie turned to look at Sonya. 'So, I was going to lend her some of Jill's spare clothes. That fierce cold wind come up so quick, didn't it?'

'Sure did. Thanks, Connie, but no need. I've brought some clothes for her,' Sonya said as she wrapped Sam in a large towel and took him aside.

'Oh, terrific,' Connie said as she went over to attend to the others.

Sonya quickly dressed him. 'Good boy, Sam. Very good boy,' she whispered to him.

Although Sam was a tall and skinny child, his appearance had not betrayed his hidden gender. Sonya never cut his long and flowing midnight-black hair. He wasn't overly shy, but a real thinker just like his mother. Sam had just had his fifth birthday when Sonya decided to introduce him to the truth about himself. Provided he could comprehend some of the broad concepts, it would make continuing to conceal his identity a lot easier. Although his circumstances were complex and he was an intelligent boy, Sonya kept her explanation as simple as possible. She didn't mention that Chad was his father – that would be too much to expect. But he understood that he would become a man, just like Chad, and that because he was not born in a farm, he needed to keep this a secret.

XXXVI

One of the large dead Sycamore trees with grey flaky bark had started to lean over the back of the house and it would only take a gusty storm to bring it down. Trees that had the life zapped out of them were scattered throughout the suburbs and continually causing problems. At least they made good firewood. Chad had the axe out and half downed the tree when he called out to Jock to grab hold of the guide rope to help steer its fall. Jock continued to ignore him and watched from a safe distance. As Chad fumed, he noticed out of the corner of his eye, the drunken sod covertly taking another swig from a bottle and hastily hiding it within a thick flowering hedge. Jock was spending more time drinking than working these days and Chad couldn't stop himself from shouting insults at him. They were embroiled in a loud argument when Sonya came running out.

'What's going on?' Sonya pleaded.

'It's Jock, drunk again, of course. How is he supposed to be helping me in that state? He can barely stand!' Chad yelled.

Jock wobbled over to a short rockery wall and slumped down against it.

The commotion had roused the kids who stood staring from the back door.

'Back inside, Sam, and take Beth with you,' Chad said.

Sonya grabbed the rope and assisted Chad in bringing the tree down. Chad had lost all patience. Jock's fanciful infatuation with fermented fluids had grown into a morbid psychosis. His disinterest grated on Chad like a mosquito buzzing at night. He tried to distance himself from Jock, but it was impossible to avoid him entirely.

We really should get rid of him, Chad thought. *I know it, but it's Sonya that needs to be convinced. In the meantime, how am I supposed to put up with him?*

Jock was groaning and rolling over trying to get up before landing on his stomach and giving up.

The washed clothes had been hanging on the line in the backyard basking in the midday warmth and were ready to be brought in. Chad collected them and stomped into the house. He placed the basket on the floor out of the way and started preparing tonight's dinner. He half-filled a large pot with water and put it on the stove to boil. Then he took handfuls of spinach from the cooler and rinsed them under the tap at the sink. Some other vegetables had to be chopped up and the bread taken out of the oven. He placed the spinach into the pot of water as it came to the boil, gave it a good stir then picked up the basket of washing and headed upstairs to sort it.

Jock stood up and urinated against a tree before heading into the kitchen. With a fuzzy head, he took it upon himself to help with the meal preparations. The pot of spinach was quite heavy and he was struggling to pick it up. He hadn't noticed Beth had come into the kitchen and was reaching up to put her cup on the bench. As he turned towards the sink to drain it, he over-balanced, wobbled and tripped, causing the molten water to splash all over her. They both fell in a tangled mess. Beth was shrieking and writhing around the floor like a fish out of water, clutching her burning face. From the parlour, Sonya came running towards her screams. Sonya swiftly pulled the wet dress off Beth and poured pot after pot of cold water over the child.

By the time Chad arrived in the kitchen, Beth was still sobbing, but not quite as hysterically.

'What the hell happened?' he asked.

'Jock's spilt boiling water all over her,' Sonya said as she examined Beth.

Sonya took Beth into Jock's adjacent bathroom and put her under the cold shower.

'It was an asid, an accida, an accident,' Jock stammered.

'Shut up. You're a slurring slob!' Chad shouted. 'A useless imbecile!'

He glared at Jock who was leaning back against the sink. As Sonya returned, suddenly Chad lunged at Jock smashing his fist into his face. Sonya gasped. She had never seen Chad so furious as she jumped in to pull Chad away and steer him towards a chair. She understood that Beth had been hurt but Chad had murder in his eyes.

'That's not going to help,' Sonya said, as Jock rubbed his bloody lip and staggered off back to his cottage.

After they let Beth soak in the cold water for nearly an hour, the poor girl was shivering uncontrollably so Chad gently got her out and wrapped her in a towel.

'Thank goodness the cold water has done an effective job at soothing the burns,' Sonya said.

Beth was marked with angry red blotches but after some pain medication, she stopped crying. Although her parents' quick thinking had saved her from serious injury, it was not enough to totally prevent her disfigurement. Beth would heal in time but she would always be left with a swirling crimson scar down one side of her face that stretched from her left cheek down to her chest.

After Sonya managed to get Beth settled in bed and Sam asleep, she entered the parlour to find Chad. She poured herself a large red wine and sat on the sofa with him. Chad was still furious.

'He has to go, Sonya,' Chad said. 'What if that had been Sam? Jock could have found out about him and then we'd be at risk of him exposing us or at least letting it slip out one day in his drunken state.'

Sonya frowned. She knew he was right.

'But …'

He cut her off. 'No. You can't defend him any longer. He's a drunk, and now even a danger to himself and us.'

'He is useless around the house and has no purpose here anymore.'

'I know you're right,' Sonya conceded with a long sigh.

'We've given him every chance and tried to help him as much as we can,' Chad said.

'Do you think so?'

'Yes,' he said.

Sonya emptied her wine glass.

'We'll ban him from the house. Demand that he stays in his cottage. In the meantime, I'll make some enquiries about what we can do with him,' Sonya said.

'Okay.' Chad looked down at his feet and shook his head. 'But I think it's got to be Area 15.'

XXXVII

With the evening meal simmering on the stove, Chad went outside to put some rubbish in the waste bin just before the dusky light faded. As he turned to go back inside, a movement somewhere to his right caught his eye. He advanced towards the old rarely used shed that stood out the back and off to the side of the main house to have a quick look around. The door was ajar so he slowly pushed it in. Nothing seemed amiss. Although watertight and weatherproof, its contents were of little value. Various lengths of timber were piled against one wall, some broken furniture stacked on the other side and an old refrigerator with a few solid but rusty gardening implements next to it. He ventured a little further and in the far corner behind a few sheets of wavy roofing iron was a curious small nest of stringy hessian bags fashioned into bedding.

For two nights Chad kept watch over the shed from the bedroom window before he went to sleep. He didn't trouble Sonya with his concerns at this stage. No point worrying her.

It was on the third night under a sickle moon that he saw a thin, dishevelled girl of about twelve or thirteen years of age nervously making her way to the garden tap. She leaned under it and took gulps of water. Squinting to keep track of her in the shadows, he watched her cautiously creeping along the fence towards the house.

Driven by growing hunger she climbed in through the open kitchen window and started helping herself to any food she could find. Chad put the light on and placed his hand on the startled girl's right shoulder. She froze but did not flinch. He called out to Sonya as he sat the girl down at the table and fixed her a plate of sandwiches and a cup of warm herbal tea.

'Who do we have here?' Sonya asked, entering the kitchen.

'Good question. She hasn't said a word,' Chad replied.

'Hello, my name is Sonya, and this is Chad. What's yours?' she said, taking a seat next to the girl.

'It's Ellie-May. Ellie-May Micklemore,' the girl replied in a timid voice through a mouthful of bread.

'Nice, to meet you, Ellie-May.'

Although they reassured her that she was safe and not in trouble, they could not get any more information from her that night, so Sonya fashioned a dress out of a new cut-down tunic for her and made up a bed for her in the parlour.

***

Chad saw Claire approaching the house as he finished cleaning the last of the front windows in the morning sunlight. She was a short, slightly built middle-aged woman with light brown hair tied in a ponytail and a consultant at the Welfare Department.

'Hello, Claire. How are you?' Chad said, after answering her knock at the front door.

'Very well, thank you, Chad,' she replied. Her thick black-rimmed glasses had a habit of slipping down her nose when she spoke.

'Please come in and wait in the parlour whilst I fetch Ms Sonya for you,' he said.

'Thank you, Chad,' she said and settled into the floral armchair by the unlit fireplace.

Sonya was nearby and entered the room with Ellie-May trailing behind. 'Hi Claire, how very nice to see you again.' They sat together on the sofa opposite Claire, separated by a small circular table.

'Hello, Sonya. And this must be Ellie-May. How are you?'

They waited in silence for a few moments.

'We've checked and there are no reports of a missing girl fitting her description anywhere in the district. Her name doesn't come up on any local register either,' Claire finally said.

'I've brought you some tea and biscuits,' Chad said as he set a shiny silver tray on the table in front of them.

'Thank you, Chad, that's very nice. We'll help ourselves.'

He closed the parlour door behind him as he left.

'Well, I've talked to everyone in the neighbourhood and no one knows her,' Sonya said, pouring three cups of tea from the pot and handing them around.

'And she's still not talking?' Claire asked, pushing her glasses back up her nose before taking a biscuit.

'She hardly speaks a word. Nothing that's going to help us find her family anyway,' Sonya answered.

Ellie-May sat silently looking at the floor, and gingerly took a sweet biscuit that Sonya offered her.

'Hmm. Well, she seems healthy, if not a little thin. Nothing a few weeks of good food won't take care of.'

'Yes, she scrubbed up alright after a wash. She is a bit scratched and bruised from living rough but generally, I think she is fine,' Sonya said.

'That's good. Well, we'll take her into the Welfare Department and if no one claims her she will be put up for adoption,' Claire said.

The girl nibbled quietly on the biscuit.

'It's a shame, she must have a family out there somewhere,' Sonya pondered.

'I know. We'll keep searching but adoption is the next best thing. There are plenty of women who would prefer to adopt than give birth,' Claire said.

When they finished their tea, Chad brought in a little bag of personal effects that they had put together for the girl. It was with a touch of sadness that after only two days they eventually had to wave goodbye to the lonely little girl named Ellie-May Micklemore.

XXXVIII

It was time for Sonya to pick up Sam and Beth from school. When she got there, it was chaos. She was greeted by thick, black, swirling smoke, intense heat and yelling. A fire had started in one of the older children's classrooms when a chemical experiment being demonstrated went horribly wrong. Several teachers were attempting to douse the hot flames with hoses. Sonya joined the other mothers who began arriving, frantically searching the groups of crying children, looking for their daughters. She found Beth safe and sound with the younger class but some girls had been taken to the Health Department. Sam was one of them. With a pounding chest and shortness of breath, Sonya quickly made her way there.

My God, what if they've examined him? she thought. 'Trying to hide him was always a risky idea, we should have known we'd never get away with it,' she said to herself.

'Connie! Where's Sam?' Sonya asked as soon as she caught up with her.

'Oh, Sonya. She's in the observation area. She's fine. Just smoke inhalation. But she's breathing normally now.'

Sonya rushed through the doors into where Sam was. When she located him, he was playing with toys with a few of his friends. The nurse assured her Sam was fine and that she could take her home.

Sonya was solemn and quiet as they left. She was so thankful she'd been given the opportunity to have children but fearful for their future. Six-year-old Beth, who had inherited her mother's slender features with long golden sunlit hair and reflective sapphire eyes. A lively little girl, who was outgoing and friendly and already showing confidence and independence even with the large scar burnt onto her face. And Sam. She looked at him, shaking her head as he ran off in front.

When they got home, Sonya told Chad all about it.

'Another close call,' he said.

'I know. We've been extremely fortunate.'

As Sam came running past, Chad said, 'Let's hope our luck doesn't run out.'

Still, no one suspected that Sam was anything other than a sweet little girl and big sister to Beth. He was dressed in the prettiest clothes and he did everything other girls did. Sonya and Chad had done such a good job so far but they had to keep going. And it was getting harder.

XXXIX

A cool breeze weaved its way across the room through the slightly raised window as Chad sat reading in the parlour when Sonya sauntered in. He glanced up at her. She was in a wistful mood, dragging her hand along the top of the sofa before walking up behind him and playfully ruffling his hair.

'Hey, what gives?' he said.

She giggled. 'Sorry, just bored.'

Chad raised an eyebrow. She walked over to the bookshelf and browsed the collection of titles.

'Aren't you supposed to be at work today?' he asked.

She shook her head mischievously with a sly grin.

He tossed his novel aside and started towards her.

'Race you to the bedroom!' she said.

She took off up the stairs, with him a few paces behind.

Neither of them had noticed Jock standing at the entry just inside the doorway to the kitchen. He spied them playfully running after each other. He begrudged being relegated to the caretaker's cottage and resented Chad even more. His jealousy had recently grown into spiteful suspicion. Once when they were out, he had wandered through their house and it was obvious to him that Chad had moved into Sonya's bedroom. They had become just a bit too complacent, even though Jock was supposed to stay in his cottage.

He quietly climbed the stairs and as he crept towards the half-closed bedroom door, he could hear them making love. He took a quick peek and sure enough they were moving around under the sheets together. As he walked away shaking his head, he thought, *How can this be if he's a Dom? Highly unlikely and illegal as well. So, he's maybe a Rec? Now I come to think of it, in all these years I've never actually seen him naked.*

It was risky, but he went back anyway. Pressing himself tightly against the wall, he slowly moved his head towards the bedroom entrance and peered through the crack between the edge of the half-open door and its frame. Soon the sheet slipped aside and Jock was left in no doubt. Chad was indeed a Rec.

'This just might be my way of getting rid of him,' a snarling Jock muttered to himself as he quietly descended the stairs.

XL

Although Jock knew he was always going to report Chad to the Sisterhood, it took a while before he built up enough courage to convince himself to go ahead. With Chad gone, Jock thought for sure Sonya would need him more than ever, and they could rekindle their earlier relationship when he first arrived and where she relied on him as one of her closest friends.

She had been so patient with me, she must really like me, he thought. He was in the backyard gathering firewood when the law enforcement team arrived at Sonya's house and he crept in the back door to find out what was happening.

They thudded heavily on the front door and shouted, 'Sonya Smith, are you home?'

Sonya and Chad came quickly.

'What is this? What do you want?' Sonya asked.

'Let us in and we'll tell you.'

They all marched into the parlour.

'We have reason to believe that your Dom, Chad, is in fact an unregistered illegal Rec,' the leader said.

'What?' Sonya gasped. 'What reason?'

'A report has been received.'

'I see.' Sonya sat on the sofa, dismayed.

'Is it true?'

Sonya and Chad looked at one another.

'There's no point lying. It's easily proved,' the leader said.

'Yes, it's true.'

'Very well. Chad will need to come with us to await his trial by the Sisterhood, which will determine his fate.' The leader looked at Chad. 'You're coming with us.'

As soon as they were gone, Sonya went to see Jock. She knew he must have reported them – who else could it possibly be? Chad was right, she should have got rid of Jock earlier. When she confronted him, he was sitting on the porch of his cottage, looking sheepish.

'Why, Jock! Why?' she shouted.

'I did it for us, Sonya. We don't need Chad. We were perfectly happy before he arrived.'

'What a fool I have been trying to help you. Chad warned me time and time again,' she said.

'I did it for you too. He was supposed to be a Dom and you were both dangerously close. He was taking advantage of you,' he pleaded futilely.

'I'm sorry, Jock, this is too much. I'm sending you to Area 15 and that's final.'

He went inside, scratching his head. His mind was buzzing wildly from swirling paradoxes. This couldn't be happening but was. It felt like a bad dream but he was wide awake. It was unbelievable but true. All he could do was pack his bag.

Sonya and the kids were waiting for Jock in the parlour as he made his way up to the house. Beth and Sam were aware he was leaving but they were too young to be told why. Sam carefully picked up a paperweight, a small fragment of ancient pink coral encased in clear glass, from the mantle above the fireplace and gave it Jock. Jock smiled at Sam and said 'thank you' then put it in his bag. He waved to Beth and regarded her crimson scar with regret.

Too late for that now, he thought as he followed Sonya out the door.

*　*　*

Neither of them spoke during the entire journey to the Health Department. When they arrived, Sonya went to the reception desk, whilst Jock took a seat in the waiting room. Sonya described Jock's uncontrollable addictions to the attendant, a pasty, thin woman not much older than herself who seemed to enjoy her job. Her cheery disposition contrasted heavily with Jock's flat expression. He was nervously tapping his foot. The attendant said there would be no problem and directed them down the adjacent hall and into the third door on the right. Jock followed Sonya into the compact office and took a seat. The clerk sitting at the desk had a little name tag on her overalls that said 'Anne'. She was already processing the application when they entered. Anne handed two copies to Sonya, one to sign and one to keep, which she folded and put in her bag. As Sonya got up to leave, she could barely look at Jock and left without saying a word.

As Anne picked up Jock's bag from the desk, his glass paperweight rolled out and fell to the floor and smashed to pieces. The small slither of twisted pink coral laid naked on the cold grey concrete. Ignoring it, Anne asked Jock to follow her. He felt faint. He gingerly arose from his chair and as he faltered, Anne quickly stepped over and supported his arm crushing the coral underfoot.

Apart from the tapping of their footsteps on the hard floor, it was eerily quiet as they walked down the bright corridor towards two large heavy doors. Through them, they passed into a large sterile room that made you feel cleansed upon entering. The intense dazzling white glare made Jock's eyes squint. It was crowded with men sitting in rows of stiff chairs facing a large shiny counter that had two sober women sitting behind it, their eyes darting about on the screens in front of them. The hush was only broken by the feverish clicking of their touch screens and the occasional painful groan from an ill man slumped in one of the seats. There were several men already being attended to at the counter.

Above the counter were the words 'Transportation Department'.

Jock and Anne waited silently for a few minutes before their turn came.

Proving that some things never change.

XLI

'Hello, Jock … Jock? Hell-oooo? It's time to go,' a perky woman said in a cheery voice whilst gently shaking him. Jock had fallen asleep in a chair whilst waiting in the Transportation Department. He was a little disorientated and wobbled as he stood. Within a few minutes, he had passed by a counter and down another corridor. Now he was on a shuttle full of old, sick-looking men, who sat silently with sullen faces.

When the humming shuttle ground to a halt, the door opened, and the men shuffled out onto the shiny white arrival platform that was so bright it hurt your eyes. The men were greeted by a smiling, happy-looking woman dressed in pure white overalls.

'Good afternoon, men, and welcome!' she exclaimed, startling Jock, and causing him to slightly stumble backwards. 'My name is Shang. Come along, men! Please, follow me!' After the jaunty instruction, the slim woman marched energetically ahead with determined purpose as Jock joined the weary group of men struggling to keep up.

As they followed her down the corridor, the light gradually faded, becoming ominously gloomier as they proceeded. The corridor ahead had a row of doors down either side. At each door, the group stopped, and their bubbly guide escorted one of the men into a single dimly lit room where a cup of water sat in the middle of a long bench seat against the far wall. As each man quietly entered, Shang said to them, 'Please, wait here. We need to arrange a few matters for you. I shall return soon,' before closing the door and locking them in.

When they arrived at the room for Jock, he turned abruptly to confront her before she had a chance to close the door and said in a firm voice, 'Is this where I get fixed?'

His bewilderment was fuelled further when she merely repeated with a grin, 'I shall return soon,' before closing the door with a solid thud, leaving Jock inside scratching his head.

He wandered over to the seat, picked up the cup and took a few sips of the tepid water before putting it down again. The liquid was sour, had a yellowish tinge and did little to relieve his dry throat. Sitting with his hands covering his face, he considered his misfortune. After being selected as a Dom and finding an amazing home to where he was now, supposedly waiting to be cured of his demons in this foreign place. The air was thick and stale and clogged his thoughts. He threw back his head, resting it against the wall and inhaled deeply with his eyes closed. He didn't open them again until he heard a sound at the door. Two women entered the room, one pushing a shiny silver, stainless-steel gurney. 'Finally, I'm going to get better,' Jock said, this time in a more confident grumble but still feeling very anxious.

Without looking at him, one of the women said, 'Yes, you are,' with a stony face and a monotone voice. Hearing her answer didn't help calm Jock, as he was certain she was lying. 'Please lie down on this,' she said, pointing to the gurney. Without hesitation, he did as she instructed. The cold metal made him shiver. Once they secured his wrists to the gurney, they started to push their way further down the same corridor again. There was no sound apart from the whirring of the gurney wheels along the concrete floor. As he stared straight up at the ceiling, he began counting the lights as they passed.

'One, two, three, four and bang!' They crashed through a pair of swinging doors that although noisy offered little resistance.

The room they entered was light, large, and packed with menacing equipment. He breathed in heavy gulps of air. In the centre, there was a smaller area enclosed by glass that was packed with men on gurneys. The gurney loaded with Jock was the last to be locked into position.

The other side of the room had what appeared to be some sort of laser gun mounted on a huge robotic arm. The two women had vanished and Jock could hear the machine humming as it raised itself to point directly at them. As he swung his head to the other side, he could see a woman standing behind a window high up in the mezzanine. She was busy pressing buttons, then suddenly she looked down and caught his glare. For a few seconds, they maintained eye contact. He opened his mouth to shout out to her just as the laser gun buzzed and a stream of painless, soft blue light engulfed him. When the hazy hue subsided, all that was left of Jock and the other men was a pile of grey dust on the metal trays, which would be used as Production Farm fertiliser. No one ever returned from Area 15.

Sonya woke and sat up suddenly with a squeal, gasping for breath, and her heart was pounding in her heaving chest. Her nightdress was saturated and the cold sweat made her shudder. She had been haunted by this nightmare ever since she'd found out the truth about Area 15. Area 15 – known by most through rumour and legend, which portrayed it as a sanctuary where the sick and feeble and even the insane could convalesce, find solace or cure. But to those in authority like Sonya, its sole purpose had always been the disposal of the unwanted, dead or alive.

XLII

Chad's trial finally arrived after months of being held in custody. He was brought before a full sitting of the Sisterhood, except for Sonya who was excluded because of her personal involvement in the matter. There was a long bench at the front of the room for the judges, with Chad at a separate pew at one end, facing an audience made up of the other Sisterhood members. As Sonya sat in the witness area, she was shocked to see Chad looking so frazzled and scared with a full face of long scraggly hair.

'All rise! This is case five on the 2064 calendar. Head Judge and Chairwoman Charlotte presiding,' said the court clerk. Charlotte led the other four judges in and took a seat at the centre of the solid timber bench. 'You may all be seated.'

'This seems like a pretty clear case to me,' Charlotte said, looking down at the notes in front of her. 'This is a man who was supposed to be a Dom, sold as Dom, but is really a Rec. There is evidence that his files and records at the Processing Department have been tampered with by someone unknown. This person could have been him. He denies this, of course, but in any event, he obviously was aware of the situation and didn't report it.' Charlotte glanced at her other judges and then out to the members. 'The defendant should be sent to Area 15,' she added.

'As his owner and only witness, do you have anything to say, Sonya Smith?' one of the other judges asked.

'Yes, your honour. Couldn't he just stay with me?'

'What sort of punishment would that be? We can't even be sure he is processed at all,' Charlotte said.

'Of course, he is. Both my daughters were born from documented embryo implantation at the clinic,' Sonya said.

'You could have just been lucky.'

'Yes, true, but his processing could be checked and redone if needed.'

'No, the Sisterhood cannot be seen to be weak. There is no excuse for falsifying records and no excuse for not reporting such an important discrepancy. Sonya, the only reason we are not sanctioning you for ignoring this issue is because of your distinguished position with us. We can appreciate you saw little harm in having a Rec.'

Sonya sat silent.

'I call for a decision. Fellow judges, please acknowledge your agreement to send the criminal to Area 15,' Charlotte said.

Sonya interjected. 'Please, there is no reason to waste a man. Can he be sent back to work in a Production Farm as penance to society?' she pleaded.

All the judges voted to send Chad to the farm except for Charlotte. Sonya had to contain her emotions; after all, he was only supposed to be a Rec. As Chad was led away, they both glanced at each other and Sonya vowed to avenge the Sisterhood and do everything she could to get him back. Charlotte was the most self-opinionated, obnoxious and spiteful individual Sonya had ever encountered.

PART III

2065 - 2084

XLIII

Sonya was pacing. She never paced. Only now she couldn't help it, walking back and forth in her room with both hands holding her stomach. There was a track being worn in the carpet. Her mind was swirling with thoughts and possibilities. With Chad locked away in a farm, she was concerned that the Sisterhood might want to investigate her children. Charlotte would already be plotting her next move and possibly still suspicious of Chad's relationship. And Sam was nearly fourteen years old, lean, lanky and already quite tall, with tanned skin, a symptom of his love for the outdoors. Sonya and Chad's efforts to keep Sam's gender hidden for all these years would soon be jeopardised by his adolescence. Shaving the sprouting soft fuzz from his maturing jawline wouldn't hide the shadow of a beard for much longer and there was no way to avoid the impending deeper tone of a prominent voice box. She stopped to look at herself in the mirror. She stretched her eyes wide open. They were streaked with red and underscored with bulky dark shadows.

The cogs in Sonya's mind turned relentlessly day and night like clockwork counting off time. She spent the night squirming in her bed plagued by mounting anxiety as she mulled over the options. She couldn't move away to hide as she was too well known as the Managing Director of the Health Department headquartered here in town, as well as her position on the Sisterhood council. It would be too obvious and her family would become fugitives.

She rolled over onto the other side of the bed and pulled up a blanket that was half on the floor.

Sam can't stay here, that's for certain. I can't say he died – deaths are reported and bodies sent to Area 15. Is he old enough to leave home on his own? she thought, still questioning herself. It was difficult to accept, but she answered, *Probably, yes.*

The winds of change were blowing strongly. Sonya resisted the thought of sending Sam on such a risky journey into uncharted territory but knew in her heart it was the only course to take; to sail away into the sunset on a voyage of self-discovery and carve out a separate life from her, at least for a while. It was a poetic way of coping with his transition from youth to maturity.

She sat up and took a sip of water from the glass on her bedside table and stared into the darkness for a while. She got up and peered out the window at the glint of moonlight reflected on the pond. 'That's it, he must run away, just like Ellie-May, for a few years anyway. All I need to decide is when,' Sonya whispered. She tried to go back to sleep but before she could, the sun had started to rise.

She went in search of Sam and found him downstairs eating breakfast.

'What's up, Mum?' he asked.

Sam's deep brown, almost black eyes didn't flinch as Sonya discussed her ideas with him. He was quick to agree, which didn't surprise her. He was a determined young man and prepared for the challenge. It was not going to be easy, living in exile being banished to the wastelands.

The next matter to consider was what to say to Beth. She was only a young girl of eleven, and too much more shock could traumatise her. Sonya just told her that Sam had decided to go adventuring for a time on her own but would visit them regularly. Whilst Sam was away, Sonya would sit down with Beth and somehow explain the bit about him really being a boy.

To create a pattern of behaviour that would reduce suspicion when he left for good, Sam pretended to run away from home a couple of times, only to return safely soon after. When Samantha went missing the first time, the neighbours had suggested organising search parties but much to everyone's relief, she returned the following day. During the second episode, there was considerably less concern. Then, of course, she came back once again.

XLIV

When the day arrived for Sam's final departure, Sonya woke early and walked into his bedroom where he was still snoring. She flung open the curtains, letting the sun pour across the room, causing him to stir and roll over.

'Come on, rise and shine, mister,' she said.

Sam sat up, vigorously rubbing his eyes and yawning.

'Today you begin your adventure to see what fate may bring,' she said as she sat down on the edge of the bed.

'Mum, what is fate?'

'Well, it's your life's story. What is meant to be happens for a reason. Everyone has a destiny, Sam,' Sonya replied.

'What do think mine is, Mum?' Sam asked.

'That's for you to discover, my son. However, I have a feeling it'll all work out for the best in the end. Now, it's time to get up. We have a big day ahead of us.'

She felt conflicted, concerned and yet content at the same time. Having lived in fear of his future for many years, it was somewhat of a relief to have the decision made, even if it meant embarking on a journey into the unknown.

They had picked up a neat rig from the market consisting of a twelve-geared bicycle with a trailer, which they kept in the hallway the past week. It was packed with as many supplies as he could manage, including a small tent, a flint, a lantern and other basic camping equipment. The heaviest item was a five-kilogram bag of quinoa which could be rationed over a couple of months. Once they were sure everything was loaded, Sonya shaved his long black locks to give him a neat, tightly cropped hairstyle. Then they ate dinner and waited.

As the daylight was fading fast, it was time to go.

'See you later, Sam. Have fun,' Beth said as they hugged. She had been surprisingly stoic, laughing at the new hairstyle and even helping with the preparations.

'Goodbye and good luck. We love you and will miss you, Sam,' Sonya said with a quivering voice.

'I'll be okay, Mum,' Sam said.

'I know you will but be careful out there. You don't know what you'll find. Make sure you keep an eye on your level of supplies and come back when you need to restock. Give yourself plenty of time.'

'Yes, Mum, I will.'

Sonya suggested it best to follow the river out of town before hitting the outskirts and venturing into the uninhabited wilderness as they gave his bike a final check. One last hug and they quietly waved him off as he disappeared down the road. It was the hardest thing Sonya had ever done.

* * *

Dressed in charcoal overalls, Sam travelled under the cover of darkness whilst the neighbourhood was ensconced in the sanctity of their homes. Sam hurried for a long time before slowing to a more leisurely pace. He followed the dim glow of the sparsely spread streetlamps down quiet streets and kept to the shadows as much as he could. The risk of being caught out was at the forefront of his mind.

He reached the deserted country beyond the borders of town. Here he could turn on the pedal-powered bicycle lights and his headlamp. His plan was to travel down the valley with the river to his left and the protection of the rocky ridge to his right. The night had settled into deep blackness and after riding for hours Sam needed to rest before daylight. In a small clearing surrounded by dead woods, he set down his backpack against a large boulder, parked his rig nearby, curled up in a blanket and fell asleep.

At daybreak, he woke to drizzling rain and ate some oats before setting off in amongst the ravines and mountainous craggy formations with scarce vegetation. Not long after, the terrain had become so rough he had to abandon his bicycle. He searched for a landmark that he could readily find whenever he returned and found a large pile of boulders with a tree trunk at its peak that stuck straight up into the air. If it had a cloth tied to the top of it, it would've looked like a flagpole. It was perfect, so he pushed the rig under a jutting outcrop and covered it as best he could with a small green tarpaulin. Now he had all his gear in his oversized backpack and a large canvas carry bag on the detached trailer that he dragged behind him.

Several weeks into his adventure, the fear of being discovered had dulled. It would take about a month travelling north before he could expect to find another town but he had no intention of going there. Instead, his focus had shifted towards finding a good campsite and exploring the area before moving on. Arriving in a sheltered hollow that the river had unhurriedly whittled through ancient rock, he stopped to pitch his tent. He got a small fire going inside a ring of stones and by the time the little metal container of water standing over it had boiled his supplies were stashed and he was cooling off in the river. Its water was lifesaving comfort.

The next day he climbed the ridge to his right that sloped high into the sky. The ascent provided a majestic view of the river as it twisted through the otherwise brown dry land and disappeared into the horizon. He wasn't surprised by the bleak and barren landscape but as he reached the peak it levelled into a sandy plateau as far as the eye could see. It would be impossible for him to continue that way so he was content to scamper back down.

After he'd finished two weeks of exploring the cave system deep in the adjacent valley, his next point of interest was the crest on the other side of the river. It was only a molehill compared to the ridge on the other side but at the top, he could see several clusters of vegetation in the distance, which made for an appealing destination. But for now, they would have to wait. He'd lost track of time but his dwindling supplies meant he was due to head back home for replenishment.

The sun rose over the clifftop and streaked across the landscape, its golden glow lighting up the red, brown and orange rock, making it look hot and fiery. But this wasn't hell – quite the opposite, and Sam was reticent to leave. He had made note of identifying markers during his trip and used them to forge his way home. The bike was where he had left it, a little dusty but in perfect working order.

Less than a month later, Sam crept to his mother's back door late at night and let himself in. The key was still under the blue ceramic pot on the second step with its prickly little cactus sporting a bulbous red flower. Sonya heard the rattle of the lock and the squeal of the hinges as Sam came in.

Sonya rushed to Sam and hugged him tightly before putting her arm around his shoulders to guide him towards the parlour. 'It's great to see you, Sam.'

'Hello, Mum,' he said.

'Thank goodness you're okay. I'll get some tea.'

They went into the kitchen and sat down whilst waiting for the water to boil.

'You look well. Tired and scruffy, but well,' Sonya said in a way only a mother could. 'Tell me all about it. What have you been doing?'

Sonya poured the tea and they settled in to talk.

Beth was still asleep when Sam eventually went upstairs to her bedroom. She was glad of his brief visit and waved goodbye to him through squinting, half-awake eyes.

Before dawn, Sam had repacked and had set off again.

XLV

He hadn't shaved since leaving his mother's place during his second trip home to restock and his face wore patchy bristles. This time, Sam was determined to push on further than he'd previously gone. As he headed towards a thick forest of trees beyond the next ridge that looked like an oasis of green in an otherwise predominantly brown world, he found sporadic bushes covered in juicy, purply blackberries. They tasted good and he collected as many as he could carry. When he arrived at a level clearing surrounded by a lot of dead trees and a few unusual small but living plants, he set up camp. He tried their leaves with some quinoa he cooked over a little fire. Some were pleasant to eat, others he spat out. His food supplies were running low again but he was careful to keep enough in reserve for a return journey home. He figured he was probably only about two days' walk from the alluring vegetation that lay beyond the next rise.

With mild morning sunrays across his tent, Sam wormed his way out and shivered. He stood unsteadily, lifted his tunic and slightly swayed whilst urgently urinating. His mind was foggy, his eyes blurry and he had trouble focussing on anything. In the distance, something barely visible moved. Although difficult to see, it was the only sign of a living being he had observed since leaving home so he studied it intensely. Unsure of what to expect, his first thoughts were to hide and watch. Glancing around frantically with his heart racing, Sam slumped to one knee before crawling behind a large fallen tree.

There was something moving and he was sure it was coming towards him. Again, trying to concentrate, he squinted into the sun. The shadowy form had the shape of a person but was huge, towering, brown and lumpy. It was groaning and growling. As it got closer, it looked as if it was made of stone. Sam felt too weak to run but he forced himself. He turned away and staggered like a wounded deer trying to escape pursuing jaws of death. He anxiously spun his head to look over his shoulder. To his horror, there was now another one. Suddenly, two of these terrifying creatures were thumping towards him. They were catching up with him. He couldn't run any faster and felt he would collapse at any moment. He tripped on an unexpected grassy tussock and tumbled in a sprawling heap, face-first into the dry dirt. Sam twisted his head to look up and momentarily a huge leg hovered over him. The heavy-looking foot started to come down He closed his eyes and waited.

After several tense seconds passed, Sam warily opened his eyes and peeked upward. He turned his head from side to side as his vision swept over the emptiness around him. He was alone. Both creatures were nowhere to be found. Sam got up, still feverishly searching around with wide-open eyes. He blinked a few times as he tried to make sense of what had happened. Then he realised he hadn't heard them leave. Perhaps they were never there. With his mind spinning out of control he questioned himself.

Was it just a stressed imagination causing him to hallucinate? He munched on some more of those delicious plump berries then laid his head on the ground and slept some more.

It was almost midday by the time hunger caused him to stir. He still felt woozy but improved a little after a plate of hot beans. He packed up camp and marched for a few hours. As he wandered down to the river to fill his bottle, his legs grew weak at the sight of another figure on the horizon. *Not again*, he thought. This one moved like a person and an emboldened Sam was determined not to shy away this time. He carefully approached the dishevelled man who wore long, thick, unkempt brown hair. The man's skin was bronzed and leathery, and what was left of his ragged tunic was tied around his waist in a careless fashion. As Sam got closer the man waved at him.

'Hello there, my good fellow,' the man said. 'What's your name?'

Sam was still uncertain and walked right up to him and touched him on the arm. Finding it tangible, he took a step back and shook his head a little.

'My name is Sam.' He gasped, timidly.

'You didn't expect to find me out here, did you?' said the man. He smiled, causing cracks to appear all over his grimy, weather-worn face. 'Tell you the truth, I never expected to see anyone out here either, although I've been watching you for a while. The name's Lector. Lex for short,' he said.

'How long have you lived here?' Sam asked, cautiously eyeing him as Lex led him up the riverbank through a passage of boulders and into a secluded little nook.

He pointed to some rocks which were positioned to resemble chairs around a table and they both sat down facing each other. 'I don't rightly remember. Must be a few years now,' Lex replied, scratching his head. 'So, what brings you out here?'

Sam glared into Lex's deep-set reddened eyes as he thought about how he could answer.

Before Sam could say anything, Lex continued, 'I used to live in a lovely little place in town, not too far from here.'

'I think I know of the town,' Sam said.

'I was their Dom, you know,' Lex added, confirmed by his barely functioning, makeshift loincloth. 'Trouble is, I was getting too old and lazy to work, and I didn't fancy going to Area 15. You know about that?' he asked, raising both eyebrows and turning to look up at Sam.

'Yeah, I do.'

'Well, you know, no one comes back from there and I didn't think that was a great idea, so I took off. Been living here ever since. Come and I'll show you around,' Lex said.

They both got up and Sam followed him with silent fascination, although he didn't think there was that much to see. They were beside a long sandstone cliff face that climbed high into the sky but was crumbly at the bottom. In front of it was the small area with scattered rocks where they had been sitting, a track through more boulders that went past the mostly dead trees near the river, and some conveniently placed craggy outcrops that were good vantage points for observation. Just when Sam was wondering how this man could survive here, they pushed their way through a thickly piled knot of dead wood, vines and branches which camouflaged the entrance to a small chilly cave. A little fire was burning at the back and Sam's eyes followed the waft of black smoke as it trailed upwards and dissipated through the crags in the cave's ceiling.

'Welcome to my home,' Lex said as he sat down against a wall on an old grubby cushion. Sam looked around and picked out another one to sit on.

'What do you eat?' Sam asked.

'It isn't easy, my lad. There are only slim pickings around here. You've probably found that out for yourself. But mainly I've got to steal from town. It's about two days return walk over that way,' Lex said, pointing to the right. 'Every other week or so I set off and bring back as many supplies as I can carry. It's risky but a man has to eat.'

Lex stood up and Sam watched the rough and gristly fellow walk over to the other side of the cold stone cavern. He pulled back a piece of dark brown cloth that Sam could barely see in the twilight glow within the cave and revealed a shelf with enough bags and containers of food to last for weeks, and some larger sacks of grain and quinoa.

'There's also plenty of wild blackberries around here but you need to know which ones are good to eat. Pick the wrong ones and they can send you mad. They make you see all sorts of weird things. Mess with your brain, they do. "Crazy berries" is what I call them,' Lex said, tapping the side of his head three times. 'What about you, what have you been living on?'

'I brought a lot of supplies with me. And I've been picking berries. Maybe some of the wrong ones too, I am guessing,' Sam replied, with a half grin.

Lex let out a hearty laugh that should have made Sam feel more at ease but didn't.

'Now, you never got around to telling me why you're out here,' Lex said. 'I must say, you look awfully young.'

'I'm nearly seventeen and I'd rather not say right now,' Sam said.

'Well, that's okay,' Lex said, interrupting the awkward silence. 'I can guess. You've escaped from a farm, huh? A young fellow like you. A fugitive just like ol' Lex.'

Lex chuckled to himself.

'You've done well. They say it's impossible to break out of a farm. You must have had some help.'

Sam sat silently.

Lex was smiling broadly and winked, then nodded his head vigorously to indicate he fully understood. 'Ah, I see. Can't say, hey? Anyway, I'm glad you're here. It's nice to have someone to talk to. It's been mighty lonely out here since ...' Lex's voice trailed off. 'You're welcome to stay for as long as you like.'

'Thank you for the offer,' Sam said. He was extremely grateful for the company but especially the food. 'I'd really like to stay here for a bit.'

Lex clapped his hands together firmly. 'Good, good. Let's have some dinner. You're looking a little gaunt. Then we'll go down to the river for a swim,' he said as he led the way.

Although Lex was trying hard to make him feel welcome during the following few days, Sam didn't intend to stay with him for long. Lex spent too much time muttering incoherently and acting peculiar, which Sam found unnerving. Just this morning Lex had offered to cook oats for them both to then make only barely enough for himself.

They started a game of checkers at Lex's suggestion. Sam took two pieces and was about to take another when Lex suddenly got up and climbed to one of the lookouts, leaving Sam sitting puzzled. Lex was so unpredictable. Sam was pouring some tea when Lex came back and offered to restart the checkers match to which Sam obliged.

'Did you see anything?' Sam asked.

Lex seemed as if he didn't hear him.

'It wasn't my idea to leave, you know,' Lex said.

'Really?' Sam responded.

'Yeah, true. I lived with a family in a massive mansion on a hill overlooking the whole district. Six women, a dozen girls and a bunch of us Doms. They even had three Recs if I recall correctly,' Lex said.

'That's a huge family,' Sam said.

'Yeah. I'd virtually grown up with another Dom called Blake. Hah, that's a double jump!' He clicked his piece twice and took two of Sam's. 'We were lifelong mates and as close as two men could be. Then one day we found out that he was being sent away. He kept getting sick. I tried to help him out, mind you. I did all my work and half his most of the time. Didn't stop them, though,' Lex said, shaking his head, looking dejected.

'That's terrible,' Sam said.

'I know it. He was mortified when he found out he was going to Area 15 so he made up his mind to escape. I knew what he was planning, of course. He told me everything. Then I started thinking. He's not that much older than me and that'll happen to me soon enough. That's when I told him I was going with him,' Lex said, pausing to take a breath.

'Well, we had it all worked out and we left together and never looked back. We literally ran for our lives and didn't stop till we got here and found this nice place to camp. We thought we would only be here a short while, but we ended up staying until ...' Lex's voice choked as he stopped to vigorously rub his dirty cheek.

Sam had let him do all the talking and seized the moment to contribute something to the conversation. 'I can see why you like it here,' he said.

'Blake got sick again and died,' continued Lex.

'Oh, I'm sorry to hear. That must have been very difficult for you,' Sam said.

'Yeah, he'd been sick before and pulled through. I just thought he'd get better.'

Sam watched him get up and slowly wander towards the river.

XLVI

About two weeks later, Lex announced that a trip to procure supplies was necessary. Sam watched him sorting through the near-empty shelving behind the curtain.

'I best go alone this time. You can come with me on the next run and I'll show you the ropes, okay?' he said as he looked at Sam for approval.

Sam nodded. 'Yeah, sure. How long will you be gone?'

'I'm usually back in a few days. Sometimes longer if I run into trouble and need to lay low for a bit,' Lex said calmly as he gathered up a khaki bag almost the size of him and slung it over his sinewy right shoulder.

'Is there much trouble?' Sam asked.

'Nah. Nothing to worry about. If someone sees me, I might have to dodge and weave, that's all. Look after the camp for us,' Lex said as he waved and marched away.

It felt good to have some time alone again. Sam could explore properly without Lex hovering around. The steep cliff face that bordered the north of the camp took his interest. A couple of hundred metres along, the passage up the side narrowed considerably and he had to shimmy along the wall to avoid falling into the deep ravine opening to his left. Loose stones made the descent into the deadwood forest so precarious he slid part of the way. On a windy day, it would be too dangerous to venture in amongst the lifeless branches that had a habit of breaking off but today was fine and calm.

There was no path to follow as he carved his way through the bracken and the aged, rough, majestic tree trunks that could fall over at any time but for now stood soaring into the cloudless sky. He was conscious of not straying too far from the camp for fear of becoming lost. The appearance of a small clearing up ahead seemed out of place amongst the dense woodland and made for a convenient point for him to turn around. As he emptied his bladder before heading back, he noticed in the dirt at his feet, what appeared to be a shiny white stone. He kneeled and dug around a little and soon discovered it was a bone fragment. Now using both hands to scratch away the dirt, he began to unearth a human skeleton buried beneath a couple of inches of loose gravel. It looked as if a lot of runoff had come through the clearing and washed most of the topsoil away from the area.

Methodically working his way past the rib cage and over the shoulder, Sam eventually found the skull. It was broken. It was smashed in as if it had been hit with severe force. He knew immediately that an injury to the head causing that much damage would be fatal. His first guess was that it was Blake but that didn't make sense. Lex had said he had buried his dead companion, who had been sick, in a beautiful spot with filtered views of the river in the alluvial soil just above its bank to the south of camp. This was nowhere near the location he had described.

It could have been someone else, Sam supposed. There were very few people in these parts, of course, but he was here, as was Lex, so it wasn't entirely impossible that someone over the years had died here. But this person was murdered and buried, so someone else must have been here with them. He had an awful suspicion that he had stumbled onto the grave of Blake and that it was something Lex didn't want him to see. Sam hastily covered the bones back up and brushed the dirt to disguise the disturbance. He also shuffled his feet to smear any footprints left behind on the track.

The next day, Lex returned with two full bags of supplies. He gave a cheery 'hello' as he walked into the campsite and saw Sam sitting on the rock in front of the cave's obscured entrance.

Sam tried to smile. 'Hi, did everything go okay?' he asked.

'Yes. Good, good. No problems at all,' Lex replied as he placed his buttocks heavily on the large flat stone opposite Sam. The bags were plonked down next to him with a thud. 'Do you want some?' Lex proffered a bottle of wine. He was sweaty and looked tired. After taking a swig, he passed it to Sam, who did likewise before handing it back.

'I'm exhausted,' Lex said. He stretched his left leg out in front and rubbed his thigh. 'I'm going to wash up then take a nap. Be a good fellow and unpack the supplies in the cave.'

Sam felt uneasy all day and sat watching Lex laid out snoring in the shade of the large overhanging crag face not far from a little fireplace where Sam was cooking a pot of food. He slept till late afternoon and by the time he awoke, Sam was swimming laps back and forth across the river. At dusk, they had a quick supper and retired to the cave for the night. Sam was tired too. Tired of thinking about yesterday's discovery.

As dawn broke, Sam had been lying awake for hours. He was up and completing his morning exercises by the time Lex came out of the cave. Lex was carrying a couple of bowls of porridge. He offered one to Sam who took it but put it down without eating one spoonful and quietly wandered down to the river. His poorly disguised cool demeanour indicated something was wrong and Lex followed him with his breakfast.

Whilst Sam took care of his morning ablutions, Lex casually asked through gulps of hot gruel, 'Is something troubling you, Sam? You've been acting different ever since I got back from town.'

Sam stood silently in the gently flowing waist-high water and turned to look at Lex, who was scraping the last bits of porridge from his bowl on the riverbank. Sam shook his head and waded back in, picked up his towel and began drying himself.

'Well, what is it? You're too quiet and you look kind of miserable,' Lex said.

The unexpected sight of Lex hovering at his right shoulder made Sam jump nervously. He hung his wet towel on a nearby berry bush, picked up his tunic and quickly flung it over his head as Lex stood facing him, waiting for a response.

Shuffling slightly back from Lex, Sam looked away from him and said, 'How did your friend die? What illness did you say he had?'

Lex was old and shrewd and immediately suspected that Sam may have found something whilst he was away.

'Ah, I didn't,' Lex replied as he went down to the water and rinsed his bowl. 'But since you're wondering, I'll tell you. There's no point trying to keep secrets if we're going to be friends, and you do want us to be friends, right?'

'Of course,' Sam replied, still staring at him.

'I had to kill him,' Lex said.

Sam stumbled backwards and gulped with a look of revulsion.

'What, you murdered him? But you said he was your friend, your life-long friend!' Sam said.

'Wait, wait, to start with I should have said he was very sick,' Lex said, holding up his hands to calm Sam. 'Please, hear me out. You see, it wasn't long after we arrived here. We were starving. Not only plain hungry but wasting away to nothing. We'd run out of food and hadn't eaten for, I can't remember exactly, but weeks. We never took enough. You were smart, you bought plenty. And see, we were wanted men; we were being hunted. We were miles from here, we kept going, had to. But we'd gone too far in the wrong direction and there was nothing out there. So, we started to head back the way we came. But it was hopeless and there was no way we were going to make it. Only got as far as here and that was it. We couldn't go any further.' Lex swallowed and took a couple of deep breaths. 'You've got to understand; we were both going to die. Both of us had talked about dying and we'd agreed that when it happened, it would be perfectly acceptable for the survivor to consume them.'

Sam stood up, glaring at him and shouted, 'You're not saying what

I think you're saying, are you?'

'Well, I got to thinking that we would both be dead soon anyway and I rightly or wrongly decided that I would kill him and eat him to keep myself alive. I know that sounds barbaric but desperation will drive a man to do things he might not otherwise do. You understand, don't you?' Lex pleaded. He slumped to the ground and sat at Sam's feet.

Sam couldn't believe his ears. It was difficult to even look at Lex but he forced himself to. 'Yes, I understand. You killed him. You're a murderer. And a cannibal! You murdered and ate your only friend!' Sam exclaimed, snarling at Lex with a pounding heart. 'Hell, how do I know that's not going to happen again? This time to me!' Sam said. He was red-faced and wide-eyed with terror and rage.

'You don't have to worry,' Lex replied in an overly condescending tone. 'It's completely different now. We have food. We're both fighting fit and besides, I enjoy our friendship. It's been awful lonely out here and I do miss Blake. I am really glad you're here, Sam,' he added.

Sam, still reeling in disbelief, nodded thoughtfully as he turned and slowly walked back to the camp. He was trying to evaluate the implications of this recent revelation, whilst listening to Lex's footsteps thudding in the dirt behind him.

'Well, aren't you going to say anything?' Lex asked as he hurried to catch up with Sam.

Sam decided to remain calm and act unperturbed. There was no point upsetting Lex right now, especially considering his violent history and his insane personality. 'Yes, it's alright. Your story sounds reasonable,' Sam replied, trying to sound appeased.

Not much was said for a while until Sam suggested that they play checkers. Lex smiled and speedily set them up. Although Sam gave Lex the impression that he had totally accepted the situation, the truth was that he was anxious and afraid. Sam's mind was ticking over and over thinking about his predicament. He didn't win one game of checkers that afternoon.

XLVII

Over the next couple of days, Sam discreetly prepared to leave, whilst keeping a watchful eye on Lex and maintaining a cheerful pretence. The weather was getting cooler and the days settled into a routine. Mornings were almost entirely spent alone at the river, either swimming, collecting berries or sometimes whittling in the breeze. Whereas most afternoons were occupied with checkers, playing cards and talking. Sam struggled with the afternoons the most but the early part of the day provided the chance to hide food and supplies in a convenient place for retrieval on leaving. He also made sure his backpack and bags were packed.

He knew there was something odd about Lex from the day he arrived and now had confirmation that he had killed and devoured his only, albeit sick, companion. And how could he expect to elicit Sam's empathy for his plight without showing any emotion himself? Perhaps he had been living rough out here alone for so long it had hardened him, Sam tried to reason in his mind, but there was no chance of trusting him. He was ready to leave.

That night he went to bed early. If he woke in the morning before Lex, he would go. A little later when Lex made his way into the cave, Sam was still awake. They both laid there for what seemed an eternity, listening to the crackle of the dying fire. Sam's eyes were feeling heavy when suddenly in the dim haze Lex spoke.

'Have you ever eaten human flesh?' Lex asked.

Sam sat up in alarm, now shaken wide awake. 'No, I haven't,' was his sharp response. He glared over to where Lex was lying, as his pulse suddenly quickened.

'Not many have, I guess,' Lex said calmly without shifting on his bedroll.

'I don't think I am likely to either,' Sam said, feeling extremely uncomfortable.

Lex went on. 'I think you would, though, if you had to,' he said as he sat up, his face now visible in the fading golden glow of the flickering flames. 'Yeah, you definitely would.'

'No, you're wrong,' Sam insisted.

Sam was visibly disturbed and got up to restoke the fire. The thought of being in the cave with Lex seemed like the worst possible place to be and it would be exceedingly more unpleasant in total darkness. Sam poked and prodded the fire with a slim, straight stick and bundled some more thicker pieces of wood onto it. Fussing over it made him concentrate on something other than their conversation. It helped him keep calm and feel somewhat less vulnerable. *This guy is definitely crazy,* he thought.

Lex, sensing Sam's agitation, said, 'Sorry, I didn't mean to offend you. Goodnight, Sam,' before settling back down and closing his eyes.

Sam was unnerved and now more determined than ever to leave in the morning. Sunrise could not come fast enough as far as he was concerned. It took a long time but eventually, he fell into a fitful sleep. He dreamt of nightmarish skeletons dancing around the fire cackling at him with jangling jaws. Suddenly, Sam was jolted awake by the sensation of close movement. He flicked on his headlamp. The glint of the metal sculpting blade first caught his eye, then he saw Lex kneeling over him, preparing to use it. Within seconds, Sam kicked out at Lex and knocked him flying across the cave.

'Get away from me, you crazy bastard!' Sam yelled. As he scrambled towards the cave entrance, he felt Lex grab hold of his right ankle, trying to pull him back.

'Come on, just a little bit off your leg. It won't hurt that much. Why won't you share?' Lex said in a deranged voice.

Sam shook loose, got to his feet and gave Lex another kick in the face. He grabbed his backpack and bag and ran as fast as he could and disappeared into the night without stopping to look back, and without picking up the hidden camping supplies.

Sam ran for hours and had lost track of how far he had travelled but he could still see the river. He was as certain as he could be that Lex was not following him, so he decided to rest and make his way down to the water. Splashing his face, he felt instantly refreshed.

The sun was already falling behind the distant mountains, casting a rosy glow and long shadows across the land so he made camp. As the light faded, he gathered some stones and placed them in a circle, pulled the flint from his backpack and started a fire. The warmth and light from the small blaze were a humble comfort. He checked his carry bag. It contained all the essentials – the tin for boiling water, quinoa, beans, flour and oats – and with the berries and roots that were more abundantly available now, he had enough to get him to the oasis of vegetation he was heading towards prior to meeting Lex.

It took three days before he reached the outskirts of the small woodland. Under the thick canopy of mostly evergreen Fig trees, he soon discovered various plants with edible leaves and roots, perfect to supplement his limited rations. Using some fallen logs, branches and fronds, he put together a crude but functional shelter that was larger and more comfortable than his tent he had left behind. After his experience with Lex, this place was paradise and provided months of bliss. However, his supplies were starting to dwindle and the vegetation, although better than nothing, by itself was insufficient to sustain him. The choices were to attempt the one-week trek back to the closest town without running into Lex or keep heading north towards the larger town, which would take at least a week longer. He chose the latter.

XLVIII

The weather had cooled but food was still a problem. For days he had found nothing of substance to eat and he was down to the last of his quinoa. Not being able to feed his shrinking muscles, he was struggling to travel more than a few hours a day before collapsing into his bedroll. He was caught in an awful conundrum – the slower he moved, the longer his journey with less to eat each day.

He rested on a large smooth shale deposit by the riverbank, staring at the sky. Coming out of a trance deep in thought, he looked up suddenly and was surprised to see his mother standing up ahead near the next bend in the river. His prayers were answered, his problems solved. Sonya would know what to do. He called to her and waved frantically. Sonya's sweet smile beamed as bright as the setting sun's reflection on the water. He moved in her direction hypnotised by her image. As he staggered closer with watery eyes and blurry vision, he stumbled and fell with flaying arms onto his chest. He picked himself up, searching for her and ignoring the painful, bloody grazes across the palms of both hands. She was still there, hazy and wavy, and she looked concerned. When he was within reach, he dived towards her with outstretched arms and fell face-first into the river. He sat up in the water and rubbed his eyes. He was alone again and he wasn't surprised.

He closed his eyes and threw his head back to the sky before dunking it under the water and holding it there for a few moments, letting his ears fill with the sounds of muffled flooding. With a loud splash, he resurfaced and felt a little better. He knew his condition was deteriorating rapidly again. He had been in this situation not long ago and it wasn't a nice feeling. He climbed out of the river and flopped onto its bank, and there lying on his back, he watched the clouds wafting overhead in the fading light. The wind had picked up and was blowing his matted wet hair across his face. He spat some trapped dirt from his mouth.

As his head fell to the left, he gazed upon a messy little nest up in one of the few growing trees about two meters from the ground.

Another mirage, he thought, but its intrigue drew him towards it. Summoning all his strength he climbed the trunk, peered inside the nest and was astonished to find five blue-and-green speckled bird's eggs. Everyone knew birds became extinct during the Insane War. He pushed four of them into his mouth and crunched them down. They tasted so good but even starving, he was mindful of leaving one. He slid down the tree and sat on the ground next to it in stunned contemplation. Just then, he saw a petite blue-and-black robin with a pointy beak flitter around the tree and land in the nest on its now one precious egg. Seeing a bird was incredible. It gave him hope. Exhausted, he rolled over and fell asleep under the dimming sky.

The wind had calmed and he was awoken by nearby voices, slicing the silence at sunrise. Startled, he sat up rapidly to listen. His eyes scanned his surroundings like two searchlights checking a prison fence. He jumped up nervously and headed in the direction of the remarkable sounds. He peered through the thick cluster of dead trees, bracken and voluminous wide and thick berry bushes and saw two women collecting wood and chatting merrily to each other. He fiercely rubbed his eyes, then shadowed them at a safe distance taking care to remain unseen. They led him through the forest of dead trees to a concealed crevice in the cliff beyond. He followed them along the narrow passage a little way before it opened into a wide hidden valley surrounded by high rocky cliffs. A strong flowing tributary of the river ran down into the valley and through the centre of it. Enriching the idyllic surroundings was the natural protection it afforded from extreme weather conditions, with the benefits of isolation.

To his amazement, after drifting around alone for nearly three years, Sam saw what looked like a well-established compact settlement or small village. His attention was first drawn to the people. There were dozens of them with varying ages from babe-in-arms to the wise and grey, and all were female. Sam could hear a cacophony of voices, a muddling mixture of talking, singing, and laughing. All the women were working whilst the youngsters played. From what he could see, they were a happy tribe.

The encampment could not be easily discovered due to its secluded location and its obscured entrance. Not that there were many people wandering around the area. It was only due to Sam's incredibly unique circumstances that he was here. Even then, had he not heard those two women talking he would have likely kept following the main branch of the river that flowed straight past and never found them.

Two young girls ran close by to where he was hiding, forcing him to crouch lower to avoid detection. He heard their frolicking footsteps as they approached the river and watched as presumably their mother followed not far behind. They undressed and jumped into the water, causing loud splashes and even louder yells as the wet cold stung their skin. The scene made him think of his mother and how much he missed her, Beth and Chad. The security of his family and the comfort of his home felt so far away.

As soon as he was sure he could move without being discovered, Sam scrambled up through some large boulders that flanked one side of the village. The overhanging escarpment contained many small caves, which would make ideal shelter. As well, the ledge was a perfect vantage point to study the clandestine community. He spent the whole day observing them, mesmerised by their activities. The younger girls were playing games and chasing each other from one end of the camp to the other. He noticed that there were no infants and none of the girls seemed younger than about ten years old. Some older women sang cheery tunes as they worked to gather berries and put them into slim woven baskets that hung from around their necks. Quite a few were preparing food or eating from bowls. The river was also a popular spot occupied by bathers, young and old, and women cleaning clothes with stones at the waterline. Although the place was busy, all were happy and relaxed. Something he yearned for.

There were dozens of little round huts with grassed roofs positioned in rings around a central courtyard. In its very middle was an impressive open fire pit with several women attending to the flames. There were also smaller fireplaces scattered around the site that looked like planets orbiting the sun. Beyond the huts were orderly gardens. A small orchard surrounded a vegetable plantation and there were large flourishing fruitful berry bushes all around. The good kind, of course, not the crazy ones. The women and girls wore pale brown sleeveless dresses not too unlike the tunics that were customarily worn by men. They were simple, plain and clean and there were no overalls to be seen. All the girls were barefoot and most wore necklaces and bracelets made with strands of colourful round beads.

Later that night whilst the tribe slept, Sam ventured into the central courtyard. He was curious and hungry. It was dark and moonless but some of the fires were still burning low, providing him with visible shadowy details of the village. As he plucked some plump fruit from a berry bush, he noticed a large charcoal-stained metal pot hanging above a fireplace. He lifted its lid and found it a quarter-full of leftover vegetable soup. He dipped the ladle in and carefully brought it to his mouth to taste it. It was still warm and felt good flowing down his throat and flooding his empty stomach. He ate some more and grabbed a few pieces of fruit that were in a sack nearby and put them in his backpack. As he quietly crept through the settlement, he peered into the occasional open entrances of some of the small dwellings he passed. The occupants were all huddled together on the ground under blankets, sleeping peacefully, and he was able to pick up a small bag of tea leaves. On the way back, he also collected some vegetables from the garden.

The escarpment provided Sam with several caves from which to choose a primary lodging and he selected one that was set back out of sight with a concealed entrance. If he were careful, he could live here, continuing to help himself to their food until he regained his strength for a homeward journey.

Over the following weeks, Sam's health returned and he was fitter than ever. Each morning he would leave early using an obscured pathway in the opposite direction to the village. He had used his time exploring the uninhabited wilderness and studying the terrain walking for days through the forest, over hills and down valleys, and into the gushing river downstream where the tributary re-joined it. When he was low on food, he entered the village at night to eat and take stock of what he needed.

Some days, Sam just surveyed the village for hours as the women and girls went about their lives, probably because he was starved of company. He never grew tired of seeing the hive of activity. As the sunlight faded, he watched the children drag themselves off to bed. The older women followed later as a few at a time retired for the night until only the last youngish stragglers had to make their way into their huts before his expedition into camp. Tonight, as he leaned over the soup pot and began eating some of the leftovers that it always held, he sensed movement behind him. Quickly he turned around, accidentally dropping the spoon. It went 'plop' before being consumed by the soup. Sam flinched at the sight of a dozen ghostly figures standing behind him silhouetted in the silvery glow of the half-moon. Their gaze felt like radiant laser beams piercing his skin.

Sam had become complacent, carelessly leaving behind evidence of his visits. The women became suspicious of his footprints and the messy dribbles left to run down the blackened sides of the soup pot, and its lid that hadn't been replaced properly. As Sam stood stunned in the dull light, his immediate thought was to run but just as he tensed his muscular legs, one woman stepped forward and spoke.

'Don't be afraid. You have nothing to fear from us. Please stay, sit down, and talk with us,' she said, in a slow calm voice.

Sam sat down and fished out the spoon from the depths of the pot. He cleaned the handle as best as he could, using the edge of his dirty old, tattered tunic, and placed it on the wobbly timber table next to him. The women all came forward to take a seat with him around the restoked fire. His time roaming the wilderness had left him with the appearance of an untamed savage. Although he had grown tall and muscular, his skin was dark and gritty, his wavy black hair was long and scraggy, and his face bore the growth of a youthful patchy beard.

'What is your name?' asked the woman who had spoken first. Her faded grey, parchment-like skin and hollowed cheeks projected the image of a wise elder of the group. She had a welcoming disposition but wore a weary smile.

He glanced up at her and said, 'I'm Samuel Smith. But people call me Sam.'

'It's nice to meet you, Sam. My name is Gloria.'

By way of introduction, she went around the circle and announced the names of the other women as they nodded to him in salutation but he was distracted by the disappointment of being caught out. He was still stewing over it when Gloria asked him where he was from.

'Sam, I asked where you are from – what brings you here,' she said, repeating herself.

He regarded her misty-coloured hair and contrasting dark probing eyes whilst thinking of what to say. Her manner was cool with the sullen greyness of a threatening tempest and calm like the stillness before a storm.

'My family couldn't keep me. I ran away and I've become lost,' Sam said. He spoke softly, sounding grave and vulnerable.

'I see,' Gloria said. 'You do look slightly bewildered. I think it would be a good idea for you to stay here with us tonight. Would you like to do that?'

Sam was surprised and said, 'Can I?'

'Of course. We have plenty of room for you. We'll put you in your very own hut for the night,' Gloria replied. 'Vicky, Jan, Penny, please find another hut tonight to make room for our guest.' The three women acknowledged the request. Gloria turned to Sam. 'Vicky will show the way if you would like to follow her,' she said, indicating to a middle-aged woman sitting directly to her right. 'We can talk more in the morning. Is that okay?'

'Yes, that would be good. Thank you very much,' Sam said as he stood and followed Vicky. Once he was settled inside the cosy hut, Vicky bid him goodnight and left. He snuggled into the bedroll and under the soft blanket. As he lay there wondering what the future held, he felt peace and contentment and murmured quietly to himself, 'We'll just have to wait and see,' before drifting off into a deep sleep.

* * *

Gloria waited until Vicky and Sam had left before continuing to chat with the remaining women. 'I expect he's probably a Domestic and his owner has fallen on hard times or had some sort of tragedy,' she said.

'Yes, I think you're right. Doms are cheap and expendable and often treated poorly. It wasn't uncommon for women to take on too many and then want to get rid of some,' Jan said.

'But why would he choose to run away and leave the only place he knew?' asked another.

'Well, it's certainly risky, but he looks incredibly young and although he seems a bit unsure of himself, he's obviously adventurous. I'd say they were getting ready to resell him and when fear got the better of him, he decided to flee. He chose one unknown path over another,' Gloria replied.

'He seemed very keen to stay with us tonight, didn't he? Do you think he can live with us if he wants to?' Penny asked.

'I don't see why not. If he's run away, there's not much risk of him going back and exposing us,' Jan said. 'The Dom that came with us when we established our village was a wonderful man and a great help to us. We all remember his efforts during the hut constructions.'

'Yes, I tend to agree, Jan,' Penny said. 'It was such a pity he died so young.'

'But Sam must be allowed to make up his own mind,' Gloria added. 'The choice is his. This was one of the main reasons we chose to shun society. To get away from the cruel and inhumane idea of keeping men locked up in farms and using others as slaves made the fight and struggle to survive out here all worthwhile.'

'I don't think there would be any harm in letting him stay,' said another.

'So, does everyone think we should offer Sam a place to stay with us?' Gloria asked, casting her eyes around the group. All the women were nodding.

'Alright then, it's agreed for now. But let's not get ahead of ourselves. We don't know much about him and he might have other plans. We'll talk with him further in the morning and if we're still happy and he wants to, we'll allow him to join us. Good night, all. Get some sleep and we will get together early tomorrow,' she said as they dispersed back to their huts.

***

Sam found a jug of water, some soap, a small mirror, a comb, scissors and a blade left by his bedside.

'Obviously, they don't appreciate the savage feral look,' he said to himself. He picked up the mirror. 'I can see why.'

He fumbled around with the comb and scissors and tidied his hair as best as he could then shaved his whiskers. A fresh brown tunic hung over a chair so he changed into it before venturing out into the emerging daylight. As he returned from the river, he was met by a group of chattering women and giggling girls. The village had never received a visitor and Sam's arrival had generated a great deal of excitement.

'Good morning, Sam!' Gloria said in a loud voice, trying to be heard over the noise.

He returned the hearty greeting.

'As you can see, news travels fast around here and you have created quite a commotion,' she said, dramatically sweeping her right arm in a broad arc.

Sam didn't expect this type of reception and blushed with embarrassment and was a little concerned that he was creating a nuisance. As the boisterous crowd gathered like a swarm of bees, Gloria put her arm around his shoulder and walked him into a larger central meeting hut. They were handed a bowl of warm oats and a spoon as they took a seat in the circle.

'I see there is actually a good-looking young man underneath all of that hair,' Gloria said with an engaging grin.

'Thanks,' he said.

'As you've probably realised by now, Sam, there are only women and girls living here. We have been without males for an awfully long time. Although, we did have one charming Dom with us when we first arrived. He was a good man and helped us considerably before he unfortunately passed away.'

'Would you like some herb tea?' Jan asked.

'Yes, please.'

'You mentioned your mistress couldn't keep you. So, did you run away from your home?' Gloria asked.

Sam took a gulp of tea and nodded silently at her.

'You know you're not supposed to do that, don't you?' she gently questioned before continuing without waiting for an answer. 'Was it just you or were there a few other Doms being sold too?'

'There was three of us,' he replied. He scraped the edges of his almost empty bowl.

Sam thought the more he agreed with whatever she said, the higher the chance they might let him stay and she had already mentioned they once had a Dom they liked.

'Well, that doesn't concern us here. Every one of us contributes to our close-knit community in some way and we all support each other,' Gloria said proudly to everyone present.

'It's nice here,' Sam said.

'We're glad you think so and you are quite welcome to stay. No one will own you and you can also leave at any time should you wish to. You will be free to work and live amongst us,' she said.

As if considering his options, Sam looked around slowly at the spellbound audience waiting patiently for his response. Having already determined that it would be a great experience to live with them at least for a while, Sam said, 'Thank you. I would very much like to,' as a wide smile crept across his face.

'You are most welcome,' Gloria said as she patted him on the back. The council gave a little cheer to show their support for the outcome before dispersing.

XLIX

Spring mornings were Sam's favourite, the fresh and bracing air, bathing whilst he had the river to himself. Once dried, he strolled back into the village to join the women who were still taking breakfast which was usually a thick porridge of boiled oats topped with brown swirls of sweet, treacle-like sauce.

Sam crunched through the acorns scattered on the ground as he approached one of the tables partly shaded with the filtered sunlight under a spreading Oak tree and asked one of the women seated if he could join them.

'Of course, please do. I'm Lily,' she said, stirring her bowl. 'And this is Nica, Olifiza and Melissa,' she said, pointing to each in turn.

'Nice to meet you all,' Sam said.

'Can you tell us a bit about yourself?' Lily asked.

Sam hesitated for a moment, thinking. This was tricky because he had no past, only Samantha did. Armed with only his mother's stories about the Production Farms, he bluffed his way. 'There isn't a lot to tell, really, because boys are raised in farms and then most go on to work in the fields tending crops. Others leave and become Doms and Recs and work in nice houses but sometimes it doesn't work out, like me,' Sam said.

'I guess so,' Lily said.

'We did play a lot of checkers. Do you know it?' Sam asked, steering the topic of discussion.

'Yeah, of course we do,' Nica said.

They talked about childhood games and activities whilst they scraped the last morsels with their spoons. Sam was finished.

'So why did you leave your *"nice house"*?' Olifiza asked after a brief pause in the conversation.

'It wasn't my choice. They couldn't keep me, so I was going one way or another whether I wanted to or not,' he answered. 'You'll have to show me where you keep the checkers.'

They got up and washed their plates in the communal cleaning trough and placed them on a table in the sun to dry. Sam was soon to discover that although the women and girls had a variety of unique personalities, they all displayed similar positive qualities and followed a charitable inherent moral code of integrity. He hadn't found anyone that he disliked; they all seemed friendly and made him feel welcome, allowing him to easily adapt to their village life.

One of his main jobs was helping to collect firewood and he also loved getting his hands dirty in the garden. Sam also put the skills he'd picked up from Chad to good use, building furniture and making repairs to the huts. When he found out that the women made their own clothes, he enthusiastically added this talent to his expanding repertoire of life skills. One of the women was showing Sam how to beat sodden strips of tree bark into sheets of woven material when Gloria came up to them.

'Would you mind coming for a walk with me, Sam?' she said.

Learning about forming, drying, cutting and stitching could wait until later. Sam handed back the wooden mallet and wiped his hands down the sides of his tunic as he stood and joined Gloria. They started strolling through the orchard towards the village courtyard.

'How are you finding life here?' she asked.

'Great. Nothing to dislike,' he replied. 'But I am wondering how this all came about. Where did you come from and why?'

'Good questions. You have an inquisitive nature,' she said, turning towards him and smiling. 'It all started when me and a dozen close friends began yearning for a simpler existence. We grew tired of the daily grind and disenchanted with the State's need to keep men in prison farms or force them to become slaves,' she said.

Sam listened quietly. *She sounds a lot like my mother,* he thought.

'We began forming plans to make our way into the unknown to see what we could find. The more we talked, the more like-minded women we found, and it didn't take long before our group had swelled to almost a hundred, many with babies or young daughters. We discreetly left our old lives behind, unannounced, never to return. We carried what equipment and stores we could and brought with us a great variety of seeds for planting. When virtually stumbling upon this fertile valley, we were quick to recognise it as the perfect place to establish ourselves.'

'It's easy to see why,' he said.

They had created a secluded, self-sustaining settlement in the wilderness and carved out an unpretentious lifestyle, unbothered by contemporary society.

'That was about ten years ago,' she added.

They sat and drank tea, chatting for another hour, before Sam got back to work.

Being a Dom was easy if he was vigilant. In his time away from chores, he would play games with the younger girls and keep everyone entertained for hours. He relished being popular and often the centre of attention. During a game of handball, he fell awkwardly to the ground, which prompted him to fashion some underwear for himself using the clothes-making equipment.

L

An unusual clamour in the village caused everyone to stir one hazy, grey morning. A twelve-year-old girl had gone missing during the night and her mother was frantically searching for her. Others hurriedly joined the distressed woman but the girl could not be found anywhere. Someone suggested that she may have wandered off sleepwalking or got up early to go exploring. It had happened on rare occasions. It was easy to become disorientated if you lost sight of the river. The women were trying to stay optimistic but before lunchtime, search parties were formed and allocated an area to comb through. At dusk, they returned without finding any sign of her. There was no way of searching beyond twilight as the light from their lanterns was too poor. They had no choice but to resume looking at dawn.

A week of constant distraught searching yielded no result. The girl had mysteriously vanished and was never seen again. He had never seen the village so miserable. The women spent days in a state of disbelief and would remain forever heartbroken by the loss of Becky. It reminded him of how he felt when Chad was taken away from him. It took a while for their period of grieving to pass, during which time Sam developed a deeper appreciation of empathy.

As the fog of despair started to clear from over the village on a cloudless night, while everyone was asleep under a blanket of stars, Sam was disturbed by a rustling noise coming from outside his hut. He brushed the crust from his eyes and peered out the door. He spotted a shadowy silhouette silently skulking around the camp, like a snake slithering over uneven-sized stones. There was a brief muffled kerfuffle and then he saw the shady figure carrying off a girl in her early teens from the hut three down from his. To raise the alarm, he shouted at the offender and charged towards them. As he got closer, Sam thought he recognised the rogue. The long scraggy hair and the makeshift loin cloth. It was Lex and he was attempting to abduct the girl. Lex had followed Sam and had been living in a secreted hole in the ground that he had dug out not far from the village.

Sam grabbed the camp's machete from its concealed location and the brightest lantern to continue the chase. Women began screaming and streaming from their huts in all directions, which intensified the utter state of turmoil. Lex dropped the squirming girl and began to run. He was faster than Sam remembered, although when living with Lex most things about him were not as they seemed. Sam was high on adrenalin, bursting with energy, and was quick and nimble enough to keep up with him.

Sam watched with a keen eye where Lex was leading him. It wasn't easy in the dark, even under the white light of the half moon, but he managed to catch sight of Lex disappearing into a hole in the ground with an almost invisible entrance hidden amongst large wedges of rock. Sam surveyed the area, taking note of his surroundings and any prominent signposts in case he had to find his way back here. In the dim lantern light, he found some bones scattered on the ground nearby. Small human bones. He gasped and fell back in horror as the realisation jolted him like a javelin hitting armour in a joust. Lex had consumed poor Becky, and Sam had caught him out hunting his next prey. The beast had been watching the village for weeks, plotting and planning his attacks, motivated by his morbid obsession to consume human flesh.

Although exhausted, the rush of agitation racing through Sam's body kept him fully alert. There was no chance he would let Lex escape. He waited at the entrance to the hole with the machete poised for the first opportunity to confront him.

Hours later, Sam could hear scratching and climbing noises coming from inside the cavern. With his eyes stinging from the sweat pouring from his brow and his heart beating like the distant war cry of a drum, he arose and got into position behind a rock from where he could surprise Lex should he emerge.

As Lex appeared, Sam brought the machete down forcefully, striking Lex's head, which cracked and spat blood onto Sam's tunic. Lex staggered sideways and Sam raised and lowered the machete again and again. Blow after blow reigned down, splattering Sam with more and more gore. His tunic was bright red, and his arms, face and hair were laced with blood and brain matter. Lex slumped over dead in a pulped mess. Sam pushed him down with his foot, and the gaping mouth in the earth swallowed the carcass whole. The moon disappeared momentarily behind a cloud as if to wink at Sam. Practically catatonic from the shock, he let the dripping machete fall from his grip and stared into the gruesome abyss unable to move for some time. Still stunned, he eventually staggered back to the village in the early hours of the morning.

All the women were asleep, apart from Jan and Penny, two of the elders who were posted on overnight watch hoping for some news of Sam. When he arrived stumbling towards them, he was bloody and shaking uncontrollably, pale, speechless and unresponsive with a chilling vacant gaze.

'Oh goodness, look at him. Oh no, he's hurt!' Jan said in a loud whisper to Penny as they both ran to meet him. They questioned him repeatedly but he couldn't speak.

'Hurry, he looks like he's going to faint,' Penny said, rushing forward with a bottle of water. After putting some water to his mouth, they placed his brawny arms over their shoulders and the two of them struggled to carry him to his hut.

'Look at the state of him,' Jan said. He was caked in congealed blood and guts and covered in scratches and cuts. They carefully laid him on the bedroll. 'He's been in a fight with that intruder no doubt.'

As Sam's head hit the pillow his eyes rolled back and then closed. 'I think he's in shock,' Penny said. 'He is out to it.'

'Help me get this filthy tunic off and check his injuries,' Jan said.

Penny got a dish of water and some towels as Jan pulled the dark-burgundy blood-soaked tunic over his head and threw it into a bucket. Penny started to sponge his face and arms as Jan removed his befouled underwear.

'Pen, look here.'

'Wait … huh?'

'Yeah, looks like we have ourselves a Rec,' Jan said.

'And all this time we thought he was a Dom.'

'Anyway, these wounds aren't that bad at all. Looks like he might have won the fight. Let's get him cleaned up and into a fresh tunic,' Penny said, resuming her work with the water and towel.

By the time they tucked him under some warm blankets, he was sleeping peacefully but they decided it best that they stay with him overnight.

At sunrise, the two women were chatting quietly next to Sam, who was still snoring. Not long after, their voices woke him and he immediately asked them what had happened. After they described his late-night arrival at the village and how they helped him into bed, he thanked them. Following a good feed, they suggested that if he felt well enough, he should talk with the council of elders.

The women gathered in the meeting hut to hear Sam. He told them about his sordid encounter with Lex and the tragic discovery of the bones. They were astonished by the tale and mortified by the terrible fate of Becky. When he conveyed the gruesome details of Lex's violent demise, the women flinched in horror but they were greatly relieved Sam had ended their ordeal and heaped praise and thanks upon him.

After everyone quietened down again Jan raised her voice and said, 'There is one other thing. We have something to tell you.'

'Yes, Jan, what is it?' Gloria asked.

'Sam's also hiding something from us,' she replied as she looked over at him sitting in the middle of the group. He shifted uncomfortably on his seat.

'And, are you going to tell us?'

'Well, we don't think he's a Dom.'

'Oh, you mean that …' Gloria said, pausing.

'Yes, he's a Rec,' Jan said.

'Well, that is a surprise,' Gloria said, casting her eyes around the gobsmacked group. As they all turned to stare at Sam, he was looking at the ground in deep thought.

'So, a Recreational. Is this true, Sam?' Gloria asked.

Sam brought his head up to look her in the eye, ignoring the mutterings of the other women. With a heavy pulse and a cloudy mind, he felt clammy. After some awkward hesitation, he stammered, 'I think, um … yes. I'm … a Rec.'

'Why are you unsure?' Gloria asked.

'Yes, yes I am,' Sam said, trying to sound more confident.

'Why didn't you say something before?' Gloria asked.

'Well, you've never had any men here apart from the Dom that you liked and now me.' His voice caught in his throat briefly. 'I guess you'll want me to leave. I never really said what I was, I just went along with your suggestions.'

'That's okay, thanks, Sam. I should think it best that you go back to your hut and rest some more,' Gloria said.

With a humble nod, Sam stood and walked out.

'This presents us with a slightly different situation, doesn't it?' Gloria said, raising her eyebrows, then twisting her mouth to the side.

One of the other women spoke up and said, 'What does it matter what he is, after all he has done for us? He is a courageous hero. Surely, he can still stay with us, can't he?'

Gloria was gazing ahead thoughtfully, her mind ticking over. 'Yes, I agree, he meant no harm,' she said. There was a steady murmuring amongst the other women.

'We've never had a Rec before, but that doesn't mean we shouldn't have one,' Penny said.

'We should put it to a vote. It could be good for some of our women,' suggested Vicky.

'It will be an interesting experiment though. We have lived here for nigh on a decade with no men and it's never been a problem. What would be the impact on the village?' Gloria asked.

'I don't think it will change anything. Why should it?' Jan replied.

'Can it be that bad?' another asked.

'I guess not,' Gloria replied. 'As long as he agrees. We should not coerce him. He must be free to choose what he wants to do. There will be no slaves here,' she added.

'Okay, we'll vote on it. Those in favour of allowing Sam to stay here as a Rec, please raise your hand,' Gloria said as she lifted her right arm. They were unanimous. 'So, it's agreed. We will put it to him and let him decide.'

Breaking into the conversation, Peggy, a middle-aged woman with dark, dry skin and fading blonde hair, stood and solemnly addressed the group in a slow deliberate voice. 'I advise caution. He is young and even with his training, he lacks experience. So, if he does agree to participate there should be some sort of management of expectations, especially initially,' she said before taking her seat again.

'Good point, Peggy,' Gloria said.

'Further to Peggy's comments, if he says yes, we should set up some sort of system,' Jan said.

'Does anyone have any ideas?' Gloria asked.

'Probably a simple diary would suffice, to keep track of engagements,' Peggy said.

'Yes, I agree, Peggy,' Gloria said. 'He can be responsible for making his own arrangements but start off slowly.'

'And we can perhaps review the situation in a month's time,' Peggy added.

'Yes, definitely,' Gloria agreed. 'Is everyone happy with the proposal?'

The other women confirmed their support.

'Okay, Jan would you please go and get Sam?' Gloria asked.

When Jan returned with Sam, he was trailing behind looking glum.

'Please take a seat, Sam,' Gloria said, pointing to the vacant space next to her. 'Sam, nothing has changed – if you want to, you can still stay with us.'

Sam looked at her in amazement. 'Really?' he asked. He was sure they would tell him to leave.

'Yes, absolutely. We like you Sam and want you to stay, and if you want, you can be a proper Rec. But only if you really want to. You're still free to do as you please when and as you like. What do you say?' Gloria asked.

Sam sat dumbfounded, caught completely unaware. With an enthusiastic smile he said, 'Yes, I would like that very much.'

'That's settled then. Jan will run through a few suggestions we have for you, whilst Vicky can spread the word amongst the women,' Gloria said.

LI

Although he'd grown accustomed to the village and was almost certain he would live here forever, he couldn't escape the nagging desire to see his family again. For now, though, any such thoughts would have to wait. He needed to focus on becoming a convincing Rec. Pretending to have Rec training was easy, thanks to the information from his mother. Sonya had explained the difference between the duties of Doms and Recs but as useful as the theory was, he still didn't have any practical experience.

A few days passed before three curious friends came knocking at Sam's hut, eager to make an appointment. Each of the women entered one at a time and he wrote their names in a small parchment diary Gloria had given him to schedule his engagements. The days were split into morning, lunchtime, and afternoon, with the first keen woman reserving that afternoon whilst the others booked the next two mornings.

When his first appointment with Melissa, a slim, freckled nineteen-year-old arrived, Sam feigned the confidence of a well-trained Rec, even though he was hiding a bundle of anxious energy. Fortunately, she was as nervous as him and didn't know what to expect either. She had taken a liking to Sam from the moment he arrived and had become a close friend. With patience, both were being guided by their virgin naivety and driven by their primal instincts. Sam straightened out the bedroll and laid some extra blankets down. Their mutual inexperience, although contributing to their slight awkwardness, also worked to relieve the intensity of the moment. They both giggled looking at each other for a moment before Melissa laid down on the makeshift nest. He watched her and as she smiled invitingly, he quickly got down and joined her.

In the following weeks, appointments became more frequent; gossip was circulating amongst the women and they were becoming more comfortable with the situation. Sam was noticing a slight nuance to his intermingling with the women. They were all still very friendly and talkative but now quite often another agenda lingered in the background of their socialising, with many conversations leading to an appointment. He wasn't concerned by this development; after all, he knew that his responsibilities had changed and it made him feel kind of special. Even those who he hadn't interacted with all that much were now making his acquaintance.

As the weeks went by, Sam was still trying to limit his engagements to one a day as recommended by the council of elders, although some days he had none, occasionally he had two or more. He had also started to make what came to be known as 'house calls', which meant he would visit the woman's hut rather than always using his own. Sometimes someone would request a special location to meet, such as a secluded part of the river. Sam started to search out spots for his outdoor encounters and he found one of his favourite places was up in the caves on the escarpment with its views to the horizon. He found the openness and freedom exhilarating. After all his life's troubles, trials, twists and turns, he felt as if he had finally worked his way through all of them.

With soaring confidence, Sam lost count of the number of times he had engaged with the various women; although if he wanted, he could count the pages in his little parchment book, which after seven weeks, was nearly full. He already had another brand-new one ready to start. He glanced through the pages showing the days of next week and there were only three vacant time slots.

They would soon be taken, he thought as he closed it and put it back on the top shelf.

His morning appointment had been very early so he played in a hotly contested handball competition for a couple of hours before heading down to the river, a little worn out and sweaty. From the water, in the distance, he saw Melissa looking intense and in earnest discussion with Gloria as they both walked off towards the meeting hut. He paused for a moment as he wondered what it could be about, then shrugged before continuing to wash his tunic.

***

'Quickly, Jan, gather the others and ask them to assemble,' Gloria said. The elders were summoned and joined Gloria and Melissa who were already seated next to each other.

'I have called you here for an important reason,' Gloria said, gravely casting her eyes around the circle of women. She stopped to look at Melissa for a moment before continuing. 'Melissa is with child.'

The group of women turned to each other and gasped with expressions of confusion and disbelief.

'Whatever do you mean – I mean, how?' Vicky asked, scratching her head.

'It must be Sam, of course,' Gloria said. 'For some inexplicable reason, he must be fertile.'

The shock reverberated around the room as the women silently glared at her.

'I know. I hardly believe it myself. It's something I've never seen. Against all possibility, he has either escaped Rec processing or escaped from a farm – both explanations are just as astonishing.'

'Oh, my goodness. So, there must be others pregnant as well,' Jan said.

'Yes, absolutely right. We'll check and see how many, but someone get Sam,' Gloria said.

Sam strolled into the hut trying to gain a hint of what was happening by reading the assembled faces. It looked serious.

'Please sit down,' Gloria said.

'You asked to see me?' Sam asked, instantly sensing the tense atmosphere.

'Yes, Sam, I did. We have something to tell you,' Gloria said.

Sam was now worried, his face changed to a concerned pout. Gloria sounded ominous and his eyes were glued to hers.

'We think Melissa is pregnant and that you are the father,' she said.

With a totally confused gaze, he said, 'I don't know what you mean.'

'Okay then. It means somehow your Rec processing may not be working properly, and because of that, you can make women pregnant through your Rec services,' Gloria said, trying to provide the simplest explanation she could.

Sam just stared at her in awe still not fully comprehending her words. 'I wasn't actually processed as a Rec,' he said.

'You weren't?' Gloria said, gently probing him further. 'Well, you weren't processed as a Dom; we know that. So that can only mean you are a Producer who escaped from a Production Farm,' she added.

'I wasn't born in a farm either,' Sam said.

'What? Wow!' Jan exclaimed as the room spontaneously erupted into several conversations.

'I see. Your story is like searching for hidden treasure, Sam, becoming more incredible with the discovery of each piece,' Gloria said.

'And you didn't think to tell us this?' Vicky asked.

'My mother told me I must keep the fact that I didn't come from a farm a secret but alas, she left out the processing and children bit,' Sam replied.

'Go on, Sam,' Gloria said. 'Can you tell us where you were born?'

'All I know is that when my mother was pregnant, she found out she was having a boy. She didn't tell me how but when she found out, she decided to keep me. I grew up disguised as a girl before I left home to come and live out here,' Sam said.

A wave of gasps resonated around the room.

'Well, we have some thinking to do. Meanwhile, let's find out how many others are in a similar condition. And Sam, if you have any other secrets, please let us know and please cancel any further appointments for now. Okay?' Gloria said.

The news spread throughout the village and to everyone's surprise, another eleven women discovered that they were in varying stages of early pregnancy. It prompted a range of reactions from uncertainty to thrilled, followed by reassurance that their children would be welcome.

After the initial confusion began to fade away, and the council of elders had time to consider their situation, they sat with Sam again.

'We know that you're a good man, Sam, and courageous and dare I say it a bit of a hero to us after that horrible business with Lex,' Gloria said.

'And we don't blame you for what's happened – you are young and inexperienced with the ways of the world and learning about yourself as much as we are,' Penny added.

'Thank you,' Sam said. 'That means a lot to me.'

'We don't view what's happened as a bad thing anyway. As we've told you, we've always considered it a travesty that the Sisterhood and their society treat men so appallingly,' Gloria said, with a reassuring smile. 'We've also been concerned for some time about our inability to have babies in the village and what that means for our future.'

Sam indicated his understanding.

'So, you see, even though we didn't realise it, you are actually helping us. It doesn't matter how we got to this point. With all the knowledge we now have, what matters is what we do with it. That's what needs to be decided and agreed upon,' Gloria said.

'Do you still want me to stay then?' Sam asked.

Gloria smiled at him. 'Yes. Yes, we do. We want to you stay here with us and your children. Not only that but we are also happy for you to continue to have more children with us if you want to,' she replied.

Sam was beaming with joy. 'Thank you so much, that's such a relief to hear!' he said, jumping up to hug her, unable to contain his delight.

The village had changed forever. They had been provided with a means of controlling their own procreation for at least a generation without the need to approach the distant and problematic Implantation Clinics. As the proliferation of pregnancies progressed, anticipation of the dawning of a new era loomed like the sun's rays on the morning horizon. The number of women with child was now twenty and rising.

Predictably the first of the pregnant women started to deliver their offspring around seven months later. Four boys and one girl arrived in rapid succession. The village had gained five noisy, pink and healthy additions to its population. There was a tremendous kindred spirit amongst everyone. Sam was very much the proud father, even though he could scarcely comprehend that they were all his children.

LII

'What's that?' Sonya wondered out loud, standing in the shower, feeling a lump under her arm. She was worried but tried to stay calm as she got dried and dressed. She had worked in the Ministry of Health long enough to know it could be a problem, especially considering she had been more tired than usual lately. She had thought she might be just working too hard.

'Oh, how I wish Chad was here,' she said to herself as she brushed her hair. 'And not locked away in that horrible prison they call a production farm.'

Her mind wandered off as she let the hand holding the brush fall to her lap and stared at her face in the mirror, thinking about Chad as she often did.

I still haven't been able to visit him since Charlotte sent him away. She and her cronies insist on no one being able to see the poor captives. Not even their mothers. What chance would I have visiting a supposed Rec? And what reason could I have without resurrecting dormant suspicions? I swear I will never give up trying to get you out, Chad. Not until my dying day. I promise you.

Straight after her Sisterhood meeting this morning, she would go to work and visit one of her colleagues to get her opinion on the lump.

***

The entire 75 members of the Sisterhood council were assembled for their monthly meeting. Rows of chairs faced the leadership committee on the stage.

'Good morning, sisters,' said Charlotte, still the Chairwoman.

The chattering women became quiet and attentive.

Jacinta reported on farm output, stock levels, numbers of female births and Producer levels before asking Sonya to file a status report on the Doms and Recs program.

Sonya provided them with the relevant statistics, noting everything was operating well. Then she added, 'But given the food supply situation is so favourable, should we be giving consideration to the release of men from the farms back into society?'

'I don't believe there is any support for the idea at this stage,' Charlotte replied.

'I can't see why not. There are other ways to limit population growth,' Sonya added.

'Alright then. We can certainly put it to a vote,' Charlotte said. 'Can I see a show of hands of those who would like to discuss the possibility?'

A few scattered hands were raised. Charlotte did a cursory count and said, 'The result clearly shows that now is not the time. Motion denied.'

'Again,' Sonya muttered.

***

'Hello, Sonya,' said Angie, one of the assessment supervisors in the Health Department.

'Hi, Angie, thanks for seeing me at short notice. I know you're busy.'

'Please, it's no trouble at all. Anything for an old friend. Take a seat.'

Sonya sat on the edge of her chair.

'Now, what seems to be the problem?' Angie asked, leaning over her desk and observing Sonya's concerned expression.

'I've been unusually and increasingly lethargic and … I've noticed this lump under my arm.'

Sonya watched her scribble some notes.

'Any nausea?'

'A little but only now and then,' Sonya admitted.

Angie placed her pencil on the desk and approached Sonya.

'Hmmm, let's take a look. Can you just raise your arms a bit for me?'

Angie felt Sonya's armpits and discovered two small lumps.

'I'll need a biopsy to confirm but it could be …'

'Lymphoma,' Sonya finished Angie's sentence.

'Yes, I'm sorry to say.'

'Damn. Cancerous lymph nodes,' Sonya said. 'I was afraid you were going to say something like that. How long do you think?'

'The good news is that it's usually a very slow disease and can stay localised for … maybe ten years, if you're lucky.'

'But of course, there's no treatment,' Sonya said.

'No. I'm afraid there isn't. When it gets, well, to the end, it'll be a trip to Area 15.'

'Okay, I understand. Thanks for your time, Angie.'

'Sorry it's not better news, Sonya.'

LIII

When Sonya came downstairs, Beth was making lunch to take to work with her.

'How's your new job going?' Sonya asked as she admired Beth's attire and how fit and well she was looking. She was immensely proud of her daughter.

Beth had recently started work within a close-knit team at the Science Department.

'It's great. We're working on some incredibly exciting research for improving our manufactured food products.'

'Sounds fascinating.'

'It is! And the people are lovely.'

'Well, I'm glad you're settling in.' Sonya walked over to the sink and rinsed her cup. 'I've been thinking. If you're interested, there is a young woman in the Health Department who specialises in cosmetic remediation. It's a relatively new area but she could take a look at your scar.'

'Yes, please, I would like that,' Beth said.

'Okay. Her name is Vamity. I'll set up a referral for you.'

'Thanks, Mum!'

Sonya smiled and nodded. 'That's what mums are for.'

***

A few days later at the Health Department, Beth was greeted by a woman slightly older and taller than herself, with tightly cropped, springy, black curls and a dark complexion that accentuated her wide, pearly-white smile.

'Hi Beth, I'm Vamity.'

'Nice to meet you.'

'Come through, I'll lead the way.'

Beth walked behind, admiring the woman's stunning beauty.

They settled into two chairs next to each other in Vamity's consulting room.

'Your mother has told me a little bit about you,' Vamity said. 'That you still live at home with her.'

'That's right. I also have a sister.'

'Really? She didn't mention that.'

'Well, she doesn't live with us anymore. She ran away.'

'Oh, that's terrible. I'm so sorry.'

'Thanks. She has been gone a long time.'

'And you've got no idea where she is?'

Beth looked away. 'No, none at all.'

After a brief silence, Beth said, 'I've recently taken a position at the Science Department – Manufactured Food Division. It's a lot of research and experimentation, but I find it very interesting.'

Vamity nodded slowly as her deep brown eyes gazed at Beth.

'I'm sure it is. I've always wondered what that stuff is that we eat. Can you make it taste any better?'

They both laughed.

'We're trying.'

'Well, my work is fairly new too,' Vamity said.

'I see. Do you think you can help me?' Beth asked.

Vamity leaned in close, tenderly took hold of Beth's jaw, and turned it to the side to examine the scar that ran down the side of her face. Beth held her breath but she didn't know why and her heart began pounding ever so faster as Vamity felt the streak of wrinkly, crimson skin. No one had ever touched it.

'I think so,' she finally said, with a reassuring smile. 'How far does it go?'

Beth undid the top buttons of her overalls and let them fall open. 'To here.' She motioned. 'Just beside my left breast.'

Vamity tenderly stroked the blemish's outline with an index finger. 'Do you mind me asking how you got it?'

'Not at all. It was from an accident when I was four.'

'Oh, how awful for you,' Vamity said.

'I was playing in the kitchen when our Dom at the time spilled boiling water on me. He was an alcoholic. So, an accident that was more than just plain old bad luck.'

'I'm sorry. That's a horrible thing to happen to you.'

'Yeah, he ended up at Area 15. I was very self-conscious of it for a long time.'

'And now?'

Beth shrugged. 'I've got used to it. But it would be nice if it was a little less noticeable.'

'Of course. I admire your courage. It would have taken a lot of inner strength to regain your confidence.'

'I guess I take after my mother.'

'What's it like being the daughter of such an influential and revered woman?'

'She's a wonderful mother and a great role model, there's no doubt about it.'

Vamity nodded slowly with a smitten smile.

'I can start you on a natural therapy that I've developed. We'll begin with the mildest version to test how you react to it and then review each week before moving on to the stronger stuff. Does that sound okay?'

'That sounds great. What does it involve?'

'It's just a lotion you apply directly to the scar. A mixture of herbs, stem cells and DNA that reduces inflammation, softens skin molecules and hopefully lightens pigmentation. We can start right away if you want. I can show you how.'

'Yes, please. I'm keen.'

Vamity went to the cupboard and brought back a small jar and began unscrewing the lid. 'Tilt your head back a bit to the right for me. You don't need much.' She put dabs of lotion all over the scar and started to gently massage it in. 'Like this,' she said.

When Vamity paused, Beth stared into her dark eyes and leaned in and placed a kiss on her full pouting lips.

'Oh, I'm sorry, you're a professional,' Beth said, withdrawing abruptly, a little flushed.

'Don't be,' Vamity said as she pulled Beth in close and kissed her back.

LIV

The yearning to see his family had morphed into an unrelenting dull ache that Sam could no longer ignore, and he finally decided the time was right to go. He'd promised his mother that he would return to see her when he could and was increasingly concerned about the anxiety back home that his extended absence had no doubt created. The village was reluctant to let him go. Especially Melissa, who was having trouble conceiving after deciding to provide a sibling for their first child.

'Don't worry, I'll be back soon,' he told her.

The journey would take under four weeks if he kept a cracking pace. He said goodbye to the women, kissed the foreheads of his babies, savoured a long kiss with Melissa, then hoisted his backpack onto his shoulders and with his other bag in hand, he set off towards the rising sun.

He clearly remembered the way, walking from dawn to dusk, cutting through the woods and the ravines and following the river. When he arrived back at Lex's old camping ground, his mind was flooded with bad but distant memories and although he stopped there for a night, his recollections were too vivid and horrible to allow him to sleep in the cave.

It was a relief to find his bike and trailer were still at the place where he'd left them, a little aged and rusty but in working condition. The rig shaved days from the trip. Under the cloak of nightfall, he once again ventured through town and back to his mother's house. When she answered the door, Sonya couldn't believe her eyes; it had been such a long time and she immediately burst into uncontrollable blubbering sobs as she reached out and threw her arms around him.

'Oh, thank goodness! You're here, you've come back!' she wailed.

'Hello, Mum.'

Upon hearing the commotion, Beth came running in.

'Come here and give your big brother a hug,' Sam said. 'Oh, wow! Your scar looks so much better.'

'I know. Thanks! I'm having some treatment done on it.'

'You look exhausted, young man, but well,' Sonya said.

'I am. I truly am and I can't wait to tell you about everything I've been doing.'

'Of course. But I'm sure you'd like to freshen up and rest a bit first,' Sonya said.

'I'll put the kettle on,' Beth said.

After bathing, Sam joined his mother and Beth in the parlour.

'You're looking a bit thin and pale, Mum, are you unwell?' Sam asked.

A little shocked by Sam's intuitive probing, Sonya smiled and said, 'Don't worry about me I'm fine, let's hear about you,' as she poured the tea.

Sam told them all about his journey and how he had stumbled across and been accepted by the village of women, although he left out the gory details of Lex.

'They abandoned society because they loathed the way it treated men, the Production Farms captivity and the imposed servitude,' he said.

'I see,' Sonya said, 'I can understand. Good on them for making a choice and taking action to support their beliefs.'

'There is one other matter,' Sam said, looking up at her. 'I have fathered a couple of dozen children. Well, forty-two, to be exact. The eldest are four years old.'

'Oh, my goodness, I'm sorry, I should have explained your fertility before you left. I was always going to when you got back but it just never seemed the right time and I didn't think to worry you, given your reclusive existence. Has it caused you problems?'

'Yes, how did they react?' Beth asked.

'I was worried at first but they were mostly pleased when they got over the shock that I could help them have children,' Sam answered.

Sonya smiled, leaned across and squeezed his hand. 'That's wonderful news. I'm so happy for you. You make me so proud,' she said, oozing with admiration. 'Tell us everything.'

After only a few hours of sleep, everyone gathered for a hearty breakfast.

'I've got some news of my own,' Beth said as she plied Sam's pancakes with extra syrup.

'Well, tell me!' Sam said.

'I'm working at the Science Department.'

'That's great. Well done. I'm so proud of you.'

'And that's not all. I met a girl last year. Her name is Vamity and we're getting married!'

'Congratulations! Oh gosh, good for you! That's even more wonderful news. I'm so glad you're happy,' he said, getting up to give her a hug.

Everyone was smiling around the table.

'Sam, you know how you were saying that the village aren't fans of the Sisterhood and their policies?' Sonya asked.

'Yes, that's right,' Sam answered.

'I've actually been trying to get the Sisterhood to begin opening up the farms for a while.'

'Really?'

'Yes. The food shortage has settled down now and there's no reason to confine the men to working in them. That level of strict population control is unnecessary.'

'What about Banshee?'

She huffed. 'That was never really an issue. We found out it disappeared years ago.'

'So, there are no real excuses for the farms to exist anymore?'

'That's right. Apart from the Sisterhood's desire to maintain control and keep men out of the way, that is.'

She got up and wandered over to the window and stared at some girls playing in the field down the road.

'Now you've got me thinking. I've known for a long time that it's nigh impossible to defeat the system with direct confrontation. That's why I've been trying to use subtle persuasion. And that's not working that well either. But …' Sonya paused, taking a moment to assemble her thoughts.

Beth and Sam sat, watching her.

She turned to look at them, 'Well maybe we could join forces with the village and together we could make changes for the better.'

'I'm not sure what you mean. Combine forces and attack?' Beth asked.

'No, as I said nothing that dramatic. Stealth is my weapon of choice.'

'We could use the village as our base of resistance,' Sam said.

'Yes,' Sonya said. 'I've been doing some investigating and in some Inner Party medical archives I found reference to a theory that it's actually possible to surgically reverse the Rec processing operation and restore their fertility.'

'There's a woman called Laura that used to work for the Inner Party's Advanced Curative Institute. I think I heard her talking about that sort of thing at the village with the council of elders when they were discussing ideas for populating the village in the future. It's obviously experimental but she thinks she could do it,' Sam said.

'Hmmm, populating the village is one thing, but I'm thinking much bigger. We're in this for the long haul. A plan that will take years, but we could start by sending Recs to the village to be reversed. They could bring more children to the village, mix the gene pool so to speak, and then when we're ready, we move onto phase two,' she said.

'What's "phase two"?'

'I'll go into that later. Best we keep it simple for now – we don't want to make it too complicated. The village will have enough to consider. Do you think you could convince the council of elders?'

'I don't see why not, if it's going to solve the problem of perpetuating the village. They've already been thinking about it anyway.'

'Good. I'll get some medical instruments for you to take. You'll also need to go with Sam too, Beth.'

Beth looked towards her, a little startled.

'Yes, Beth. I want you to go with Sam and make a detailed map along the way. After talking with the elders, you'll come back to me with their decision. We'll run through the details before you leave.'

LV

During their journey to the village, they carefully documented every landscape formation, each twist in the river and any tree or cave that provided a pointer for their map. Along the way, Sam also told Beth about his earlier experiences with near starvation, wild berries and hallucinations and showed her where he had left Lex.

As they came through the unfolding natural pathway carved into the ageless cliffs, they were greeted by a swelling chorus of cheers. Beth shook her head as she marvelled at the sight and followed Sam who introduced her to the women as they approached.

Melissa ran to Sam and gave him a huge hug and a fervid, lingering kiss before stepping back and looking Beth up and down.

'This is my sister, Beth,' Sam said.

'Oh. I'm pleased to meet you, Beth,' Melissa said.

After cleaning up and then devouring a hearty meal washed down with a good wine, they were ready to sit with the council of elders.

'Do you think Laura can reverse the Rec Processing procedure?' Sam asked.

'We talked about it a while ago and she wasn't sure,' Gloria replied.

'Would you be interested in trying it?

'Why do you ask?'

'My mum, Sonya, would like to send some Recs here to find out if it can be done. If it works, the village could establish more broader families and secure its future. I've started it, but we can't all be related,' Sam said.

'I can definitely see merit in the idea,' Gloria said.

'Our inability to have children has been weighing on our minds, growing heavier as time passes and this would provide a longer-term solution,' Vicky said.

'The village wouldn't have to rely on Sam so much,' Melissa added.

'As with all of these types of decisions, we should put it to a vote,' Gloria said.

After a brief discussion, the council unanimously agreed to go ahead with the plan. A few days later Beth left for home, testing the veracity of her mapping skills.

***

'Sam, can I please see you tonight?' Melissa asked. 'I know you're busy, but I thought our little Jimmy would have a brother or sister, or both, by now.'

He leaned in and gave her a kiss. 'I'm sorry. I haven't meant to ignore you.'

'If you're as serious about this as I am, you'd agree that we're not together enough.'

'I know. But you do realise how busy I've been and probably will be for some time yet.'

'Yes, of course, I do. But I hate having to make appointments with you all the time!'

'Well, move in with me and you won't have to,' Sam said.

'Really?' she said incredulously. 'Are you sure?'

'Yes. Definitely,' he answered with a glowing grin.

She threw her arms around him and they passionately kissed in a warm embrace.

***

When Beth made it back, Sonya was overjoyed with her news. It couldn't have been better.

'Let's make a list of the Recs that are our close friends and trust enough to approach,' Sonya said as she sat with Beth at the dining room table, finishing off a bottle of wine after dinner. 'We can begin by subtly exploring their attitudes and then provide a few pieces of vague information about what we are proposing.' She tipped her glass up and finished it before picking up the bottle for a refill.

'There would be a least a dozen, probably double, that I can think of to start with,' Beth said. 'And I know Vamity and her mother want to help us.'

'Then, if we're comfortable that they are genuinely interested, we'll go into the details of their relocation to the women's village, and their opportunity to become fathers,' Sonya said.

'And what a profound opportunity it is,' Beth said, wistfully thinking of Chad.

Sonya looked at Beth and nodded. 'I know.'

Beth admired her mother's determined yet weary, grey-tinged face. Sonya tired easily these days and said 'goodnight'. Beth watched as she methodically climbed the stairs clutching the banister. When Sonya had divulged to her that she was sick, she implored her not to worry, that it would take years and that she would be an elderly woman before it took her. But Beth couldn't help thinking that lately, her mum was starting to look a lot older.

Within weeks they successfully recruited their first group of ten Recs. They were provided with instructions on what to pack and where to assemble. At dusk on the date of departure, Beth met them on the outside of town, not far from the start of the trail. She explained their copy of the map. 'Someone must come back as soon as the results of the reversal procedure are known,' she told them before wishing them luck.

* * *

'Mum, I want to tell you about the exciting discovery we have made at work,' Beth said.

'Go on.'

'We've found a new ingredient to include in the manufactured protein sustenance. It's called Mono-sodium, Tri-oxolite, Benzotip.'

'Okay … What's it do?'

'It increases the nutritional content by two-fold and actually improves the taste.'

'Really, that's fantastic! How far along is the testing?'

'It's coming along. We shouldn't be too far off having a product ready for trial. But we're confident that it's just a formality.'

'That sounds very positive. Do you want me to let the Sisterhood know?'

'Yes. My supervisor told me to ask you.'

'Okay. I will. The next meeting isn't too far away.'

***

Sonya and Beth endured nearly two months of anxiously waiting to hear from the village before Beth's sleep was disturbed by a gentle tapping on her bedroom window in the cold quiet darkness just prior to dawn.

'That's great!' Sonya said after Beth had called her into the parlour to meet with the messenger who conveyed the news that the reversal procedure worked, confirming that the Recs were responsible for multiple pregnancies in the village.

The energised duo swung into action, recruiting more candidates for relocation. Their recruitment continued at a steady pace and dozens of others were enlisted. 'I'm off to the auctions now, Beth,' Sonya called out. She was organising purchases for the village. Beth waved as Sonya closed the door behind her.

LVI

'You'll have to hurry, or you'll be late!' Beth yelled from the kitchen.

Sonya was carelessly scrambling downstairs. 'I know, thanks, dear,' she said, grabbing a few gulps of tea as she pulled on her overcoat on her way out the front door. 'See you later.' She was heading to the Sisterhood's monthly meeting.

As Sonya entered, she checked her watch and much to her surprise had arrived with five minutes to spare. When general business was called, Sonya motioned to speak.

'I want to tell the sisters about the exciting and revolutionary results being achieved by the Science Department which will effectively solve any lingering anxieties about food shortages. I believe it could lead to the relaxation of the Production Farms.'

'What results might those be?' Charlotte asked.

'A new additive that doubles the nutritional value of the manufactured protein sustenance.'

'That all sounds well and good but has it been tested?'

'It's in the final stages now and it looks very promising,' Sonya answered.

'Yes but we've heard many, many promises before that turn into nothing and testing can take years,' Charlotte said with a dismissive hand gesture. 'I don't really think we have time for this now. We have much more pressing issues to discuss. Thank you anyway, Sonya.'

Sonya snarled silently in her seat.

The main item on the agenda that Charlotte was referring to was the growing incidence of Recs disappearing from their homes. However, their discussion raised more questions than answers which calmed Sonya's concerns. It meant the measures she had taken to conceal her involvement were working. They really didn't have a clue. But they resolved to tighten up the supervision of Recs and implement regular reporting and recently developed surveillance systems that would make it much more difficult for Sonya and her family to continue their current operations. Sonya supported the imposition of the new rules which helped to deflect any unwelcome suspicion that might be directed towards her. Besides, she had more important matters to attend to.

***

'I can't believe the Sisterhood disregarded our impressive work so blatantly,' Beth said as she sat down next to her mother. She was relaxing in the afternoon sun, drinking tea beside their favourite tall, fork-trunked Elm tree not far from their pond. 'It just seems crazy.'

'I agree but it's what I've come to expect by now,' Sonya said.

'It's so infuriating but mostly disappointing. It really makes me want to go up to them and shake them around!' Beth enthused.

Sonya sympathised with her daughter's frustration. 'You know, I haven't had a holiday for years and I'm thinking of paying Sam's village a visit. Would you come with me?'

'Yes, of course, Mother,' Beth replied before crunching on a cookie.

'Thanks, dear. Do you think Vamity will mind staying behind to look after the place for us?'

'I'm sure she'll be fine,' Beth answered.

'Good,' Sonya said, pausing to take a sip of tea. She looked at Beth with a mysterious smirk. 'Yes, I think it's time for phase two.'

LVII

When they arrived looking tired and relieved, Sam was in the orchard picking fruit. Vicky came running up to him yelling, 'Sam! Sam! Your mother and sister are here!'

Sam almost fell off the ladder and managed to kick over a basket of oranges as he scrambled towards the central courtyard where he found his mother and Beth flanked by villagers.

'Mum!' he cried as a path was cleared for him.

Tears flowed freely down Sonya's weary but happy smiling face.

'It's so good to see you!' she said.

Sam hugged them both. 'Come, you must need some food and rest,' he said, taking the bag from her. They followed him into the meeting hut and he introduced them to Gloria and the council of elders. Gloria was pleased to meet the woman who had done such a fine job of raising Sam.

After washing up, Sonya and Beth retired early for the evening and slept soundly the entire night. The sounds of chatting and laughing brought them out of their huts and into the brisk chill of an Autumn morning. Sam gave his mother a guided tour of the place and she was thrilled to meet her grandchildren who ranged in age from babies unable to crawl to seven-year-old children skipping around in front of her. He also introduced her to Melissa who was heavily pregnant with their second child.

'We're so glad you were able to offer your assistance to us,' Gloria said during Sonya's meeting with Sam, Beth, and the elders, some with male partners.

'And thank you for taking such good care of my son and welcoming him into your community,' Sonya said.

'The pleasure was all ours,' Gloria said. 'And now I'd like you to meet Laura. She performed the successful Rec reversal operations.'

'Great to meet you, Sonya,' Laura said.

'Likewise, you are very talented,' Sonya said.

'Thank you.'

Sonya shifted in her seat and looked around the room before focussing on Gloria. 'I'm hoping we can continue working together.'

'Of course, but in what way?' Gloria asked.

'It's no small thing. I'd like your help to further undermine the Sisterhood, dismantle their policies and the Production Farms, and ultimately free all men,' Sonya replied.

'Good gracious! You are one determined woman. Now I know where Sam gets his drive from. As ambitious as it sounds, we'd love to hear more!' Gloria said, leaning forward. 'Please, go on.'

'Well. I'd like to increase the number of Rec reversal conversions that you're doing here.'

'We will be able to accommodate some more men but how many are we talking about?'

'They won't all be staying here. I'm hoping many will go back to the towns and we can match them up with women who want the opportunity of having children with the right man. With the new shortcuts Beth found, it's only about two weeks between here and my place.'

'Oh, I see.'

'We'll require support. I think it would also be beneficial to have some of the already converted men and women from the village go back into society and establish families there if they wanted to. The women willing to help us will need to infiltrate the farms, the auction houses, and the processing and records departments. I've got things started but if this grows, more trustworthy people will have to be involved. The Sisterhood are already making it difficult to continue moving Recs out here the way we have been.'

'Have you thought about the risks involved?' Penny asked. 'I mean, what if we get caught?'

'There is no denying that if we're not careful there will be consequences. Those discovered will be without doubt sent to Area 15. But I have given this a lot of thought and if I for one moment didn't believe it was feasible, I wouldn't be suggesting it,' Sonya said.

'There is a lot at stake, though if it works even somewhat, the ramifications for society are huge,' Gloria said.

'What about identity papers for the women? They'll need to have some sort of documentation if they are going to find houses and apply for jobs,' Penny asked.

'They will hide at my place on arrival. I'll organise their credentials and once they find somewhere to live, Beth and I will help them gain access to the job application process,' Sonya said.

'I'm going to need some help though,' Laura said, with a concerned frown.

'Of course,' Sonya said. 'I'd like to think that you can train a team to work with you. Do you think that is possible?'

'Yes, I guess so. There should be a few volunteers willing to learn,' Laura replied. 'We can make sutures and ferment our "crazy" berries to make anaesthetic but what about medical instruments?'

'I've bought several sets with me,' Sonya said.

'It's worth trying,' Gloria said. 'What does everyone else think?'

The group voted in favour of Sonya's proposal. She stood and went around the circle from person to person, individually shaking their hands and thanking them.

'I have a fairly good idea of who we need and where they need to be so we can get to work on selecting the first group of women and men that are prepared to get involved over the next few days,' Sonya said.

The volunteers filed one by one into the meeting hut to discuss matters with Sonya, Sam and Beth. The trio chose those they felt could fill the various strategic positions within the departments. Sam ensured the travellers would have sufficient provisions in their backpacks and Beth supplied the village with plenty of copies of her map. The following week, the group of a dozen women and men were ready for Sonya and Beth to lead the expedition homeward.

LVIII

As they entered the outskirts of town, Sonya sent Beth to scout ahead to make sure the way forward was clear. In groups of four or five, they secreted along the backstreets then in amongst the acreages and finally into the sanctity of Sonya's house. Their living quarters were a little crowded during those first couple of weeks, but once Sonya's contacts had prepared the necessary identity documents for the women and their partners, Beth, who had taken up a new job at the Records Department, co-ordinated their resettlement. Vamity helped organise the search for suitable accommodation that they could move into through her recently acquired position in the Housing Department. They also quickly found women willing to match with the men from the first batch of singles that came back from the village.

After their relocation was settled, they commenced infiltration. Sonya made enquiries about the availability of promotions and key roles requiring new staff and even created some new job openings. Many of her applicants were armed with her endorsement and on several occasions, Sonya was able to be part of the interviews and selection panels. For positions considered crucial, she ensured the entire short-list of candidates consisted of women from the village.

A shuttle parked in the Production Farm was rapidly being filled by a procession of Recs, eager to start their new lives. When the last of them boarded, one of Sonya's specially planted drivers closed the shuttle door and signalled the gatekeeper. The huge creaking portcullis retracted slowly upward allowing them to pass. The passengers had no idea that they had veered off course and were no longer heading towards the auction house. Although they had come to a halt in a secluded suburban side street, they still had no inclination.

It wasn't until the driver told them that they had been specially chosen to undertake a mission that their chattering subsided. 'Don't be concerned and don't ask me too many questions,' said the driver. As they sat waiting, she distributed some fruit and water. When it was time to disembark, they were greeted by women who separated them into groups of three or four and escorted them in different directions only to end up together again at the agreed meeting place at dusk. Beth took the men to the start of the trail, where she handed them over to a guide with a map and supplies to enable their trek to the village.

Dozens of shuttles, which were selected from those leaving the farms, followed this routine that the team had practised to the point of clockwork precision. With every group of Recs sent to the village, a message went with them detailing how many women and men should return in the next group.

As well as the physical process interventions, the infiltrated departments had their records altered and adjusted to cope with the irregularities. The Sisterhood's increased surveillance of Recs in homes was rendered ineffective as the new method of moving Recs prior to auction bypassed their recently tightened integrity measures.

In a matter of months, the results of Sonya's groundwork started rippling through society. Beth and Vamity arranged for the stream of available converted Recs to be surreptitiously introduced to women seeking male partners, and if they were compatible assisted with all the documentation and formalities.

LIX

The inevitable occurrence of hundreds of pregnancies and births followed, causing outrage amongst the Sisterhood. As Chief Administrator of the Recs and Doms Program, they naturally turned to Sonya to lead an enquiry into the unexplained fertility of Recs.

Over the next twelve months, Sonya made sure that the progress of the investigation remained slow and occasionally completely stalled but always reported to the Sisterhood that matters were in hand. At one stage she announced at a meeting that a breakdown had been identified in the processing procedure and that everything was back on track. But it wasn't.

As more months went by with increasing numbers of births to Recs, the Sisterhood also had to contend with the dilemma that although *seemingly* surprised, all of the new mothers chose to defy their orders and were keeping their sons rather than surrendering them to the farms. There was an undeniable groundswell of women who were drawn towards the ideal of natural procreation and knowing the father of their children. Society was becoming overwhelmed by the tidal wave of emotion ingrained in the family unit. Another emergency meeting of the Sisterhood was convened.

'Sisters, sisters, please settle! We need to get started,' Charlotte said, beckoning those assembled with her raised arms. 'We still have a growing problem with the Recs and it's getting out of control.'

'Sonya, what have you go to say about it?' Susan said.

'I'm sorry. I don't know what's happened. By all accounts, everything was supposed to be working correctly again. I can only suggest that we re-open another more thorough investigation,' Sonya said.

'More thorough? Sonya, with all due respect, your previous effort was a complete and utter disaster!' Charlotte declared.

Sonya sat silently, looking concerned and miserable.

'We must stop the Rec Program immediately, even just temporarily, until we find out what's happening,' Charlotte said, looking directly at Sonya.

The rest of the group turned towards her as well, bracing themselves for an adverse reaction to the suggestion.

But Sonya nodded and as if resigned to the fact, quietly said, 'I agree.'

There was a moment's silence.

'Okay, then so be it. The Rec Program is halted forthwith. Orders to be issued immediately,' Charlotte commanded.

When the meeting was over, Connie approached Charlotte who was still packing her notes at the front of the room.

****

'Charlotte, have you got a minute?'

'Sure, Connie, what is it?'

'You don't think you're being a bit harsh on Sonya, do you?' Connie asked. 'I mean, she does have good intentions.'

Charlotte's eyes locked onto Connie's as she leaned towards her and said, 'I'll tell you something, Connie, something I have never told anyone else. Before the Insane War, I was gang-raped as a teenager by a group of men I didn't know and who were never punished for it.'

'Oh God, that's awful, Charlotte. I'm so sorry.'

'Yes. And as well, I got pregnant.'

Connie had turned white.

'With twin girls, and then I lost both in a miscarriage at eighteen weeks.'

Connie gasped and recoiled in horror.

Charlotte maintained her steely glare as she nodded. 'Trust me. Keeping men locked up is the only way women can control their reproduction and live without fear. Women like Sonya will never understand. We need to get her out of the way so that we can thoroughly investigate what's happening without any of her, shall we say, interference.'

***

Sonya left the meeting with a satisfied grin. Not only did voting for the cessation of new Recs being released help to diffuse any distrust of her that the Sisterhood might be harbouring, it would undoubtedly create more chaos. Societal unrest was already fermenting due to the Sisterhood's feeble attempts to dismantle families and removing the ability to acquire Recs would further escalate frustration and cause market distortions. It also promised the additional benefit of sowing complacency within the Sisterhood by allowing them to think that they had at least temporarily stymied the problem.

But it was too late, Sonya was always one step ahead of them. Just as she had modified the original plan of sending Recs from their owner's homes to the village, the diversion of newly released farm Recs for conversion and assimilation with willing women had long been discontinued. With the help of Laura and Beth, Sonya and her flourishing network had used the last few years to establish vast teams of homebased clinicians in towns capable of reversing Rec infertility in procedures carried out within a day.

Sonya's scheme began experiencing exponential growth as women everywhere took advantage of the clandestine opportunity. The Sisterhood's attempts to thwart the disruption were successfully stifled by Sonya's cleverly integrated and highly effective operatives that had permeated and entrenched themselves throughout the entire system.

LX

Gosh, when Connie asked me to come around to her place tonight, she sounded awfully worried, Sonya thought as she made her way to her best friend's house after dinner.

'Sonya, please come in,' Connie said. 'Do you want a drink?'

'Will I need one?'

'I think we both do.'

'Make mine a large then.'

'White wine okay?'

'Perfect. Thanks.'

They sat sipping their fully charged glasses. Sonya reclined in the comfy chair and admired the simple décore.

'Now what is it you needed to see me about?' Sonya asked.

Connie put her glass down on the little table beside her and turned to Sonya.

'It's Charlotte. She wants you out of the way so the Sisterhood can investigate the Rec problem, without, as she put it, your interference.'

'I see. I'm not overly surprised. We've never seen eye to eye but she makes it personal.'

'For sure. Believe me when I tell you it is very personal to her. She is never going to change. She can't.'

Sonya studied her gloomy expression.

'Not only that – there are rumours circulating the Health

Department that you had something to do with the problem with the Recs,' Connie said.

'Is there any proof?'

'Not as far as I know but we've been friends a long time and I just thought you should know.'

'You do have something to do with it, don't you?'

'Yes. But it's best I don't tell you anymore.'

'It's okay, Sonya, I'm on your side in this. Please remember that.'

'Thanks, Connie, I really appreciate it.'

Sonya wasn't too concerned. The Sisterhood probe wasn't likely to find anything to implicate her in the turmoil. Besides, the tentacles of the network she had created were now spread and deep-rooted, working seamlessly throughout the whole structure of society.

***

Sonya looked in the mirror at her sunken grey eyes and thinning neck, acutely aware of her declining mortality. The cancer was in there, as always, eating away at her and growing fatter. Vamity placed their meals on the table as Beth pushed Sonya's chair in for her as she sat.

The uncomfortable silence as they ate was broken when Sonya said, 'I've decided to retire, girls. It's all getting too much for me.'

'Really?' Beth wasn't that surprised, even though she made it sound like it.

'Yes, well I'm not getting any younger. I'm only two months shy of turning sixty,' she said.

'I suppose so. I can't believe it's 2080 myself. Where does the time go?' Beth said, chewing her food.

Sonya shrugged and gave a half grin. 'I'm going to tell the department tomorrow morning and make an announcement at the Sisterhood meeting being held later in the afternoon,' she replied as she pushed around some boiled potatoes on her plate with her fork.

***

When Sonya returned to the Health Department to announce her retirement and hand over her affairs, she was approached by Connie. A plaque was to be commissioned to recognise Sonya's contribution and years of service. Although she wasn't in the mood for ceremonies and memorials, she accepted the honour with good grace.

Later that day, when Charlotte opened the Sisterhood meeting, she was more sharp and abrupt than usual and Sonya could immediately sense her confrontational demeanour.

'I want to get straight to business this morning, sisters,' Charlotte said with a determined scowl. 'I move a motion that Sonya be stood down whilst we launch an independent investigation into the entire Recreational Program.'

'That sounds like an accusation, Charlotte,' Sonya said.

'Maybe it is.'

The others were all staring at Sonya.

'Well, it doesn't bother me. I'm happy to vote in favour of your motion,' Sonya responded, further inflating the other women's admiration for her.

'Good. All those in favour of the motion for Sonya to stand aside as the Chief Administrator of the Rec and Dom Program during the investigation please raise your right hand,' Charlotte said.

Sonya was the first to raise her hand and the others followed, resulting in the motion passing unanimously.

'But I'd also like to move a motion of my own,' Sonya said, casting her eyes around the room. 'Good leaders never blame or chastise people for doing their best, especially in difficult circumstances where assistance is rarely offered. Great leaders take responsibility for the successes under their watch and more importantly, for the failures. I move that Charlotte be replaced as Chairwoman and expelled from the Sisterhood. She has proven to be a grossly incompetent leader and presided over a disastrous breakdown in society. She has mishandled this crisis from the beginning in a most spiteful and vindicative manner that defiles the Sisterhood and caused irreparable damage to our credibility and authority.'

Charlotte was incensed. 'How dare you!' she yelled.

'Why? I have the right,' Sonya spat back.

Susan, the deputy Chairwoman, nodded in agreement. 'I'm sorry, Charlotte, it's perfectly valid. All those in favour of the motion for Charlotte to be expelled from the Sisterhood, please raise your right hand.'

The motion was affirmed unanimously.

Charlotte was fuming with rage and her face turned bright red. She stood up and stormed out the door.

After the fevered excitement faded, Sonya stood to address the meeting.

'Thank you for your support, everyone. I also came here today with another announcement. I'm retiring. From the Health Department and the Sisterhood. My health isn't that good, and I feel like it's the right time for me to step down and let someone younger and more energetic take over from me. So, this will be my last meeting. I wish you well with the investigation.'

The women glanced around at each other in stunned silence.

* * *

Soon after, Sonya met the members of the Sisterhood and a bunch of family friends, ex-colleagues and other assorted spectators on the front steps of the Health Department. Connie's speech mentioned that 'they were paying tribute to a very deserving and hard-working woman' and concluded with her leading the appreciative audience in three cheers. Sonya stepped forward to draw the string to cast aside the little curtain covering the shiny metal sign. As she did so, she stumbled slightly, and Connie took hold of her arm to steady her. Sonya smiled at the crowd and responded with a heartfelt thank you and a brief reply. Her work had never been a chore, always a pleasure. Connie looked Sonya in the eye and whispered, 'Goodbye and good luck with everything, old friend.'

As soon as she was home, Sonya, Beth and Vamity finalised their plans to relocate to Sam's village. With Sonya's declining health and the looming investigation, they would leave as soon as possible. Vamity's mother would stay and look after the house.

LXI

Their journey took almost two weeks longer than usual. Sonya was only able to travel part of the day before she had to rest her exhausted body. Her illness was making its presence known and sapping her reserves of strength. Beth had concerns that she might not make it so she was greatly relieved when they finally came within sight of the little fork in the river that led to the hidden passage through the rocky hills.

Making their way gradually to the courtyard, they rested on a bench under the shade of a gnarled old fig tree. Sam came to greet them and tried hard not to look shocked by his mother's sickly pallor and frail posture.

'What a pleasant surprise, it's great to see you here,' Sam said, giving them all a hug. He supported his mother as the group continued to walk. 'Come inside whilst I organise some refreshments.'

'So, what news do you have for me?' Sam asked.

Sonya looked over to Beth, then to Sam. 'I've retired, Sam, and I've decided to live here from now on.'

'That's great to hear. I think it will be good for you,' he said.

'It's up to you now, Sam. You and Beth have to take over for me.'

'Is everything still running to plan?' Sam asked.

'Yes, there are thousands of men now living with their families and with the will of the people, I doubt the Sisterhood can stop it,' Sonya said.

'That's excellent news,' he said as some lemonade was brought over to them. Beth helped herself to the jug and poured four cups.

'We now have some allies in the Sisterhood too.'

'That's incredible. You're incredible. Rest now, Mother, you deserve it,' Sam said.

'Sam, you have to find Chad for me and get him out.'

'We will, Mum. Don't worry. It won't be much longer.'

Sonya moved into a hut near Sam's, and Beth and Vamity's wasn't far away either. This was her home now, with time spent pottering around the village and getting to know her grandchildren who blessed her with their youthful lust for life. She also passed on her knowledge to Sam and he took over her role of co-ordinating and fostering their network operatives. Sam and Beth continuously travelled back and forth between the village and towns over the next few years to quell any disruptions that might hinder the dismantling of the Sisterhood's popularity and power, and Sonya always looked forward to hearing of their progress.

The embossed silver handle of Sonya's dark mahogany walking cane hit the hardwood floor with a clunk as she knocked it from its resting spot. Gingerly she leaned down to pick it up then tidied her thin silver hair with a few strokes of her hand. She hunched over the stick as she slowly made her way to the meeting room. Sam had just this morning returned to report to her, Beth, Vamity and the council of elders. The progress of societal structural reform they had achieved in the last decade was beyond what anyone of them could have imagined. The number of families now numbered in the tens of thousands scattered far and wide, across the States.

'You've done well, Sam,' Sonya said as they walked back to her hut, one arm leaning on the walking stick, the other firmly supported by Sam.

'Thank you, Mum.'

'And I'm so glad that I managed to live long enough to witness it.'

'Oh, you've got plenty of years ahead.'

'Sam, I haven't talked of years for a while, nor months. It's weeks now, and one day at a time.' She paused to take a couple of deep breaths.

'And in just a few more days, Melissa will give birth to another precious grandchild.'

LXII

The Production Farm was eerily quiet during the cool still morning.

'Have you noticed that there's only been about half the normal number of staff over the past few days?' Chad asked Harry, one of his mates.

'Yeah, the guys have been talking about it.'

'There's definitely something funny going on. The staff that are here are edgy and huddled in deep discussion.'

'Look, the gates are opening!'

The men started to gather in the courtyard as a large group of armed women marched into the compound and corralled the outnumbered and unresisting farm staff into a corner.

'Attention Producers! Please listen. This farm's status is forthwith changed to "Liberated". That means you are free to leave if you want. You are free to stay if you want. And you are free to come and go as you please. The gates will not be closing ever again. You can choose what you want to do. I repeat, the gates will be left open.'

After a moment of disbelief, some of the men began cheering and yelling, slapping backs and throwing their arms around each other. Some men chose to stay. 'Where will we go?' they asked. 'Someone has to look after the crops,' others reasoned.

'What about Banshee?' Harry asked.

'Don't worry about it. I've been out there and it's not a problem, believe me,' Chad replied.

'Are you going then?'

'Yes. See you later, I'm going home,' Chad said as he took off through the gates.

Chad was overwhelmed with emotion as he finally approached Sonya's house. He raced up the familiar path, panting, and banged on the door that he had painted green many years ago, yelling out, 'Sonya! Sonya! It's me, Chad!'

A strange woman answered it and Chad took a step back.

'I'm sorry. I'm looking for Sonya,' Chad said.

'I'm afraid she isn't here.'

'Oh, well, do you know where she is? I'm Chad, I used to live here with her and Beth and Sam.'

'You'd better come in, there's quite a bit to explain,' she said.

He followed her into the parlour.

'Beth is married to my daughter Vamity. I'm Fatima.'

'Nice to meet you. So where is everyone?'

'A lot has happened since you've been away. Sam discovered a village in the wastelands and Sonya, Beth and Vamity are living there.'

'Do you know how I can get there?' he asked.

'I have a map,' she replied. 'I'll need to pack you some supplies as well. It's about a two-week hike from here.'

Fatima told Chad as much as she could about what he had missed whilst in the farm before he left for the village.

LXIII

Beth, Melissa and her new baby named Brien were visiting Sonya when Sam walked in and greeted them.

'Hello, Mum,' Sam said, leaning in to kiss her cold forehead. By now he'd become accustomed to the noticeable decline in his mother's health each time he visited.

'Hello, dear, how lovely to see you,' Sonya said, trying to sound upbeat as he came in with a few kids trailing behind. She loved seeing her grandchildren, more so whilst struggling with the final stages of the debilitating illness that had been slowly gnawing away at her. She was in bed breathing slowly and methodically with a conscious laboured effort. The white sheet pulled up around her neck gave her a ghostly appearance.

As she lay with her head propped against a soft pillow, Sonya smiled weakly at the children as they passed by. She raised a trembling hand to gently scratch her face as she glanced down at two little boys playing with toys on the floor near her bed. Her thin wispy hair looked like silver strands of thread and her skin was almost translucent.

'Look how they play. It's so delightful. Their life is just starting, whilst mine is just ending,' Sonya said. She spoke softly and wistfully. Her mind was sharp but her diseased body frail and withered.

'I'll go and put Brien down for his nap and leave you with Sam and Beth for a while,' Melissa said. 'Do you need anything?'

'No, thank you, dear. I'm fine.'

'Okay, goodbye. I'll be back soon. See you, Sam,'

'Bye, Melissa.'

Beth went to separate the two boys who had started squabbling over something.

'It's happening, Mum. The Sisterhood's stranglehold on society is unravelling faster than ever.'

She smiled weakly.

'Who would have thought?' he said, pausing to tenderly stroke her face. 'In the year 2084, the third and final phase has begun, with the dismantling of the Production Farms underway. The Sisterhood are overwhelmed by the surge of our supporters and have given up resisting. The gates are opening, and the first farm Producers are being released. Our soldiers are winning,' Sam said.

Beth watched him reach over to the cup of water by the bed. He brought it carefully to their mother's mouth for her to take a slow sip and dabbed the dribbles with a handkerchief.

'And what's more exciting is that with the help of our allies, the Sisterhood will soon be replaced by a popularly elected government, and they want me to stand as a candidate for first President,' he added.

'That is great news, Sam.' She stopped to take a breath. Unlike her youthful health, her ambitions had never evaporated. 'I knew you could do it.' She turned her gaze towards him. 'I've always trusted fate.'

He smiled whilst looking deeply into her glassy, yellowing eyes.

She continued. 'All those years ago, I pushed my way onto the Sisterhood's steering committees and made sure that Recs were not emasculated the way Doms were. But it wasn't until I found Chad that our destiny started to become clearer.'

Sam continued to gaze at her, spellbound, as he absorbed the meaning of the words she forced from her mouth. 'Yes, Chad was your father, and Beth's.' She took another sip of water.

'And then Ellie-May Micklemore came along. You were only young. Do you remember her?'

'Not that much. Wasn't she the runaway?'

'Yes, that's her. Whilst she was with us, she told me about the women's renegade commune in the wastelands where she'd lived. She was hopelessly lost and couldn't even recall the direction she'd come, so we agreed it best to keep quiet about it for the sake of her people.'

Sonya closed her eyes to take a deep breath, then looked back at him and continued.

'Naturally, I could never be sure the commune would still be there all those years later but at least I knew there was a possibility something like it could exist somewhere out there. If anyone could find it, you could. I always hoped you'd discover such a welcoming place. And I always hoped you'd have your own children one day.'

She managed a feeble smile as she gently nodded her head.

'You've accomplished more than I could ever have imagined. You were always destined for greatness.'

Sam looked up at the tired man who had suddenly appeared, standing in the doorway.

'Father! You made it!' he exclaimed.

A wrinkled smile crept across Chad's face as Sam and Beth ran towards him and gave him an almighty hug.

'Is that really you, Chad, my love?' gasped Sonya.

He went to her and looked deeply into her eyes and said, 'Yes it's me,' as he gently kissed her.

She blinked a couple of times and said, 'I'm so sorry I could never visit you. I wasn't allowed. But my prayers are finally answered. Thank goodness you are safe. You are free and you are here with your family.'

Sonya took a few shallow breaths and reached out to take Sam's hand as they all stood by with watery eyes. 'I love you all very much and always will.'

Sam nodded as she continued.

'I can leave happy and content, knowing the fight is over; knowing I have a wonderful family with wonderful lives ...'

'Mum, stop that. You're not going anywhere.'

A single tear fell down his cheek.

'We did it, my son, we did it,' she said, and with one last long deep sigh, she closed her eyes.

'Goodbye, Mum. I love you.'

As he held her hand that had guided so many, her pulse faded away.

Sonya Smith 2020 – 2084.

She would be buried at the village.

She would not be sent to Area 15.

EPILOGUE

Thousands of families were living in the village, which was now a small township called Sonyaville with a thriving community where sprightly girls and boys were playing, laughing, learning and simply growing up together. An efficient shuttle service now connected it to the city, which had forged the progress of many houses, shops, schools and extensive agricultural operations.

The sight of several diaries piled on a shelf in a corner of Sam's house, relics of a bygone era that he had never got around to throwing away, reminded him of Gloria. It had been such a long time since he had seen her, he made a special effort to visit. As he approached her place, he could see Gloria sitting in the sun on her front porch which had an elevated outlook over the town square.

'Good morning, Gloria,' Sam called out as he strolled towards her.

'Morning to you, Sam. Lovely to see you and you're just in time for a cup of tea.'

'Wonderful. Thank you,' Sam said as the old lady slowly came back with a cup and filled it with tea from the pot on the table as he sat down next to her.

'We have come a long way since you arrived, Sam. So much has changed,' Gloria said as they both sat absorbing the expansive view.

'In a good way, I hope,' Sam said, breaking into a friendly smile.

'Of course, Sam. The village will never look back on better times than those that we are living right now. The history being made, thanks to you and the help of dear Sonya, will endure the test of time,' she said.

Sam could feel the weight of her words on his shoulders as she spoke in such a profound tone. He was always so caught up in life's activities and his busy schedule that he never properly reflected on what his fate had delivered. Not only to himself but to all the lives he had influenced. The women, the children, the village, the State, they were the reason for his, and of course his mother's, existence. Sonyaville was a beacon of peace and harmony and symbolised inherent order within a world that had been knocked over and turned upside down by cataclysmic man-made disasters. It was as if Sonya had picked up the fragile globe, placed it upright and set it spinning correctly again.

A short while later, as Sam sat by his mother's grave, resting on the hill overlooking the town, he turned his head towards the south and stared at the distant horizon. He thought of his childhood home that seemed like two lifetimes ago. Somehow, after many false stops and starts, he had finally found his true place, his purpose, his destiny. He felt he must be the luckiest man in the world as he pondered over the trials he had endured. His life had been one long pretence, a trail of deception and subterfuge. From home living as Samantha to pretending to be a Dom, the charades were over now that society was freed of its shackles. In the end, as the secrets were snuffed, the truth had been good to Sam.

The old tan backpack that he had carried from home long ago sat beside him. It was the only tangible reminder of his childhood that he possessed. He reached inside it, took out a water bottle then rummaged around the bottom of it, trying to pick up some loose berries. Although he had looked in the backpack countless times over the years, he had completely forgotten about the zipped compartment discreetly concealed within its lining. Its obscured opening was tucked under a flap of material stitched at the top. As he fumbled with the bag on his knees, he opened the sealed pocket and brought out a copy of an old book. His mother must have brought it with her and stowed it there for him to find.

The dark brown leather cover had crackled gold lettering across the top that said, 'The Holy Bible'. It was in remarkably good condition for something that appeared to be over a hundred years old. Inside the cover, there was a faded and barely legible, scrawled signature. Sam squinted and moved it closer to his face. Tilting it towards the sunlight, he read in a soft voice,

'Winston Smith 2024'

He knew that name. There was a well-worn crease in the book's spine that marked a place where it would open instinctively, as if begging him to look at it. He placed it on his lap and let it fall open.

Under the bright morning rays, he stared down at the pages of Matthew Chapter 5, Verse 5, and heavily underlined in dark ink were the words, 'Blessed are the meek, for they shall inherit the earth'. Sam nodded his head and smiled.

THE END